THE
ARABIAN NIGHTS

The Forty Robbers return to their cave

THE
ARABIAN NIGHTS

Edited by ANNA TWEED

Illustrated by
CASPAR EMERSON AND LEON D'EMO

Contents

Illustrations

Introduction

"THE Book of a Thousand Nights and a Night," as it is called in the original, is of unknown authorship, nor can we tell with any exactness when the stories took the form of a printed volume. Some light is thrown on their probable date by the fact that there are but three allusions to coffee in the tales, and only once or twice any mention of tobacco; and in neither the case of coffee nor tobacco are these references believed to belong to the ancient text. Coffee was not in general use in the East until the fourteenth century, and the usual supposition is that tobacco was introduced from America. These things and certain other details make it seem likely that the stories were written after the year 900 and before the year 1400.

They were first made known to Europe by a French Orientalist named Galland. His translation was published in Paris at intervals between the years 1704 and 1717. By many persons the books were credited to the genius of Galland himself, and his statement that they were by an unknown Arabian author was thought to be a hoax. They attained a greater popularity than any other books of the time, and the gay young men of Paris used to gather in groups at night beneath Galland's windows and sing and shout until he appeared. Then after saluting him with a round of applause they would cry: "O, you, who know such fine stories and can tell them so well, tell us one now."

Under the title of "The Arabian Nights' Entertainments" the stories were soon famous throughout Europe; and few books have been translated into so many different languages or given delight to so large a number of readers. From their very first appearance in English they have been accorded a foremost place in the ranks of imaginative literature. They are pure narratives with no object except to please or amuse, yet with a very real value for their portrayal of Oriental life. The reader is transported into a wonderland of marvellous palaces, beautiful women, powerful magicians, and exquisite repasts, and the descriptions captivate the senses with their Eastern richness and splendor. We have been reading them for two hundred years, but the passing of time does not in the least dim their lustre nor dull the pleasure that is to be found in them. Indeed, these tales form one of the few books destined always to be young—one of the elemental books to which every succeeding generation returns with fresh enjoyment.

Not only is the "Arabian Nights" one of the world's greatest story books in its power to interest and charm, but it is also one of the greatest in its bulk. In its complete form it would make more than twenty volumes the size of the present one. This "Golden Book" is a selection of the most attractive of the tales for young readers. Various texts have been drawn from and combined to form what is believed to be an exceptionally clear and vivacious treatment of the narratives.

The Arabian Nights

I

THE SULTAN'S VOW

AMONG the ancient Persian monarchs was a certain illustrious sultan who was said to be the best monarch of his time. He was beloved by his subjects for his wisdom and prudence, and feared by his enemies for his courage and for the hardy and well-trained army of which he was the leader. This sultan had two sons, the elder called Shahriar, and the younger Shahzeman, both equally good and deserving of praise. But when the old sultan died at the end of a long and glorious reign, Shahriar became ruler of the entire realm in his stead. Shahzeman was not, however, in the least envious, and a friendly contest then arose between him and his brother as to which could best promote the other's happiness. The younger did all he could to show his loyalty and affection, while the new sultan loaded him with all possible honors, and presently bestowed on him the kingdom of Great Tartary. This made it necessary for the brothers to separate, and Shahzeman journeyed to Samarcand, the chief city of his empire and there dwelt.

After a separation of ten years Shahriar became so anxious to see his brother that he sent his grand vizier with a splendid embassy to invite the King of Tartary to visit his court. As soon as Shahzeman was informed of the approach of the vizier, he went to meet him, accompanied by all his ministers, and inquired after the health of the sultan, his brother. The vizier answered such questions as the monarch chose to ask, and then told the purpose of his coming.

"Sage vizier," said the king, "it is impossible that the wish of the sultan to see me can exceed my desire of again beholding him. You have arrived at a happy moment. My kingdom is tranquil, and in a few days' time I will be ready to depart with you. Meanwhile pitch your tents on this spot, and I will order every refreshment and accommodation for you and your whole train."

In about a week Shahzeman had arranged all his affairs, and he and such officers as he had appointed to attend him, left the city one evening and camped near the tents of his brother's ambassador. This they did that they might start promptly on their journey early the following morning. After a little while the king concluded to return to the city in order to once more see the queen whom he tenderly loved. He went back to the palace privately and was greatly amazed to find the queen in the company of another man whom it was plain she loved better than himself. In the fierceness of his indignation he drew his cimeter and with two rapid strokes slew his unfaithful consort and her companion.

He then went from the city as privately as he entered it and returned to the camp. Not a word did he say to anyone of what had happened, and at dawn the next day the tents were taken down and the march toward Persia was begun to the sound of drums and other instruments of music. The whole troop was filled with joy except the king, who could think of nothing but his queen's death, and he was silent and sorrowful during the entire journey.

When he approached the capital of Persia, he perceived the Sultan Shahriar and all his court coming out to greet him. As soon as the two parties met, the brothers alighted and embraced each other, and after a thousand expressions of regard, they remounted and entered the city amidst the shouts of the multitude. A palace had been prepared for Shahzeman, which was only separated from the sultan's own palace by a garden, and thither he was conducted.

Shahriar left the King of Tartary to himself long enough for him to bathe and change his clothing, and afterward they seated themselves on a sofa and conversed for a long time. They supped together and continued their conversation, and not until the night was far advanced did Shahriar leave his brother to repose.

Shahzeman retired to his couch, but the grief, which the presence of the sultan had for a while made him forget, now returned with doubled force. Every circumstance of his queen's death came into his mind and kept him awake. Such a look of sorrow did this impress on his countenance that the next morning the sultan could not fail to remark it. The sultan did all he could to amuse his brother but the most splendid entertainments only served to increase Shahzeman's melancholy.

One morning when Shahriar had given orders for a grand hunting party at a distance of two days' journey from the city, Shahzeman requested permission to remain in his palace, excusing himself on account of a slight illness. The sultan was quite willing he should do as he chose, but he himself went with all his court to partake of the sport.

After the hunting party had gone, the King of Tartary sat alone in his apartment mourning over the calamity that had befallen him. As he sat thus grieving, he looked out of the open window down on the beautiful garden of the palace. Presently he observed the sultana, the beloved wife of his brother, come into the garden and meet a man with whom she held an affectionate and secret conversation. Evidently they were lovers. When Shahzeman witnessed this interview he determined within himself that he would no longer grieve over a misfortune which came to other husbands as

well as to himself. He ordered supper to be brought
and ate with a better appetite than he had shown since
his departure from Samarcand. He even enjoyed the
fine concert that was performed while he was at the
table.

Shahriar returned from hunting at the close of the
second day and was delighted to find his brother so
much more cheerful than when he went away. He
urged him to explain the cause of his former sorrow,
and the King of Tartary related the whole story of his
wife's misconduct, and of the severe punishment he
had visited on her.

Shahriar expressed a full approval of what his
brother had done and said in conclusion: "If I had
been in your place, I would not have been contented
with taking away the life of one woman. I would have
sacrificed a thousand. Surely, your fate is most singu-
lar. Since, however, it has pleased God to afford you
consolation, which doubtless is as well founded as the
cause of your grief, inform me, I beg, of that also."

Then Shahzeman revealed the faithlessness of the
sultana. Shahriar's rage over her conduct knew no
bounds. Not only did he sentence her to death, but he
solemnly vowed that in future, after his brother's departure, he would marry a new wife each night and
command her to be beheaded in the morning.

When Shahzeman was gone, the sultan began to put
into operation his unhappy oath. Every evening he

married the daughter of one of his subjects, and the next morning she was ordered out to execution. It was the duty of the grand vizier to provide the brides and see that the wives were killed. He was a kind-hearted man to whom this horrid injustice caused the keenest regret, but he was obliged to submit to the sultan's orders on peril of losing his own life. The monarch's cruelty spread a panic of universal fear through the city, and everywhere there were cries and lamentations. So instead of the praises and blessings which had hitherto been bestowed on the monarch, all his subjects poured out curses on his head.

The grand vizier had two daughters, the elder of whom was called Sheherazade, and the younger Dinarzade. Sheherazade was clever and courageous to a remarkable degree. She had read much, and never forgot anything she either read or heard. Moreover, her beauty excelled that of any other maiden in the entire realm of Persia.

One day, when the grand vizier was talking to this elder daughter, of whom he was passionately fond, she said: "Father, I have a favor to ask of you. Every day you have to provide a fresh wife for the sultan. I implore you to allow me to have the honor of being his next bride."

"Have you lost your senses?" cried the grand vizier. "You know very well the penalty."

"Yes," she replied, "but that does not deter me from my purpose. I have a plan for putting an end to the barbarous practice of the sultan. If I fail, my death will be glorious; and if I succeed I shall have done my country a great service."

Nothing the vizier could say served to shake his daughter's decision, and at last he yielded to her entreaties, and went sadly to the palace to announce to the sultan that Sheherazade would be his bride the following evening.

"Is it possible," said the astonished sultan, "that you are willing to sacrifice your own daughter?"

"Sir," replied the vizier, "she has herself made the offer. The dreadful fate that hangs over her does not alarm her. She resigns her life for the honor of being the consort of your Majesty."

"Vizier," said the sultan, "do not deceive yourself with any fancy that she will fare differently from those who have preceded her. Be assured that when I deliver her into your charge tomorrow, it will be with an order to strike off her head. If you attempt to disobey my command, your own head will be the forfeit."

"Though I am her father," answered the vizier, "I promise that you shall be obeyed."

When the grand vizier returned to Sheherazade she thanked him warmly for yielding to her wishes, and tried to console him in his grief by saying she hoped the outcome of her venture would be so fortunate that he would never repent having allowed her to marry the sultan.

Before Sheherazade went to the palace, she called her sister aside and said: "I am to become the bride of the sultan this very evening. As soon as I have been presented to his Highness, I shall entreat him to allow you to sleep near the bridal chamber that in the morning I may see you without delay and enjoy for the last time your company. If I obtain this favor, as I expect, re-member I shall awake you an hour before daybreak, and you must come in and say: 'My sister, I beg you to tell me one of those delightful stories you know.'

"I will immediately begin one, and I flatter myself that by means of my story-telling I shall free the realm from the terror that now overwhelms it."

Dinarzade promised to do what her sister requested and as soon as this matter had been arranged the vizier conducted Sheherazade to the palace where he left her with the sultan. Shahriar was charmed with her beauty; and he was quite ready to listen when she said she had a request to make.

"Sir," said she, "I have a sister whom I dearly love. Grant me the favor of allowing her to pass the night in an apartment adjoining ours, that we may see each other in the morning, and once more take a tender farewell."

Shahriar consented to the petition, and sent for Dinarzade. On the morrow Sheherazade awoke about an hour before day, and called to her sister, who soon came into the royal chamber. After greeting each other, Dinarzade said: "My dear sister, if you are willing, I entreat you to relate to me one of the charming stories you know. It will alas! be the last time I shall have that pleasure."

Sheherazade turned to the sultan and said: "Will your highness permit me to do as my sister asks?"

"Freely," he answered. So Sheherazade began.

II

THE MERCHANT AND THE GENIE

THERE was once a merchant who possessed great wealth in land, merchandise, and ready money. His business made it necessary that he should occasionally go on long journeys and he sometimes had to pass through regions that were very barren and lonely. It was therefore his custom to take with him a small bag full of dates and biscuits, lest he should suffer from hunger when he was in an uninhabited region. One day he mounted his horse, and started for a distant city. He arrived without any mishap at his destination, and as soon as he had finished his business set out to return.

On the fourth day of his homeward trip he went aside from the road to rest under some trees, for the heat of the sun was very great. At the foot of one of the trees was a spring of clear, cool water, and after tying his horse he sat down beside this spring to eat some food from his little store. While eating he amused himself by throwing around the stones of the fruit, and when he had satisfied his hunger he washed his hands, his face and his feet, and repeated a prayer, like a good Mohammedan.

He was still on his knees when he saw an aged genie, of great stature, advancing toward him with a cimeter in his hand. "Arise that I may kill you!" cried the genie in a terrible voice. "You have caused the death of my son."

As he finished uttering these words he gave a frightful yell. The merchant, quite as much terrified at the hideous face of the monster as at his words, responded tremblingly: "How can I have slain your son? I do not know him, nor have I seen him."

"Did you not, on your arrival here, sit down and take some dates from your wallet?" the giant asked; "and after eating them, did you not throw the stones about?"

"That is all true," replied the merchant. "I do not deny it."

"Well then," said the genie, "I tell you that you have killed my son; for while you were throwing the stones my son passed by. One of them struck him in the eye and caused his death."

"Oh, sir, forgive me!" cried the merchant.

"I shall show you neither forgiveness nor mercy," responded the genie. "Is it not just that he who has inflicted death should suffer it?"

"Yet surely, even if I have inflicted death," said the merchant, "I have done so innocently, and therefore I entreat you to pardon me and allow me to live."

"No, no," cried the genie, "I must destroy you."

So saying, he seized the merchant, threw him on the ground, and lifted his cimeter to strike off his head.

Sheherazade, at this instant, perceiving that the day had dawned, and knowing that the sultan rose early to pray and then to hold a council, ceased speaking.

"What a wonderful story!" said Dinarzade.

"The rest is still more wonderful," declared Sheherazade, "as you would agree, if the sultan would consent that I should live another day, and in the morning permit me to continue the relation."

Shahriar who had listened to the story with much pleasure, decided to defer the execution of Sheherazade until the morrow that he might hear the conclusion of the narrative. He now arose, and having prayed, went to the council.

All this time the grand vizier was in a terrible state of anxiety. He was unable to sleep, and he passed the night lamenting the approaching fate of his daughter. Great was his surprise when the sultan entered the council chamber without giving him the horrible order he expected.

The sultan spent the day, as usual, in regulating the affairs of his kingdom, and on the approach of night, retired with Sheherazade to his apartment.

On the next morning he did not wait for Sheherezade to ask permission to continue her story, but said: "Finish the tale of the genie and the merchant. I am curious to hear the end of it."*

She immediately went on as follows:

When the merchant saw that the genie was determined to slay him, he said: "One word more, I entreat you. Grant me a little delay. I ask only that you allow me to go home and bid farewell to my wife and children. Afterward I will return to this spot and submit myself to your pleasure."

"But if I grant you the delay you ask I am afraid you will not come back," said the genie.

"I give you my word of honor," responded the merchant, "that I will come back without fail."

"How long do you require?" asked the genie.

"I ask you for a year's grace," answered the merchant. "A twelvemonth from this day you will find me here under these trees ready to give myself up."

"Let God be witness of the promise you have made me," said the genie.

"Again I swear," said the merchant, "and you may rely on my oath."

Then the genie left him near the spring and disappeared.

As soon as the merchant had recovered a little from his fright he mounted his horse and resumed his journey.

---

*The sultana relates a fragment of a story each morning, and she never fails to break off in a most interesting part. This induces the sultan to spare her life another day that he may hear the end of the tale on which she is engaged. The thousand and one interruptions are omitted in the present edition.

At length he reached his home where he was received with the greatest joy by his wife and children. But when he told them of his promise to the genie, his wife uttered the most lamentable groans and tore her hair and beat her breast, and the children made the house resound with their grief.

The next day the merchant began to settle his affairs. He paid his debts, gave alms to the poor and presents to his friends and provided for his family. The year passed quickly, and the merchant, mindful of his oath, was obliged to depart. He arrived at the destined spot on the very day he had promised. While he sat beside the spring waiting for the genie, there appeared an old man leading a deer. The newcomer saluted the merchant respectfully and inquired what brought him to that desert place. So the merchant satisfied the old man's curiosity.

"This is a most marvellous affair," said the old man. "I would like to witness your interview with the genie."

Scarcely had he finished speaking when another old man, accompanied by two black dogs, came in sight. The newcomer greeted the other two and asked what they were doing there. So the old man with the deer repeated the tale of the merchant, and the second old man decided that he, too, would remain to see what would happen.

Soon they perceived in the distance a thick smoke like a cloud of dust raised by the wind. This smoke came nearer and nearer, and then it suddenly vanished, and they saw the genie. Cimeter in hand he approached the merchant and grasped his arm.

The merchant and his two companions began to weep and lament; but the old man with the deer hastily controlled his terror and kneeled at the monster's feet. "Lord Genie," said he, "I humbly entreat you to suspend your rage and listen to me. I wish to tell you my story and that of the deer, which you see; and if you find it more wonderful than the adventure of the merchant, whose life you intend to take, I hope you will grant me one-half of the body of this unfortunate man."

After meditating some time, the genie said: "Very well, I agree to your proposal."

III

THE OLD MAN AND THE DEER

THE deer that you see with me, Lord Genie, is my wife. After I married her we lived together thirty years without having any children. At the end of that time I adopted the son of a slave woman, intending to make him my heir. My wife, however, took a great dislike to both the slave woman and the child.

When my adopted son was grown to be a young man I was obliged to go on a journey, and I intrusted him and his mother to my wife's keeping. While I was absent my wife studied magic and became sufficiently expert to change the slave and my adopted son into a cow and a calf. Then she sent them to my farm to be fed and taken care of by my steward.

As soon as I returned I inquired after the lad and his mother. "Your slave is dead," my wife declared, "and it is more than two months since I have seen your son; nor do I know where he is."

I was grieved to hear of my slave's death, but as my son had only disappeared, I flattered myself that he would soon be found. Eight months passed, however, and I failed to get any tidings of him.

In order to celebrate a holy festival, which was then

approaching, I ordered my steward to bring me the fattest cow I possessed for a sacrifice. He did so. After binding the cow, I was about to kill her when she began to low most piteously, and I saw that her eyes were streaming with tears. This seemed to me so extraordinary that I could not but feel compassion for her, and was unable to give the fatal blow. I therefore ordered her to be led away and another brought.

My wife, who was present, scoffed at my compassion, and opposed my order. So I said to the steward: "Make the sacrifice yourself. I cannot, for the lamentations and tears of the animal have overcome me."

The steward promptly killed her. On removing the skin I was vexed to find hardly anything but bones, though she had appeared very fat. "Such a creature will not serve our purpose," said I to the steward. "If you have a fat calf bring that in her place."

He soon returned with a remarkably fine calf, which, as soon as it perceived me, made so great an effort to come to me, that it broke its cord. Then it ran to where I was, knelt at my feet, and acted as if it wished to excite my pity and to beg me not to take its life. Indeed, it turned its eyes, filled with tears, so persuasively on me that I had no power to execute my intention of killing it.

"Wife," said I, "I will not sacrifice this calf. I wish to favor it."

My wife tried every means to induce me to alter my

mind, but I continued firm in my resolution. Another calf was killed, and this one was led away.

The next morning my steward informed me that his daughter, who had some knowledge of magic, wished to see me. When she was admitted to my presence she told me that, during my absence, my wife had turned the slave and my son into a cow and a calf. "You have already sacrificed the cow," said she, "but I will restore your son to his natural self, if you will give him to me for a husband, and allow me to punish your wife as her cruelty deserves."

To these proposals I gave my consent and we immediately went to the stable where the calf was kept. The damsel then took a vessel of water, pronounced over it some words I did not understand, and threw the water on the calf, which instantly became a young man once more.

"My son! my dear son!" I exclaimed, kissing him in a transport of joy; "this damsel has rescued you from a terrible enchantment. To reward her I have promised that you will be her husband, and I am sure that your gratitude will prompt you to fulfil this promise."

He consented joyfully, but before they were married the young girl changed my wife into the deer you see before you. My son long ago became a widower, and is now travelling. Many years have passed since I have heard anything of him. I have therefore set out to search for him, and as I did not wish to trust my wife to the care of other people, I am taking her with me.

This is the story of myself and the deer. Can anything be more wonderful?

"It is so marvellous a story," said the genie, "that I grant you a half of the body of this merchant."

Now the second old man, who led the two black dogs said to the genie: "I, too, would like to relate my story; and I feel sure that you will find it even more astonishing than the one to which you have just been listening. If so, I ask that you grant me also a half of the merchant's body."

To this the genie agreed, and the old man began.

IV

THE SECOND OLD MAN AND THE TWO DOGS

THESE two black dogs and myself are three brothers. Our father, when he died, left us each one thousand sequins.* This sum enabled us to start in business as merchants, and we each opened a shop. But in a short time my eldest brother resolved to travel and trade in foreign countries. With this intention he sold all he had and bought merchandise suited to the journey he was about to make. He set out and was away a whole year. At the end of that time a beggar came to my shop.

"Good day," I said.

"Good day," he responded. "Is it possible you do not recognize me?"

Then I looked at him closely and saw he was my eldest brother. I made him come into my house, and asked him how he had fared in his enterprise.

"Do not question me," he said. "It would only renew my trouble to tell of all the misfortunes that have befallen me and brought me to this condition in the year I have been away."

I paid him every attention and gave him my best clothing. Then I examined my accounts, and when I

---

*A sequin was a gold coin worth about $2.25.

found that I had doubled my capital, I gave my brother half, saying: "Now, brother, you can forget your losses."

He accepted the thousand sequins with joy, and once more established himself in a shop.

Some time afterward my second brother wished also to sell his business and travel. I did all I could to dissuade him, but it was of no use. He joined a caravan and set out. At the end of a year he came back in the same state as our elder brother. But I took care of him, and as I had prospered, I gave him also a thousand sequins and helped him to reopen his shop.

My brothers were not content, however, to be simply shopkeepers, and they frequently proposed to me that we should all three make a voyage for the purpose of traffic. At first I refused to go. "You travelled," I said, "and what did you gain?"

But at the end of five years I yielded to their repeated requests. When we consulted about the merchandise to be bought for the voyage I discovered that nothing remained of the thousand sequins I had given to each. I did not reproach them. On the contrary, as my capital had increased to six thousand sequins, I again gave them each one thousand. I kept a like sum myself and buried the other three thousand in a corner of my house, so that if our voyage proved unsuccessful we might be able to console ourselves and begin in business anew. We bought goods, loaded a vessel with them, and set forth with a favorable wind.

After two months' sailing we arrived at a port where we disembarked and traded to great advantage. I, in particular, sold my merchandise so profitably that I gained ten for one.

While we were preparing to start on our return voyage, I chanced to meet on the seashore a woman of great beauty, but very poorly dressed. She came up to me, kissed my hand, and urged me most earnestly to permit her to be my wife. I stated many objections to such a plan; but she begged so hard, and promised to be such a good wife, that at last I consented. Then I provided some handsome dresses for her, and we were married. The vessel was by that time ready to sail and we went on board and the voyage began.

In the days that followed I found my wife possessed so many good qualities that I loved her every day more and more. Meanwhile, my brothers, who had not traded so profitably as I, were not only jealous of my prosperity, but were envious because of my happy marriage. They even plotted against my life; and one night they seized my wife and I, while we slept, and threw us into the sea. My wife, however, was a fairy, and she did not let me drown, but carried me to an island.

As soon as the day dawned she said to me: "When I saw you on the seashore, just before your vessel was ready to sail, I took a great fancy to you, and decided to test the goodness of your heart. So I presented myself before you in the disguise you saw. You acted most generously, and I am glad I have been able to reward you by saving your life. But I am very angry with your brothers, and I shall not be satisfied until they have been punished."

I thanked the fairy for her great kindness to me. "But, madam," said I, "I entreat you to pardon my brothers."

She questioned me about my past relations with them and I told her just what I had done for each. My account only increased her wrath, and she said: "I must fly after these ungrateful wretches. They shall not escape the fate they deserve. I will sink their vessel and send them to the bottom of the sea."

"Beautiful lady," said I, "for heaven's sake, moderate your indignation, and do not execute so dreadful an intention. Remember they are still my brothers, and that I am bound to return good for evil."

My words somewhat appeased her anger, and instead of following my brothers' vessel, she caught me up and in a moment transported me from the island where we were to the entrance of my own house. There she left me, and I opened the door and dug up the three thousand sequins which I had hidden. Afterward I went to my shop and received the congratulations of the merchants of the neighborhood on my safe return. When I went home I perceived two black dogs at the door of my house, and as soon as they saw me approaching they came to meet me with a strange air of sorrow and submission. I could not imagine what their actions meant, but just then the fairy appeared and said: "Be not surprised at seeing the two dogs. They are your brothers."

My blood ran cold on hearing this, and I inquired by what power they had been transformed into that state.

"It is I who have done it," replied the fairy, "and I have sunk their ship. They shall remain dogs for ten years."

Then after telling me where I could find her she vanished. The ten years are now nearly passed, and I am travelling to the place which is her abode.

This is my story, O Lord Genie. Do you not think it is a most extraordinary one?

"Yes," replied the genie, "I confess it is very wonderful, and I therefore grant you the other half of this merchant's body. You and your companion with the deer can dispose of him as you please."

So saying, the genie disappeared to the great joy of the merchant and the two old men. The merchant did not fail to bestow many thanks on his liberators, and then each went on his way. In due time the merchant reached home, where he was warmly welcomed, and spent the remainder of his days with his family in happiness and tranquillity.

V

THE STORY OF THE FISHERMAN

THERE was once an aged fisherman who was so poor that he could scarcely manage to support his wife and three children. One morning, when he had resorted to the seashore as usual to fish, he cast his net and drew it to land four times in succession feeling assured each time from the resistance and weight that he had secured an excellent draught of fish. But he only found on the first haul the carcass of a donkey; and his net was badly broken by the burden. After mending the breaks he tried again, and this time drew in a big wicker basket filled with sand and mud.

He was much annoyed. "O Fortune!" he cried, "do not trifle thus with a poor, hardworking fisherman."

But his third haul resulted no better. He simply drew in his net filled with stones and shells. Almost in despair he threw his net for the fourth time. Again he supposed he had caught a great quantity of fish, and he pulled the net forth with as much difficulty as before. Nevertheless, not a fish was there in it, but instead a heavy copper vase, closed and fastened with lead, on which was the impression of a seal. "This vase at least is a thing of some value," said the fisherman joyfully. "I will sell it to a metal-worker, and with the money I get for it I will buy a measure of wheat."

He examined the vase on all sides, and he shook it, but could hear nothing; and yet the impression of the seal on the lead made him think it was filled with something valuable. To find out whether he was right in his surmise, he took his knife, and with a little trouble got the vase open. Then he turned it upside down and was much surprised that nothing came out. So he set the vase on the ground and was attentively observing it when there issued from it so dense a smoke that he was obliged to step back a few paces. This smoke by degrees rose far up toward the sky and spread over both the water and the shore, appearing like a thick mist. After it had all come out of the vase it gathered into a solid body and took the shape of a genie of gigantic size.

At sight of this terrible-looking monster, the fisherman wanted to run away, but he was too frightened to move a step. The genie turned his eyes toward the fisherman and said: "Humble yourself before me. I intend to kill you."

"For what reason will you kill me?" asked the fisherman. "Have you already forgotten that I set you at liberty?"

"No," answered the genie; "but that will not prevent me from destroying you, and I will only grant you one favor."

The fisherman

"And pray what is that?" said the fisherman.

"It is to permit you to choose the manner of your death," replied the genie. "I am a spirit who, thousands of years ago rebelled against God. Solomon, the wise king of Israel, inclosed me in this copper vase as a punishment, and put his seal on the leaden cover. This done, he had the vase cast into the sea.

"During the first century of my captivity, I vowed that if anyone should free me before a hundred years were passed, I would make him rich. During the second century I vowed that I would give all the treasures in the world to my deliverer. During the third I promised to make my liberator a most powerful monarch, and to grant him three wishes every day. These centuries passed away, and I was still in the vase. Then, enraged at my long captivity, I swore that I would without mercy kill whoever should in future release me, as a revenge for not being set free sooner, and that the only favor I would grant him should be to choose the manner of his death. Since, therefore, you have delivered me, select whatever kind of death you please."

The fisherman was greatly distressed. "Alas!" he cried, "have pity on me. Remember what I have done for you."

"Let us lose no time," responded the genie. "Your arguments avail not. Tell me how you wish to die."

Necessity is the mother of invention, and the fisherman thought of a stratagem. "Since I cannot escape death," said he, "I submit to my fate; but before I name the sort of death I choose answer me truly a question I am going to put to you."

"Ask what you will and make haste," said the genie.

"My question is this," said the fisherman: "Dare you to swear that you were really in this vase? It cannot contain one of your feet. How then could it hold your entire body?"

"I swear to you, notwithstanding," replied the genie, "that I was in the vase. Will you not believe me?"

"No," declared the fisherman, "I shall not believe you unless I see you return into it."

Immediately the form of the genie began to change into smoke, and the smoke had presently spread over both the shore and the sea. Then it collected and began to enter the vase, and it continued to do so in a slow and equal manner till nothing remained outside. A voice was now heard from the vase saying: "Well, unbelieving fisherman, here I am where I was before. You see I spoke only the truth."

Instead of answering, the fisherman seized the leaden cover and put it on the vase. "Genie!" he shouted, "it is now your turn to beg for mercy. I shall throw you again into the sea, and I will build a house on the shore, in which I will live to warn all fishermen who come here not to fish up such a wicked genie as you are, who vows to kill the man that sets him at liberty."

The genie tried for a long time in vain to rouse the

fisherman's pity. "You are too treacherous for me to trust you," the fisherman affirmed. "I would deserve to lose my life if I put myself in your power a second time."

So saying, he grasped the vase and was about to throw it back into the water when the genie cried: "One word more, fisherman; I will teach you how to be rich."

"I would listen to you," said the fisherman, "were there any credit to be given to your word. Swear to me by the great name of God that you will faithfully perform what you promise, and I will open the vase. I do not believe you will dare to break such an oath."

The genie promised, and the fisherman took off the covering of the vase. Instantly the smoke ascended, and the genie resumed his natural form and kicked the vase into the sea. Then he turned to the fisherman and said: "Take your net and follow me. I will show you that I intend to keep my word."

They passed over the top of a mountain and descended to a vast plain where they at length came to a lake situated between four small hills. "Fisherman," said the genie, "throw your net and catch fish."

The fisherman could see a great number of fish in the water, and he was surprised to observe that they were of four different colors—white, red, blue and yellow. He threw his net and caught one of each color. As he had never seen any fish like them he admired them greatly and he was pleased to think how much money they would bring.

"Carry these fish to the palace," said the genie, "and present them to the sultan, and he will give you more money than you ever before handled in all your life. You may come every day to fish in this lake, but beware of casting your net more than once each day. This is my advice, and if you follow it exactly you will do well."

When the genie finished speaking he struck his foot on the ground, which immediately opened in a wide crack, swallowed him up and then closed.

The fisherman walked back to the town and presented his fish at the sultan's palace. They were so unusual that they were promptly shown to the sultan himself. He observed the four fish attentively, and after admiring them for a long time said to his grand vizier: "Take these fish to the cook. I think they must be as good to eat as they are beautiful; and give the fisherman four hundred pieces of gold."

The vizier first paid the fisherman, who joyfully hastened home to use the gold in relieving the wants of his family. After the fisherman had gone his way the vizier carried the four fish to the cook. She soon had them cleaned, and then put them on the fire in a frying-pan. When she thought them sufficiently done on one side she turned them over. At that moment, wonderful to relate, the wall of the kitchen opened, and a young lady of marvellous beauty appeared. She was dressed in a satin robe embroidered with flowers, and wore gold bracelets and a necklace of large pearls, and she held a rod in her hand. The cook, greatly amazed, remained motionless, while the lady moved toward the frying-pan, struck one of the fish with her rod, and said: "Fish, fish, are you doing your duty?"

Then the four fish raised themselves up and said very distinctly: "Yes, yes, if you reckon, we reckon. If you pay your debts, we pay ours. If you fly we conquer and are content."

When they had spoken these words the damsel overturned the frying-pan, and entered the opening in the wall, which at once closed and left no mark to show where it had been.

The cook, as soon as she had recovered from her fright, went to take up the fish, but these had fallen into the ashes. They were as black as coals and not fit to be sent to the sultan. At this she began to weep and lament, saying: "Alas! what will become of me. No one will believe me when I tell what I have seen, and the sultan will be very angry."

While she was thus distressed, the grand vizier entered the kitchen and asked if the fish were ready. The cook then related all that had taken place; but when the vizier returned to the sultan, instead of telling what had really happened, he invented an excuse that satisfied his royal master, and sent to the fisherman for four more fish. These the fisherman promised to bring the next morning.

He set out before dawn and went to the lake. Then

he cast his net, and drawing it out found four fish like those he had taken the day previous, each of a different color. Without further delay he plodded back to the city, and carried the fish to the grand vizier, who paid him handsomely and took them to the kitchen. There the vizier shut himself up with the cook, and she prepared the fish for frying and put them on the fire. The grand vizier then witnessed an exact repetition of all that the cook had told him.

"This is too extraordinary to be kept from the sultan's ears," he said. "I will go and inform him of the wonder."

The sultan was much surprised and wished to see the marvel himself. So he sent for the fisherman, and said to him: "Can you bring me four more such fish?"

The fisherman said he could, and early the next day, he went again to the lake. Just as hitherto, he caught four fish of different colors at the first throw of his net, and then he hastened with them to the palace. The sultan expressed the greatest pleasure at seeing them, and ordered four hundred more pieces of money to be given to the fisherman.

Then he shut himself up with the grand vizier in a room that contained everything necessary for frying the fish. The vizier put them on the fire in a pan, and as soon as they were done on one side he turned them on the other. Immediately the wall of the room opened, but instead of the beautiful lady, there appeared a black man of gigantic stature dressed like a slave, and holding a large green staff in his hand. He advanced to the frying-pan, and touching one of the fish with his rod, he cried out in a terrible voice: "Fish, fish, are you doing your duty?"

At these words all the fish lifted up their heads and said: "Yes, yes, we are. If you reckon, we reckon. If you pay your debts, we pay ours. If you fly, we conquer and are content."

Then the black man overturned the frying-pan into the fire and entered the aperture in the wall, which at once closed, and the wall appeared as it did before.

"These fish signify some mystery that I must clear up," said the sultan.

He sent for the fisherman and asked him where the fish came from; and when he learned that they had been caught in a lake not more than three hours' journey from the palace, he commanded all his court to mount horses and set out for the place, with the fisherman as a guide. After they arrived at the lake, and the sultan had observed the fish in it with great admiration, he demanded of his courtiers if it were possible they had never seen this lake, which was within so short a distance of the city. They all said they had never so much as heard of it, though they had often hunted in the vicinity.

"I am not less astonished than you at this novelty," said he, "and I am resolved not to return to my palace till I have learned how this lake came here, and why the fish in it are of four colors."

He then ordered his court to encamp on its borders. When night came the sultan called his vizier, and said: "My mind is much disturbed. The only way to gain information is to seek it, and I intend to go from the camp quite alone this night and see what I can find out. I trust you to keep my departure a profound secret. Remain in my tent, and when my courtiers present themselves at the entrance tomorrow morning, send them away. Say I wish to be alone, and day by day make the same report till I come back."

The grand vizier tried to persuade the sultan not to go, but he pleaded in vain.

VI

THE YOUNG KING OF THE BLACK ISLES

THAT very night, as soon as everything in the camp was quiet, the sultan took his cimeter and left the tent. He passed over one of the small hills and descended to the plain beyond. When the sun rose he found himself near a grand palace built of polished black marble. Delighted that he had so soon encountered something worthy of investigation he went to the front of the palace and knocked at the gate. He waited for some time without getting any response. "If this palace is deserted," said he, "I have nothing to fear; and if it is inhabited, I have wherewith to defend myself."

The gate was not locked, and he passed through it into a spacious court. There he shouted as loud as he could, but received no answer. He then went into a superb hall, in the middle of which was a large fountain with a lion of massive gold at each corner. The sultan wandered a long time from room to room, until, being tired with walking, he sat down on a veranda which faced toward a garden full of all kinds of flowers and shrubs. Suddenly a plaintive voice from within the palace reached his ears. He listened attentively and heard these melancholy words: "Oh that I could die, for I am too unhappy to wish to live any longer!"

The sultan immediately rose and went toward the spot whence the voice issued, and drawing a door-curtain aside saw a young man very richly dressed seated on a sort of throne. The sultan approached and saluted him, and the young man bowed but did not get up. "My lord, I would rise to receive you," he said, "if I was able to do so. As I am not, I trust you will pardon my apparent lack of courtesy."

"Whatever may be your motive for not rising," responded the sultan, "I willingly accept your apologies. I come to offer you help. But first tell me the meaning of the lake in this vicinity where the fish are of four different colors, and explain also why you are thus alone in this great palace."

Instead of answering these questions the young man lifted his robe so the sultan perceived he was a living man only to his waist, and that thence to his feet he was changed into black marble.

"What you show me," said the sultan, "fills me with horror. I am impatient to hear your history. Pray relate it."

"I willingly comply," said the young man. "This is the kingdom of the Black Isles of which my father was the ruler. After his death I succeeded him, and within a short time I married. My wife and I lived happily together for five years, when I began to perceive that she no longer loved me.

"One day, after dinner, she went to the garden, and I lay down on a sofa to have a nap. Two of her servant maids came and sat, one at my head and the other at my feet, with fans in their hands to moderate the heat and to prevent the flies disturbing me. They thought I was asleep, and engaged in a whispered conversation, but as I had only closed my eyes I heard all they said.

"'Is not the queen wrong,' observed one to the other, 'not to love so amiable a person as our master?'

"'Certainly,' was the reply, 'and I cannot understand why she goes out every night and leaves him. Does he not know of it?'

"'How could he?' resumed the first. 'She mixes in his drink, every evening, the juice of a certain herb, which makes him sleep all night so soundly that she has time to go wherever she likes; and when at break of day she returns, she rouses him by the smell of some scent she puts under his nostrils.'

"I pretended to awake without having heard the conversation. That night, before I went to bed, the queen presented to me the cup of water which it was usual for me to take, but instead of drinking it, I approached an open window and threw out the water without her observing what I did. I then returned the cup into her hands, that she might believe I had drunk the contents. We soon retired to rest, and, shortly after, supposing that I was asleep, she got up, dressed herself and left the chamber. A few moments later there came to my ears the sound of a door closing softly behind her as she went out of the palace.

"I at once arose, dressed in haste, took my cimeter, and followed her so quickly that I soon had almost overtaken her and could hear the sound of her feet before me. With stealthy steps I walked after her until she entered a little wood, the paths of which were guarded by thick hedgerows. Here she was joined by a man, and from behind a hedgerow I listened while she offered to fly with him to another land. Enraged at this I leaped forth from my concealment, and struck him with my cimeter. He fell, and I retired in haste and secrecy to the palace.

"Although I had inflicted a mortal wound, yet the queen by her enchantments contrived to preserve in her lover a trance-like existence which could neither be called death nor life. On her return to our chamber she was absorbed in grief, and when the day dawned she requested my permission to build a tomb for herself on the grounds of the palace.

"I consented, and she built a stately edifice which she called the Palace of Tears. After it was finished, she caused her lover to be conveyed thither, and there she wept and bewailed over him daily. Presently I went myself to the tomb the queen had built. She was addressing the inanimate body in words of passionate

affection. This made me lose all patience, and I drew
my cimeter to punish her. But she turned on me with
a disdainful smile, pronounced some magic words, and
added: 'By my enchantments, I command you to
become half marble.'

"Immediately I became what I now am. As soon
as this cruel sorceress had thus transformed me she had
me conveyed to this apartment, and then destroyed my
capital by reducing the site of it to the lake and desert
plain you have seen. The fish of four colors in the lake
are the four kinds of inhabitants of different religions
which the city contained. The white are the Moham-
medans, the red the Fire Worshippers, the blue the
Christians, and the yellow the Jews. To add to my
affliction, the enchantress comes every day and gives
me on my naked back a hundred lashes with a whip."

When the young king finished his narrative he could
not restrain his tears, and the sultan was himself greatly
affected. "Where is this wicked woman?" asked the
sultan.

"I do not know where she stays," answered the king,
"but every day, after she has beaten me she goes to see
if her lover is any better."

"Unfortunate king," said the sultan, "I will do
what I can to revenge you."

The sultan then proceeded to the Palace of Tears,
which he found lighted with a great number of torches
of white wax, and perfumed by a delicious scent issuing

from several censers of fine gold. He drew his cimeter and destroyed the remnant of life left in the queen's lover and then dragged the body to the outer court and threw it into a well. That done, he lay down on the couch the lover had occupied, placed his cimeter under the covering, and waited for the enchantress to appear.

Shortly afterward, the queen arrived in the apartment of the young king, who at her approach filled the palace with his lamentations and begged her to take pity on him. She, however, ceased not to beat him till she had completed the hundred blows. Next she went to the Palace of Tears. "Alas!" she cried, addressing the person on the couch, whom she supposed was her lover, "will you always, light of my life, preserve this silence?"

The sultan, lowering his voice as if in great weakness, spoke a few words.

"My dear lord!" exclaimed the sorceress joyfully, "is it really your voice that I hear?"

"Wretched woman," responded the sultan, "are you worthy of an answer?"

"What! Do you reproach me?" said the queen.

"The cries, the tears, the groans of your husband, whom you every day beat so cruelly, prevent my rest," answered the supposed lover. "I should have long since recovered the use of my tongue if you had disenchanted him."

The enchantress and the young king

"I am ready to obey your commands," said she. "Would you have me restore him?"

"Yes," replied the sultan, "make haste and set him at liberty that I may no longer be disturbed by his moanings."

The queen at once left the Palace of Tears, and taking a vessel of water went to the apartment where the young king was. "Reassume your natural form," said she, throwing the water over him.

Immediately the marble limbs of the king became flesh, and he rose with all possible joy. "Go from this palace and never return," ordered the enchantress.

So he retired and hid himself. Meanwhile the queen returned to the Palace of Tears, and still fancying that she spoke to her lover said: "I have done as you wished me to do."

"What you have done yet is not sufficient to cure me," said the sultan, disguising his voice as before. "The fish every midnight raise their heads out of the lake and cry for vengeance against you and me. This is what delays my cure. Go speedily and restore everything to its former state. When you return I will give you my hand and you shall help me to rise."

The enchantress hurried away to the border of the lake, took a little water in her hand and scattered it about. She had no sooner done this and pronounced certain words than the city appeared, and the fish became men, women and children, and the houses and shops and everything were restored to the same condition as before the enchantment. Now the sorceress hastened back to the Palace of Tears. "Dear heart!" she cried, on entering, "I have done all you required of me. Give me your hand and arise."

He reached forth his hand and she helped him to his feet, when, without a moment's warning, he slew her with a blow of his cimeter. Then he went and joined the young king of the Black Isles. "Rejoice," said he, "you have nothing more to fear. Your cruel enemy is dead; and now I will go back to my capital, which I am glad to find is so near yours."

"So near mine!" exclaimed the King of the Black Isles. "Potent monarch to whom I owe so much, do you really think that you are near your capital?"

"Yes," replied the sultan, "it is not more than two or three hours' journey from here."

"It is a whole year's journey," the king declared. "I do indeed believe you came hither in the time you mention, but, since my domain has been disenchanted, things are different."

"Can you not go with me?" asked the sultan. "I promise you a hearty welcome at my capital and you shall have as much honor and respect shown you as if you were in your own kingdom."

"I will follow you to the ends of the earth," declared the young king.

"Your decision to accompany me gives me great

happiness," said the sultan, "and as I have no children I intend to adopt you and make you my heir and successor."

After a few days of preparation they began their journey, taking with them a hundred camels laden with riches from the treasury of the young king. For a twelve-month they were on the way, and then they arrived at the sultan's capital where they were received by the inhabitants with every sign of joy. The next day the sultan assembled his court and announced to them his intention of adopting the King of the Black Isles. Then he bestowed presents on all, according to each person's rank and station; nor did he forget the fisherman, but made him and his family happy and comfortable for the rest of their days.

VII

PRINCE AHMED AND THE FAIRY

THERE was a sultan of India who had three sons and a niece. The eldest son was called Houssain, the second Ali, and the youngest Ahmed. The name of their cousin was Nouronnihar. She was the daughter of a favorite brother of the sultan who had died young, and she had been brought up in the palace from childhood. Her wit and beauty were admired by all who knew her, and as soon as she arrived at a proper age the sultan began to arrange that she should become the wife of the ruler of a neighboring kingdom. However, while the negotiations were still pending, he found that his three sons loved the princess, and each wished to marry her. The discovery caused him great grief—not because their wishes were contrary to his own plans for her future, but because of the discord this mutual passion would be likely to occasion among them.

He was quite willing that one of his sons should marry the princess, but with all three eager to wed her he was puzzled what to do. At last he spoke to each of them separately, and urged them to let the princess herself decide which she would have for her husband; or that all should agree to resign their claims to her and allow her to marry a stranger. But they obstinately refused to do either the one thing or the other.

The sultan therefore had them all appear before him, and said: "My sons, since I have not been able to persuade you in this matter, and as I have no wish to use my authority to give the princess to one in preference to another, I have thought of a plan to solve the difficulty. It will please you all and preserve harmony among you, if you will listen to my advice. I suggest that you travel into different countries, and my niece shall marry him who brings home to me the most extraordinary rarity. For the purchase of the rarity and the expense of travelling I will give you each a sufficient sum of money."

The three princes cheerfully consented to this proposal, and each flattered himself that fortune would prove favorable to him and that the princess would become his wife. Preparations for the journey were at once begun, and early the next morning they left the city, each dressed like a merchant, well mounted and equipped, and attended by a trusty officer. They proceeded the first day's journey together, and when evening came they stopped at an inn. While they were at supper they agreed to travel for a twelve-month and then to meet at that inn, and return to their father's court in company. The next morning by break of day, after they had embraced and wished each other a safe journey, they mounted their horses and each took a different road.

Prince Houssain bent his course toward the coast of India; and after three months' travelling with various caravans, sometimes over deserts and barren mountains, and sometimes through populous and fertile countries, arrived at Bisnagar.* He engaged lodgings at an inn and went to the bazaars where merchants of all kinds had their places of business. The multitude of shops and the wealth of goods they contained surprised him very much. He was especially delighted with the wares displayed by the goldsmiths and jewellers, and was fairly dazzled by the lustre of the pearls, diamonds, rubies, emeralds, and other precious stones exposed for sale.

After Prince Houssain had gone through a number of streets, a merchant who saw that he was fatigued, invited him to sit down in front of his shop. He had scarcely accepted this invitation when a crier appeared, having on his arm a piece of carpet, about six feet square, which he offered at forty purses. The prince called to the crier and asked to see the carpet. When he had examined it he told the crier he could not comprehend why so small a piece of carpet and one of so indifferent an appearance, should be held at so high a price, unless it had some extraordinary quality of which he was ignorant.

*Now called Baroda, a city in India about two hundred miles north of Bombay.

"You have guessed the reason," responded the crier. "Whoever sits on this piece of carpet may be transported in an instant wherever he desires to be."

"If the carpet has the virtue you attribute to it," said Houssain, "I will buy it and not think forty purses too high a price."

"Sir," said the crier, "I have told you the truth, and with the permission of the master of this shop, we will go into his rear apartment, where I will spread the carpet. When we have both sat down on it, and you have wished to be transported to your room at the inn, if we are not conveyed thither I will not ask you to buy."

The prince accepted the conditions and they went into the back shop. There they both sat down on the carpet, and as soon as the prince had formed a wish to be transported to his room at the inn he found that the carpet had conveyed him and his companion thither. This proof of the virtue of the carpet was sufficiently convincing, and he counted to the crier forty purses of gold, and gave him twenty pieces for himself.

In this manner Prince Houssain became the possessor of the carpet, and he was overjoyed that he had found so rare a curiosity, for he did not doubt it would gain him the hand of Nouronnihar. That his younger brothers should find anything to be compared with it seemed impossible. If he chose, he could sit on the carpet and be at the place of meeting that very day; but as he would be obliged to wait there for his brothers until the time they had agreed on, he decided to remain at Bisnagar. After a time, however, having seen all the wonders of the city, he wished to be nearer his dear Princess Nouronnihar. So he spread the carpet and had it transport him and his attendant to the inn where he and his brothers were to meet. There he passed for a merchant till their arrival.

Prince Ali, the second brother, joined a caravan and travelled into Persia. After being four months on the way, he arrived at Shiraz, the capital, and the next morning he went for a walk into that quarter of the town where the jewellers had their shops. While he was there he was not a little surprised to see a crier, who held in his hand an ivory tube, about a foot in length, and about an inch thick, which he offered at forty purses. Ali's first thought was that the crier must be crazy, and he asked him what he meant by charging such a sum of money for a tube that seemed to be a thing of no value.

"Sir," said the crier, "you are not the only person who takes me for a madman on account of this tube. You shall judge for yourself whether I am or not, when I have told you its peculiar power. By looking through it, you can see whatever object you wish to behold."

The crier handed him the tube, and Ali looked through, wishing at the same time to see the sultan his father. He immediately beheld him in perfect health, sitting on his throne in the midst of his council. Next he wished to see the Princess Nouronnihar, and instantly beheld her laughing in a gay humor with her women about her.

Prince Ali wanted no other proof to persuade him that this tube was the most valuable thing in the world, and he said to the crier: "I am very sorry that I have entertained so wrong an opinion of you, but I hope to make amends by purchasing the tube, and I will give you the price you ask."

The prince then took the crier to the inn where he lodged, counted out the money and received the tube. He was overjoyed at his bargain and felt certain that his brothers would not find anything so wonderful. Therefore the Princess Nouronnihar must be the recompense of his fatigue and trouble. He now thought of nothing but seeing whatever was curious in Shiraz and thereabouts, until the caravan with which he came was ready to return to the Indies. When the caravan departed he went with it and arrived happily without any accident at the inn where he and his brothers had agreed to meet. There he found Prince Houssain, and both waited for Prince Ahmed.

Prince Ahmed had chosen to go to Samarcand, and the day after his arrival, he went, as his brothers had done, to the streets where the merchants had their shops. While walking about there, he heard a crier offer at forty purses, an artificial apple, which he carried in his hand. The prince stopped the crier, and said to him: "Let me see that apple, and tell me what virtue it possesses to be valued at so high a rate."

"Sir," said the crier, "if you look at the outside of this apple, it is not very remarkable, but if you consider the benefits it can confer, you will agree that it is invaluable. It cures all sick persons of every disease, and even patients who are dying are restored to perfect health. This it does merely by the patient's smelling it."

"If I may believe you," responded Prince Ahmed, "the person who possesses such an apple is master of a great treasure; but how am I to know that you do not err in the high praises you bestow on it?"

"The truth of what I say is known by the whole city," declared the crier. "Ask any of these merchants. You will find several of them will tell you they would not now be alive, had they not made use of this excellent remedy."

While the crier was detailing to Prince Ahmed the merits of the artificial apple, many persons gathered round them, and confirmed what he declared; and one among the rest said he had a friend dangerously ill, whose life was despaired of. Here was a favorable opportunity to show the apple's power, and Prince Ahmed told the crier he would give forty purses for the apple, if it cured this sick person.

"Come, sir," said the crier, "let us go and make the experiment, and the apple shall be yours."

The experiment succeeded, and the prince at once counted out to the crier forty purses and received the apple. In the days that followed he spent his time in

seeing all that was curious at Samarcand and roundabout. When a caravan presently set out for the Indies
he joined it and arrived in perfect health at the inn
where the Princes Houssain and Ali waited for him.

The brothers embraced with tenderness, and com-
plimented each other on the happiness of meeting in
safety after being parted a whole year. Houssain then
said: "We shall have time enough hereafter to describe
our travels. Let us show each other at once the curiosities we have brought, that we may ourselves judge to
which of us the sultan, our father, is likely to give the
preference. I will tell you that the rarity I have brought
from Bisnagar is the carpet on which I sit. It looks
ordinary, yet its virtues are wonderful. Whoever sits
on it, and desires to be transported to any place, be it
ever so distant, is immediately carried thither. To
return here I made no use of any conveyance except
this marvellous carpet, for which I paid forty purses.
I expect now that you will tell me whether the rarities
you have brought are to be compared with mine."

Prince Ali spoke next. "I acknowledge, brother,"
said he, "that your carpet is a most surprising curiosity,
but I have secured an ivory tube which I think is no
less worthy. I acknowledge that it appears commonplace, yet it cost me forty purses, and I am as well
satisfied with my purchase as you are with yours; for
on looking in at one end of this tube you can see what-

ever you wish to behold. I would have you make a trial of it yourself."

Houssain took the tube, and wished to see the Princess Nouronnihar. To the great surprise of his brothers they saw his countenance suddenly express extraordinary alarm and affliction. "Alas!" cried he, "to what purpose have we undertaken such long and fatiguing journeys, with the hope of being rewarded by the hand of our charming cousin? In a few moments the lovely princess will breathe her last. I see her in bed, surrounded by her women, who are all weeping and evidently expect her death. Take the tube, Ali. Behold yourself the miserable state she is in, and mingle your tears with mine."

Prince Ali received the tube and after having looked through it with the deepest grief presented it to Ahmed, and he likewise perceived the sad sight which so much concerned them all.

"Brothers," said Ahmed, "the princess is indeed at death's door, but it is possible that we may yet preserve her life. This apple which you see cost the same as the carpet and the tube; and it has the surprising power of restoring a sick person to health by its smell, whatever be the malady."

"Let us transport ourselves instantly into the chamber of the princess by means of my carpet," said Prince Houssain, "and Ahmed shall try the effect on her of his wonderful apple. Come, lose no time. Be seated on the carpet at once. It is large enough to hold us all."

Ali and Ahmed sat down by Houssain and the carpet immediately conveyed them to the chamber of the sick princess. They were not recognized at first, and the attendants in the room were greatly alarmed at the sudden appearance of three strange men in their midst. The guards were about to attack them when the princes made known who they were.

Ahmed then went to Nouronnihar's bedside, and put the apple to her nostrils. Instantly she opened her eyes, sat up and asked to be dressed. She appeared perfectly well, and as if she had awakened out of a sound sleep. Her women informed her that she was indebted to the three princes, and particularly to Prince Ahmed for the sudden recovery of her health. She expressed her joy at seeing them, and thanked them all, but especially Prince Ahmed.

The three young men now retired and went to present themselves to their father. They found he had already been informed of their arrival and by what means the princess had been so suddenly cured. He received them with the greatest joy, both for their return and the wonderful recovery of his niece, whom he loved as if she had been his own daughter. When the greetings were over the princes showed the rarities they had brought, and, after extolling their virtues, begged the sultan to declare which son should have Nouronnihar for a wife.

The sultan remained some time silent, considering what answer he should make. At last he said: "I would declare for one of you, my sons, if I could do so with justice. You have illustrated very effectively the value of the rarities you found. To the artificial apple the princess is indebted for her cure; but let me ask you, Ahmed, whether you could have contrived to cure her if Ali's tube had not revealed the danger she was in, and if Houssain's carpet had not brought you to her so swiftly? Your tube, Ali, made known to you and your brothers the illness of your cousin; but you must grant that this would not have saved her without the apple and the carpet. As for you, Houssain, your carpet was an essential means for effecting her cure; but it would have been of little use, if you had not been acquainted with her illness by Ali's tube, or if Ahmed had not applied his artificial apple. Therefore, my sons, as none of the rarities you secured has preference over the others, I cannot grant the princess to any one of you. The only satisfaction you have gained from your travels is the happiness of having equally contributed to restore her to health.

"This being the case, I must resort to other means to determine the choice; and there is time between now and night to do it. Each of you go and get a bow and arrow, and repair to the great plain where the horses are exercised. I will soon join you, and will give the Princess Nouronnihar to him who shoots farthest."

The three princes had nothing to say against the decision of the sultan, and promptly provided themselves with bows and arrows. Then they went to the plain followed by a great concourse of people.

As soon as the sultan arrived Prince Houssain shot his arrow. Prince Ali shot next, and his arrow went much beyond Houssain's. The last to shoot was Prince Ahmed; but it so happened that nobody saw where his arrow fell; and notwithstanding all the search made by him and by the spectators it was not to be found. So the sultan determined in favor of Prince Ali, and gave orders to prepare for his and Nouronnihar's wedding. This was celebrated a few days later with great magnificence.

Prince Houssain would not honor the festivities with his presence. His love for the princess was so sincere and ardent that he could not endure to see her marry another. In short, such was his grief that he left the court, renounced all right of succession to the crown, and became a hermit.

Nor did Prince Ahmed go to the wedding, but on the day it occurred he went to the plain where the archery contest had taken place. He could not imagine what had become of his arrow, and he was resolved to search for it again. Starting where his brothers' arrows were picked up, he walked straight on looking carefully on both sides as he advanced. He went so far that he began to conclude his labor was in vain; yet he kept on till he came to some steep craggy rocks, which prevented any farther progress.

At the foot of these rocks he perceived an arrow, which, to his great astonishment, he found was the same he had shot. "Certainly," he said to himself, "neither I nor any other man could shoot an arrow so far. There is some mystery in this; and perhaps fortune, to make amends for depriving me of what I thought the greatest happiness of my life, may have reserved a richer blessing for my comfort."

On looking around, the prince beheld in a wall of rock, close at hand, an iron door. It was closed, but when he pushed against it, the door opened and revealed a staircase. Down this the prince walked expecting presently to be in pitch darkness; but he soon came forth into a spacious and brilliantly lighted cavern where was a splendid palace. While he stood gazing at the palace a lady of majestic air advanced toward him. She was adorned with a wealth of jewels and attended by a troop of ladies, who were scarcely less magnificently dressed than their mistress.

When Ahmed saw the lady, he hastened forward to greet her; but she addressed him first, saying: "Welcome, Prince Ahmed."

It was no small surprise to the prince to have his name spoken in this strange place, and by a lady whom he had never seen before. "Madam," said he, "I thank you heartily for your assurance that I am welcome. I

Prince Ahmed enters the underground palace

feared my imprudent curiosity had led me to penetrate too far. But, may I, without giving offence ask by what chance you know me?"

"Prince," said the lady, "let us go into the palace, and there I will gratify your curiosity."

She led the way into a noble hall and sat down on a sofa. At her request the prince also seated himself, and she said: "You know that the world is inhabited by genies as well as by men. I am a fairy, the daughter of one of the most powerful of these genies, and my name is Periebanou. Your love and your travels are well known to me, and the artificial apple you bought at Samarcand, the carpet Prince Houssain purchased at Bisnagar, and the tube Prince Ali brought from Shiraz were of my contrivance. You seemed to me worthy of a better fate than to marry the Princess Nouronnihar. Therefore I caused your arrow to fly out of sight and strike against the rocks near which you found it. You now have the chance to avail yourself of a favorable opportunity to make you happy."

The fairy pronounced her last words with a different tone, and after looking tenderly at the prince, sat with downcast eyes and a modest blush on her cheeks. It was not difficult for him to comprehend what happiness she meant, and he said: "If I could have the pleasure of making you the partner of my life, I would think myself the most blest of men."

"Then you are my husband," responded the Periebanou, "and I am your wife; for our fairy marriages are contracted with no other ceremonies than a mutual consent. I will give orders for the preparation of our wedding feast which will be served this evening, and while it is being made ready I will show you my palace."

The fairy led Ahmed through many beautiful apartments, where he saw diamonds, rubies, emeralds, and all sorts of fine jewels and precious marbles, and the richest of furniture. At last he and the fairy entered a hall adorned with an infinite number of wax candles perfumed with amber. Here were tables loaded with tempting viands and delicious drinks, and the prince sat down with the fairy and her attendants to enjoy the feast. While they ate and drank they were entertained by singing and the music of many harmonious instruments. After the dessert, which consisted of the choicest fruits and sweetmeats, Periebanou and Prince Ahmed rose and went to a dais provided with cushions of fine silk, curiously embroidered. There they sat while a numerous company of genies and fairies danced before them.

Every day spent with Periebanou was a continued feast and merrymaking, for she was always providing new delicacies, new concerts and new diversions. If Ahmed had lived a thousand years among men he could not have experienced as much enjoyment as was his in a few short months with Periebanou. There was nothing at his father's court comparable to the happiness he enjoyed with her. Nevertheless, at the end of a half year he felt a great desire to visit the sultan and know how he was. He mentioned his wish to Perie-banou, who was much alarmed, lest this was only an excuse to leave her, and she entreated him to forego his intention.

"My queen," responded the prince, "I had not thought that my request would displease you. It was made simply out of respect to my father, who no doubt believes I am dead. Since, however, you do not wish to have me go and comfort him by the assurance that I am alive, I will deny myself the pleasure, for there is nothing to which I would not submit to gratify you."

The fairy heard the prince say this with extreme satisfaction.

Meanwhile, the Sultan of the Indies, in the midst of the rejoicings on account of the marriage of Prince Ali and the Princess Nouronnihar, was deeply afflicted at the disappearance of his other two sons. He soon learned of the resolution of Prince Houssain to turn hermit, but as Houssain was alive and well, his father gradually became reconciled to his absence. A diligent search was made after Ahmed, and messengers were despatched to all the provinces of the kingdom, with orders to the governors to apprehend him and oblige him to return to the court. But these efforts did not have the desired success, and the sultan's affliction increased rather than diminished. "Vizier," he one day said, "you know I always loved Ahmed the most of any of my sons. My grief is so heavy at his strange absence that I shall sink under it. If, therefore, you have any regard for my life, I beg you to assist me, and find out where he is."

The grand vizier, anxious to give his master some ease, proposed to consult a sorceress, of whom he had heard many wonders, and he suggested that she should be summoned at once to the palace. To this plan the sultan consented, the sorceress came, and the grand vizier brought her into the presence of the ruler.

"Can you tell me by your art what has become of my son, Ahmed?" asked the sultan. "If he is alive where is he? What is he doing? May I hope ever to see him again."

"Sir," replied the sorceress, "if you will allow me till tomorrow, I will endeavor to satisfy you."

The sultan granted her the time for which she asked, and promised to recompense her richly if his son was found by her means.

On the following day she returned and said to the sultan: "Sir, I have been able to discover nothing more than that Prince Ahmed is alive. Where he is I cannot tell;" and with this answer the sultan was obliged to be content.

Prince Ahmed steadily adhered to his resolution not again to ask permission to leave the fairy Periebanou, but he frequently talked about his father, and she perceived that he still wished to see him. At length, being assured of the sincerity of his affection for her she said to him: "Prince, I grant you leave to visit the sultan your father, on condition that your absence shall not be long. You can go when you please; but first let me advise you not to inform him of our marriage, nor the place of our residence. Beg him to be contented with knowing that you are happy, and that the only purpose of your visit is to make him easy respecting your fate."

Prince Ahmed expressed to Periebanou his gratitude, and she summoned twenty horsemen, well-mounted and equipped to attend him. A charger, which was most richly caparisoned, and as beautiful a creature as any in the sultan's stables was brought for the prince himself, and he set forward on his journey.

As it was no great distance to his father's capital, Prince Ahmed soon arrived there. The people received him with shouts of rejoicing and followed him in crowds to the palace, where the sultan embraced him affectionately, complaining at the same time of the sorrow his long absence had occasioned.

"Sir," said Prince Ahmed, "I was much distressed by my failure to win the Princess Nouronnihar, and had no desire to be present at her wedding festivities. The loss of my arrow also dwelt continually in my mind, and I resolved to search for it. I therefore returned to the plain and walked from the spot where I stood to shoot fully a league in the direction the arrow sped. The

strongest archer could not have sent a shaft that distance, and I was about to abandon my quest when I
saw an arrow near the foot of the rocks at the far side
of the plain. I took it up and knew it to be the
one I had shot. Instead of blaming your Majesty for
declaring in favor of my brother Ali, I was certain there
was a mystery in what had happened that would prove
to my advantage. Such has been the case, but as to
revealing this mystery, I beg you will not be offended
if I remain silent. Be satisfied to know that I am happy.
To tell you this and relieve your anxiety, was the motive
which brought me hither. I must soon return, and the
only favor I ask is permission to come occasionally to
pay my respects and inquire after your health."

"Son," responded the sultan, "I wish to penetrate
no further into your secrets. I can only say that your
presence has restored to me the joy I have not felt for
a long time. You shall always be welcome when you
can come to visit me."

Prince Ahmed stayed three days at his father's court,
and on the fourth returned to the fairy Periebanou. A
month later the fairy herself proposed that he should
again visit his father. "Go to him tomorrow," said
she, "and in the future visit him once a month."

The next day the prince started with the same attendants as before, but much more magnificently mounted
and dressed, and was received by the sultan with joy
and satisfaction. For several months he continued to

make these visits, but always in a richer and finer equipage.

At last the sultan's councillors, who judged of Prince Ahmed's power by the splendor of his appearance, sought to make the sultan jealous of his son. They represented that it was but common prudence to discover where the prince dwelt and how he could afford to live so sumptuously, since he had no revenue assigned for his expenses. "Sir," said they, "he seems to make his visits only to insult you by affecting more grandeur than you yourself show. It is to be feared that he may inveigle himself into the people's favor and dethrone you. The danger is all the greater because he cannot reside far from the capital; for the clothing and weapons of his attendants are always quite free from the dust of travel, and their horses look as if they had only been walked out. We should think ourselves wanting in our duty if we did not make these humble remonstrances; and we trust that for your own preservation your Majesty will take such measures as you may think advisable."

"I do not believe my son Ahmed is so wicked as you would persuade me he is," declared the sultan, "but I am obliged to you for your advice, and do not doubt that it proceeds from your loyalty to me."

Nevertheless, such was the impression his courtiers' words had made on his mind, that he was much alarmed, and he resolved to have Prince Ahmed watched. So he sent privately for the sorceress, and she was introduced by a secret door into his apartment. "You told me the truth," said he, "when you assured me that my son Ahmed was alive. He now comes to my court every month, but I can not learn from him where he resides. I believe you are capable of discovering his secret. He is with me at the present time, but will depart in the morning. I require you to watch him. Find out whither he retires, and bring me information."

The sorceress left the sultan, and knowing the place where Prince Ahmed found his arrow, went immediately thither, and concealed herself near the rocks.

At daybreak, the next morning, the prince left the sultan's court, and the sorceress presently saw him coming. He and his attendants rode straight to the rocks and suddenly disappeared. The rocks were so steep and high that they were an impassable barrier to anyone either on horseback or on foot, and the sorceress concluded that the prince and his retinue had entered some cavern. She explored the vicinity where she had lost sight of them, but notwithstanding all her diligence, could perceive no opening; for the fairy Periebanou had by her magic made the iron door invisible to all except those she favored. The sorceress was obliged to abandon her search without learning anything further, and she went to give the sultan an account of what she had seen.

He was very well pleased with her conduct, and to

encourage her to persevere in her efforts to obtain the information he wished he gave her a diamond of great value.

She knew that Prince Ahmed would again visit his father in a month's time, and shortly before he was expected she once more resorted to the foot of the craggy precipice where she had seen him disappear. It was her intention, when he came forth, to pretend that she was seriously hurt. This she thought would arouse his pity and he would have her conveyed into his underground retreat.

The next morning Prince Ahmed and his attendants went out at the iron door on their journey to the capital; but at the base of the rocks they saw a woman lying, and she was moaning as if in great pain. Ahmed stopped his horse, and asked her what was the matter and whether he could do anything to ease her.

She turned her eyes toward him, without lifting her head, and answered in broken words and sighs as if she could hardly fetch her breath: "I was going to the capital city, but was taken with so violent a fever that my strength failed me. So I was forced to lie down here far from any habitation, and without the least hope of obtaining help."

"Good woman," responded Prince Ahmed, "you are not so far from habitations as you imagine. You shall be carried at once to a place near by where all possible care will be taken of you, and where you will undoubtedly be speedily cured, Only get up, and you shall mount behind one of my attendants."

At these words the sorceress made many pretended efforts to rise, and then fell back as if exhausted. So two men of the prince's retinue alighted, lifted her in their arms and placed her behind one of their companions. Then the entire procession turned back and entered the iron door. As soon as Prince Ahmed came into the outer court of the fairy's palace he sent her word that he wanted to speak with her, and she came with all imaginable haste, curious to know what had brought him back so unexpectedly. "Princess," said he, "I desire you would have compassion on this good woman whom I found overcome with sickness. Render her the assistance which she needs, and do not send her on her way until she is restored to health and strength."

The fairy, who had her eyes fixed on the sorceress all the time the prince was speaking, ordered two of her women to take her from the men who supported her, and carry her to an apartment in the palace. "Make her comfortable there," she ordered, "and give her as good care as you would me."

While the two women were executing the fairy's commands, she went up to Prince Ahmed, and in a whisper said: "This woman is not as sick as she pretends to be. Unless I am much mistaken she is sent hither on purpose to cause you great trouble. But I will deliver you out of all the snares that shall be laid for you. Go now on your journey."

"As I do not remember I ever did, or designed to do, anybody an injury," said Ahmed, "I cannot believe anyone has a thought of injuring me. But even if they have, I shall not forbear doing good whenever I have an opportunity."

So saying, he set forward again for his father's capital. The sultan received him as usual and concealed whatever anxiety he felt arising from the suspicions suggested by his favorites.

In the meantime the sorceress had been conveyed into a very fine and richly furnished apartment where her attendants laid her on a sofa and put over her a quilt of embroidered brocade and a coverlet of cloth of gold. One of the women went out and soon returned with a china cup full of a certain liquor, which she presented to the sorceress, saying: "Drink this. It is the water of the Fountain of Lions, and a sure remedy. You will feel the effect of it very quickly."

The sorceress drank the liquor and the attendants left the apartment. When they returned an hour later they found her sitting up. "Oh, the admirable potion!" she exclaimed. "It has wrought its cure and I am now well enough to continue my journey."

After the two attendants had expressed their pleasure at the promptness of her recovery, they conducted her through several superb apartments into a large hall, the most magnificently furnished of all the rooms in the palace. Periebanou was seated in this hall on a throne of massive gold, enriched with diamonds, rubies, and pearls of extraordinary size, and attended by a great number of beautiful fairies, all richly clothed. At the sight of this splendor, the sorceress was so dazzled and amazed that she could not open her lips to thank the fairy as she intended.

"I hope you find your strength fully restored," said Periebanou; "and I am glad I had an opportunity to do you a kindness. No doubt you wish to resume your journey now, and I will not detain you."

The old sorceress, who had not power or courage to say a word, prostrated herself with her head on the carpet that covered the foot of the throne, and then was conducted by her two attendants to the iron door through which she had been brought by Prince Ahmed. After she had thanked them they opened it and wished her a pleasant journey.

As soon as the door closed behind her the sorceress turned to observe it, that she might know it again, but all in vain, for it was invisible to her. Except for this circumstance, she was very well satisfied with her success, and she hurried away to relate to the sultan all that had happened.

He at once had her admitted to his apartment, and when she finished her narrative she said: "What does your Majesty think of the marvellous riches of this fairy? Perhaps you rejoice at the good fortune of your son. But for my part I shudder when I consider the misfortune which may happen to you. Is it not quite likely that the fairy, by her caresses and attractions, will inspire your son with the design to take from you your throne?"

The sultan had the sorceress follow him to his council chamber, and repeat her story before the council. When they had heard her to the end, one of the councillors, addressing the sultan said: "In my opinion the prince should be arrested. He is now in your Majesty's power, and delay is dangerous."

This suggestion was unanimously applauded by the other councillors; but the sorceress said: "If you detain the prince you must likewise detain his retinue. They are, however, all genies. Will they not at once escape by the power they possess of rendering themselves invisible? Then they will transport themselves to the fairy and give her an account of the insult offered her husband, which she surely will not let go unrevenged. Would it not be wiser to turn the prince's union with the fairy to your advantage by imposing on him such difficult tasks that the fairy will tire of aiding him and presently send him away. For a first request I think you might ask him to procure you a tent, which can be carried in a man's hand, and yet be large enough to shelter your whole army."

When the sorceress had finished her speech, the

sultan asked his favorites if they had anything better to propose. As they were all silent, he determined to follow her advice.

The next morning the sultan spoke to the prince, saying: "My son, I congratulate you on your marriage to a fairy, who I hear is worthy of your love. It is my earnest wish that you use your influence with her to do me a great service. You know to what an expense I am put, every time I engage in war, to provide mules, camels, and other beasts of burden to carry the tents that are needed for shelter. But I am confident that you can easily procure from your wife a tent that can be carried in a man's hand, and yet which will protect my whole army. Pray oblige me in this matter."

Prince Ahmed was greatly troubled by his father's request, which he feared would be impossible for even so powerful a being as the fairy to grant. "Sir," said he, "though I know not how the mystery of my marriage has been revealed to you, I cannot deny the correctness of your information. I will ask of my wife the favor you desire, but I do not promise to obtain it. If I fail to come again to pay my respects you can know that I have not succeeded in my petition."

"I see that you are not aware of the influence a husband has over his wife," commented the sultan. "She would show that her love for you was very slight if, with the power she possesses as a fairy, she should refuse so trifling a request as the one I have begged you to make."

But Prince Ahmed was far from being satisfied that this fairly represented the case; and so great was his vexation that he left the court two days sooner than usual.

Hitherto he had always returned to the fairy with a gay countenance. Now, however, he was melancholy and moody. The fairy asked the cause of this change, and he reluctantly confessed that the sultan had discovered the secret of his abode and marriage, though by what means he could not tell.

"Do you not recall the old woman on whom you had compassion?" said the fairy. "She was a spy of the sultan's, and she has informed him of all she saw and heard. But the mere knowledge of my abode by your father would not so trouble you. There is something else which is the cause of your grief and vexation."

"It is even as you say," acknowledged the prince. "My father doubts my fidelity to him unless I can provide a tent large enough to shelter his entire army, and small enough to carry in his hand."

"Prince," responded the fairy, "what the sultan requests is only a trifle, and I take pleasure in granting this favor."

Then the fairy sent for her treasurer and asked her to bring the largest tent from the treasury. The treasurer soon returned with a small case in her hand which

she gave to her mistress. Prince Ahmed fancied the
fairy must be bantering him. She immediately perceived his look of incredulity and exclaimed: "What!
do you think I jest with you? I will show you that I
am in earnest."

So she ordered the treasurer to set the tent up that
the prince might judge whether the sultan would think
it large enough. Then the treasurer led the way out of
the palace to a great open space and set up the tent,
and the prince declared it was large enough to shelter
two armies as numerous as that of his father. After the
tent had been reduced to its first size it was given to the
prince. He waited only till the next day, and then
mounted his horse and went with his usual attendants
to the court of the sultan.

His father, who was sure there could be no such tent
as he had asked for, was greatly surprised at his son's
speedy return. He took the tent, and after he had admired its smallness he had it set up, and found it large
enough to cover with ease his whole army.

The sultan expressed great obligation to the prince
for so noble a present, and desired him to convey his
thanks to the fairy. But in his secret bosom he felt
greater jealousy than ever of his son. Therefore, still
intent on Prince Ahmed's ruin, he went to consult the
sorceress, and she advised him to ask the prince to bring
him some of the water of the Fountain of Lions.

That evening, when the sultan was surrounded as

usual by his court, the prince came among the rest to pay his respects. "Son," said the sultan, "I esteem the tent you have obtained for me the most valuable article in my treasury; but you must procure one thing more which will be no less agreeable to me. I am informed that the fairy, your wife, makes use of a certain water called the Water of the Fountain of Lions, which cures all sorts of diseases. As my health is doubtless dear to you, I trust you will ask her for a bottle of the water and bring it to me that I may use it when I have occasion. Do me this important service, and complete the duty of a good son toward a tender father."

Prince Ahmed, who had believed that the sultan would be satisfied with so remarkable and useful a tent as the one he had brought, and that he would not impose any new task on him which might hazard the fairy's displeasure, was thunderstruck at this request. After a long silence he said: "There is nothing I would not do to help prolong your life; but I wish it might be by other means, and I dare not promise to bring the water. All I can do is to assure you that I will request it of the fairy; though I shall do so with as great reluctance as I asked for the tent."

The next morning Prince Ahmed returned to the fairy, Periebanou, and related all that had passed at his father's court. "I regret this further request of the sultan's," said he in closing, "and I shall not in the least blame you if you refuse to gratify him."

"No, no," said the fairy, "I will comply with his wishes. He evidently consults the sorceress; but whatever advice she gives him, he shall find no fault with you or me. There is much wickedness in this new demand, for the Fountain of Lions is situated in the middle of a court of a great castle, the entrance to which is guarded by four fierce lions, two of which sleep while the other two are awake. But let not that frighten you. I will supply you with means to pass them safely."

The fairy took up a ball of thread and passed it to Ahmed, saying: "Take this with you and a bottle to fill with the water. You must have a horse to ride, and you must lead another horse loaded with a sheep cut into four quarters. Set out early in the morning, and when you have passed the iron gate throw before you the ball of thread, which will roll till it reaches the gates of the castle. Follow it and you will find the gates open, and you will see the four lions. The two that are awake will, by their roaring, rouse the other two. Be not alarmed, but throw each of them a quarter of the sheep, and then clap spurs to your horse and ride to the fountain. Fill your bottle without alighting, and return as speedily as you can. The lions will be so busy eating they will let you pass unmolested."

Prince Ahmed set out at dawn the next morning and carefully followed the fairy's directions. The ball of thread rolled along before him and showed him the way, and presently he arrived at the gate of the castle, where

he distributed the quarters of mutton among the four
lions, passed at a gallop through the midst of them,
and filled his bottle at the fountain. Then, without a
moment's delay, he galloped back through the gate.
He was continuing his return journey at a rapid pace
and congratulating himself on the safe accomplishment
of his mission when he observed two of the lions coming
after him. In great alarm he drew his cimeter and
made ready to defend himself. But as he went forward he saw one of the lions turn out of the road to
pass him, and its actions showed that it did not intend
to do him any harm, and only wanted to go before him.
The other followed behind. He therefore put his cimeter into its scabbard. Guarded in this manner he arrived at the capital of the Indies; and the lions never
left him till they had conducted him to the gates of the
sultan's palace. Then they returned the way they had
come, though not without alarming all who saw them,
in spite of the fact that they walked gently and showed
no signs of fierceness.

A number of officers came to attend the prince while
he dismounted, and they conducted him into the sultan's council chamber where the monarch was surrounded by his favorites. Ahmed approached the
throne, laid the bottle at the sultan's feet and kissed the
rich tapestry which covered his footstool. "I have
brought the water you so much desired," said he; "but

I wish you such a degree of health that you will never have occasion to use it."

After the prince had concluded his compliment, the sultan responded: "Son, I am greatly obliged to you for this valuable present, and also for braving the danger to which you exposed yourself on my account in getting it."

Outwardly the sultan showed all the demonstrations of great joy, but secretly he was more jealous than ever, and he retired to an inner apartment and sent for the sorceress. When he consulted with her she contrived a new request for him to make; and the next day the sultan said to his son: "I have one thing yet to ask of you, after which I shall expect nothing more. I wish you to bring me a man not over a foot and a half high, whose beard is thirty feet long, and who carries on his shoulder a bar of iron which he uses as a quarterstaff."

The prince hastened back to Periebanou and told her of his father's latest demand. "This is a more difficult thing to grant than the two former requests," said he; "for I cannot imagine there is such a man in the world. Without doubt the sultan seeks my ruin."

"Do not alarm yourself, prince," said the fairy. "You ran a risk in fetching the water of the Fountain of Lions for your father, but there is no danger in finding this man. He is my brother, Shaibar. However, I warn you that he is a person of violent temper whose resentment kindles at the slightest offence. On the other hand, he is so good as to oblige anyone who shows him a kindness. I will send for him, but prepare yourself not to be frightened at his extraordinary figure."

"What! my queen," exclaimed Ahmed, "do you say this Shaibar is your brother? Let him be ever so ugly or deformed, I shall love and honor him as your near relative."

The fairy ordered a fire to be lighted in a gold chafing-dish on the porch of her palace. Then she took some incense and threw it into the flames. A thick cloud of smoke arose, and after a few moments the fairy said to Prince Ahmed: "There comes my brother."

He had just entered the palace gate. When he joined them, he looked at the prince with a glance that chilled Ahmed's very soul, and asked Periebanou who that man was. She replied: "He is a son of the Sultan of the Indies, and he is my husband. I did not invite you to my wedding, because you were engaged in a distant expedition, from which I have since heard with pleasure that you returned victorious. It is on my husband's account that I have taken the liberty now to call for you."

At these words Shaibar looked at Ahmed favorably and said: "It is enough for me to know that he is your husband. Wherein can I serve him?"

"The sultan, his father, has a curiosity to see you," Periebanou answered, "and if you will favor him in this matter my husband will guide you to the sultan's court."

"I will go with him whenever he is ready," responded Shaibar.

The next morning he and Ahmed set out to visit the sultan. When they arrived at the gates of the capital, the people, as soon as they saw Shaibar, either hid themselves in their shops and houses and shut their doors, or they took to their heels and communicated their fear to all they met. So Shaibar and Ahmed, as they went along, found all the streets and squares desolate. They presently came to the palace, where the guards, instead of preventing Shaibar from entering, ran away and stayed not to look behind them. Thus he and the prince advanced without any obstacle to the council-hall, where the sultan was seated on his throne surrounded by his councillors.

Shaibar haughtily approached the sultan, and without waiting for Ahmed to present him, said: "You have sent for me. What do you wish?"

The sultan, instead of answering, put his hands before his eyes to exclude the sight of so terrible an object. At this uncivil reception Shaibar was much enraged. "Will you not speak?" he shouted, and swinging aloft his mighty iron bar he gave the sultan a crushing blow that laid him lifeless on the floor.

This he did before Prince Ahmed had any chance to interfere. Then he destroyed all the councillors except the grand vizier, whom he only spared at the earnest entreaty of the prince. After he had completed this frightful execution he went out into the courtyard, and confronting the grand vizier said: "I well know that a certain sorceress stirred up the sultan to demand my presence here. Let her be brought before me."

The grand vizier immediately sent for her, and as soon as she arrived Shaibar slew her with his iron bar, saying: "Learn the consequences of giving wicked advice."

Then he turned to the vizier and said: "One more thing I require of you. Prince Ahmed, my brother-in-law, must be instantly acknowledged as Sultan of India."

All who were present cheerfully assented to this proposal and made the air ring with cries of: "Long live Sultan Ahmed!"

In a short time the whole city echoed with these same words. Shaibar had the prince clothed in the royal vestments, and he was duly installed. Then Shaibar went after his sister Periebanou and fetched her to the city in great pomp and caused her to be acknowledged as Sultana.

The new sultan gave to Prince Ali and the Princess Nouronnihar a very considerable province, and he sent an officer to Houssain to acquaint him with the change in affairs and offer him any province he might choose. But that prince was so happy in his solitude that he bade the officer to thank his brother for his kindness, and say that the only favor he desired was the privilege of living retired in the place he had selected for his retreat.

VIII

THE ENCHANTED HORSE

IT was one of the festival days of spring in the city of Shiraz, and the Emperor of Persia had been taking part in the magnificent pageants prepared by his subjects. The sun was setting and he was about to retire, when a Hindu appeared before him leading an artificial horse that was so finely modelled it at first seemed a living animal. The Hindu prostrated himself, and said: "Sir, this horse is a great wonder. Whenever I mount it, I have only to wish myself transported to some special place, and the horse carries me thither in a marvellously short time. With the bridle rein in my hand I can easily guide it in any direction that suits my pleasure. I will gladly prove the truth of what I say if you will allow me to do so."

The Emperor of Persia, who was interested in everything that was curious, and who had never before heard of a horse with such qualities, bade the Hindu mount the animal and show what it could do. Instantly the owner of the horse put his foot in the stirrup and vaulted into the saddle with admirable agility. "Whither would you have me go?" he asked.

"Do you see that mountain?" said the emperor, pointing to a huge mass that towered into the sky about three leagues from Shiraz. "Ride your horse there and bring me thence a leaf of a palm tree."

The words were hardly spoken when the Hindu turned a peg on the horse's neck, and the creature instantly rose from the ground into the air and was soon beyond the sight of even the sharpest eyes. Within less than a quarter of an hour the waiting multitude saw him returning with the palm leaf in his hand; but before he descended he took two or three turns in the air amid the acclamations of all the people. Then he guided his horse to the spot whence he had set out, dismounted and laid the leaf at the feet of the emperor.

The monarch, who had viewed with surprise and admiration the astonishing flight of the horse, greatly desired to posses the creature. "I will buy the horse of you," said he to the Hindu. "Name your price."

"Sir," responded the Hindu, "there is only one condition on which I will consent to part with my horse, and that is the gift of the princess your daughter as my wife."

A shout of laughter burst from the courtiers when they heard this extravagant proposal. Prince Feroze-shah, the emperor's eldest son and heir was too indignant to join in this laughter. "I hope you will refuse so insolent a demand," said he to his father, "and that you will not allow this juggler to fancy for a single moment that he can thus become allied to one of the most powerful monarchs in the world."

"My son," said the emperor, "I will not grant the Hindu's request; and perhaps he does not make the proposal seriously. No doubt I can arrange other terms with him. But before I bargain further, I would be glad to have you try the horse and give me your opinion of it."

The Hindu offered no objection when the prince told him of the wish the emperor had expressed, and they went together to the horse and the Hindu helped Ferozeshah to mount. As soon as the prince had his feet in the stirrups, without staying for advice, he turned the peg he had seen the Hindu use, and instantly the horse darted into the air. In a few moments neither horse nor prince was to be seen. The Hindu, alarmed at what had happened, prostrated himself before the emperor, and said: "Sir, you must have noticed your son's impatience. It was that which prevented me from giving him directions how to manage the horse and make it return to the place from which it started. I implore you not to punish me for what was not my fault."

"But why did you not call to the prince the moment he ascended?" demanded the emperor in a burst of anxiety and wrath.

"The horse flew away with such rapidity," said the Hindu, "and I was so astonished, that your son was out of sight before I recovered my speech. But it is not unlikely that when he finds himself at a loss what to do, he will perceive a second peg. As soon as he turns that the horse will descend toward the ground."

"But even if he sees the other peg and makes a right use of it," said the emperor, "what is to hinder the horse from descending straight into the sea, or dashing its rider to pieces on the rocks?"

"Have no fears, your Highness," responded the Hindu, "the horse has the gift of passing over seas without ever falling into them, and of carrying its rider wherever he wishes to go."

"Your head shall answer for my son's life if he does not return safe," declared the emperor.

He then ordered his officers to seize the Hindu and throw him into prison.

Meanwhile the prince was carried through the air with surprising speed. In an hour's time he had ascended so high that he could not distinguish any object on the earth distinctly. Even the mountains and plains all looked the same. He now began to think of going back, and imagined he might do this by turning the peg the opposite way. To his surprise and horror he found that, turn as he might, the horse continued to ascend and he felt as if he was getting so near the sky that he would soon hit his head against it. Then he realized what a grievous mistake he had made in not having learned to guide the steed before he mounted.

He examined the horse's head and neck with attention until he discovered behind the right ear another peg, smaller than the first. This he turned, and to his intense joy observed that the horse began to descend. It went earthward in the same oblique manner as it had risen, but more slowly.

Night had overshadowed that part of the world, and as the prince could see nothing, he could not choose what place he would go to, and was obliged to let the bridle rein lie idly on the horse's neck. He awaited the outcome patiently, yet with a good deal of anxiety. At last, however, the horse gently alighted on the ground, and the prince dismounted very faint and hungry, for he had eaten nothing since early morning. He found himself on the terrace of a splendid palace, and after groping about for a time in the darkness, he reached a staircase which led to an apartment, the door of which was half open.

The prince went up the steps and stopped to listen. He could hear the breathing of some people who were fast asleep, and he looked in. The room was dimly lighted, and he saw a row of black slaves sleeping, each with a naked cimeter beside him.* This guard made it evident that the apartment was the ante-room to the chamber of some queen or princess. Ferozeshah advanced on tiptoe, passed the attendants without wak-

---

*It was customary to protect the apartments of ladies of wealth or high station by a guard of black slaves.

ing them, and by drawing aside a curtain he entered the chamber beyond. It contained many couches, one of them on a raised dais, and the rest on the floor. A princess slept on the dais and her women on the other couches. The prince crept softly toward the dais, and gazing on the sleeper saw that she was more beautiful than any woman he had ever before beheld. But fascinated though he was, he realized the danger of his position, and was well aware that any sudden exclamation or noise on his part would awake the guards and cause his certain death.

So he sank quietly on his knees beside the princess and gently twitched her sleeve. She opened her eyes, and seeing before her a handsome young man, was speechless with astonishment.

The prince availed himself of this favorable moment, to make a low obeisance and say: "Beautiful princess, by a most wonderful adventure, you see here the son of the Emperor of Persia, a suppliant for your protection. A few hours ago I was in my father's court; but now I am in an unknown land in danger of my life."

The princess was the eldest daughter of the King of Bengal, who had built this palace at a short distance from his capital that his daughter might enjoy the country air. "Prince," said she, "you are not in a barbarous country, and have no need to be uneasy. Hospitality and humanity are to be found in the kingdom of Bengal as well as in Persia. I grant you the protection for which you ask."

The prince was about to thank her for her goodness, but she added quickly: "Though I am very curious to learn by what means you have travelled here so speedily, and by what enchantment you have passed my guards, I know that you must want some refreshment. I will therefore have my attendants show you to an apartment where food will be brought to you and you can eat and rest yourself after your fatigue."

By this time the attendants of the princess were all awake and listening to the conversation. At a sign from their mistress they each took one of the wax candles with which the room was lighted, and conducted the prince to a handsome chamber, where they brought him a supper. When he had eaten as much as he wanted, they removed the trays and left him to enjoy the sweets of repose.

The next day the princess prepared to give the prince another interview, and in expectation of seeing him, she took more pains in dressing than she ever had before. She tried her women's patience by making them do and undo her hair several times; and she adorned her head, neck, arms and waist with the finest and largest diamonds she possessed. After she had consulted her glass, and asked her women if anything was wanting in her attire, she sent one of them to tell the Prince of Persia that she would make him a visit.

When the messenger arrived at the room of the prince he was just leaving it to ask if he might be allowed to pay his homage to the princess. But on learning her intentions he returned to his apartment and eagerly awaited her coming. She soon appeared, and after mutual compliments they sat down on a sofa, and the prince related to her the wonders of the magic horse, and all about his journey through the air, and how he happened to enter her chamber. Then he thanked her for her kind reception, and expressed a wish to return and relieve the anxiety of the emperor, his father.

"I cannot approve of your going so soon," said the princess. "Grant me at least the favor of a little longer acquaintance. Since you have chanced to alight in the kingdom of Bengal, I desire that you should stay long enough to be able, when you go back to Persia, to give a satisfactory account of what you may see here."

The prince could not well refuse to do as she asked, and the princess spared no effort to render his stay agreeable by all the amusements she could devise. There was a constant round of concerts and feasts in the gardens, and hunting parties. Two whole months the Prince of Persia abandoned himself to the pleasures contrived for him by the Princess of Bengal. But at last he declared seriously that he could not stay longer and begged her to give him leave to return to his father. "Were it not for fear of offending you," said he in conclusion, "I would ask the favor of taking you along with me; for my life can not be happy when separated from you, and I promise that my father will gladly consent to our marriage."

The princess made no answer to this address, but her silence and her downcast eyes spoke for her and informed him that she had no objection to accompanying him. The only doubt she had was as to whether the prince knew well enough how to govern the horse. She dreaded lest they might find themselves in the same difficulty as when he made his former journey. But the prince assured her she might trust herself with him, for after the experience he had acquired, he defied the Hindu himself to manage the horse better. She therefore thought only of arranging for their flight so secretly that nobody belonging to the palace should have the least suspicion of their design.

A little before daybreak the next morning, when all the attendants were asleep, she met the prince on the terrace of the palace. The prince turned the horse's head toward Persia, they mounted, and as soon as the princess was well settled with her arms about his waist for her better security, he turned the peg. Up went the horse into the air, and travelling with its accustomed speed it carried its riders in two hours' time within sight of Shiraz. The prince decided not to alight in the city, but directed his course to his father's summer palace at a little distance from the capital. There his horse gently descended to the earth, and he led the princess into a handsome apartment and told her to rest while he went to inform his father of their arrival and prepare a reception worthy of her rank.

He then ordered one of the emperor's horses brought from the stables and set out for the city, where he was welcomed with shouts of joy by the people, who had long lost all hope of seeing him again. On reaching the palace he found the emperor surrounded by his councillors, all dressed in the deepest mourning. The monarch received his son with tears of surprise and delight, and asked him to relate his adventures.

In response the prince told of the embarrassment and danger he was in when the Hindu's horse ascended into the air, and how he had arrived at last at the Princess of Bengal's palace, and of his kind reception there. He frankly confessed that the lady's charms had won his heart and induced him to linger with her, and that not only did he love her, but she loved him. "Sir," said he in conclusion, "I gave my royal word that you would not refuse your consent to our marriage, and so persuaded her to return with me on the Hindu's horse. She is now in your summer palace, where she is waiting anxiously to be assured that I have not promised in vain."

"My son," said the emperor embracing him, "gladly do I consent to your marriage, and I will hasten to pay my respects to the princess and thank her for the benefits she has conferred on you. She shall return with me and we will celebrate your wedding this very day."

The emperor now ordered that the Hindu should be released from prison and brought before him. His commands were obeyed, and the Hindu was led into his presence, surrounded by guards. "I have kept you locked up," said the emperor, "so that in case my son failed to return, your life should pay the penalty. Thanks be to God, he has now come back. Go, take your horse, and never let me see your face again."

The Hindu hastily quitted the presence of the emperor, but he paused as soon as he was safely out of the palace to inquire of a guard where the prince had been all this time and what he had been doing. In response the guard told him the whole story, and how the Princess of Bengal was in the summer palace where the prince had left her, expecting some message from the emperor.

This suggested to the Hindu an opportunity for revenge. He hastened to the summer palace and informed the doorkeeper that he had been sent by the emperor to fetch the Princess of Bengal to the capital on the enchanted horse.

The doorkeeper recognized the Hindu, for he had seen him on the day that he exhibited his wonderful steed before the emperor, and he was of course aware of his imprisonment and the reason for it. Now that he saw him at liberty he gave credit to what the Hindu

said and took him into the presence of the Princess of
Bengal. She at once consented to go with him, and he,
overjoyed at the ease with which he had accomplished
his villainy, mounted his enchanted horse, and with the
assistance of the doorkeeper, took the princess up behind him. Then he turned the peg and instantly the
horse rose into the air.

At the same time the Emperor of Persia, attended by
his court, was on the road to the summer palace, and
the prince had gone on ahead to prepare the princess
to receive his father. The Hindu, in order to make his
revenge all the sweeter, appeared over their heads with
his prize. When the emperor saw the horse and its
riders he stopped short with astonishment and horror.
His affliction was the more acute, because it was not
in his power to punish this affront. He loaded the
Hindu with a thousand curses, as did also the courtiers
who were witnesses of the fellow's insolence and
treachery.

The rider of the enchanted horse heard them quite
unmoved, knowing that he was perfectly safe, and he
presently continued on his way. There was nothing
for the emperor to do then except to return, mortified
and angry, to his palace. But the distress of the monarch was not to be compared with that of Prince
Ferozeshah when he saw the object of his passionate
devotion being borne rapidly away. He was speechless
with grief and remorse at not having guarded her bet-

ter, and he rode on, melancholy and broken-hearted, to the summer palace.

The sight of the prince coming dejected and alone, showed the doorkeeper of what folly he had been guilty in believing the artful Hindu. He flung himself at the prince's feet with tears in his eyes and begged for pardon.

"Rise," said the prince, "I do not impute the loss of my princess to you, but to my own want of precaution. Fetch me the costume of a dervish,* but let no one know for whom you are getting it."

Not far from the summer palace was a dervish convent, the superior of which was the doorkeeper's friend. From him the desired clothing was readily obtained and carried to Prince Ferozeshah, who immediately put it on. Thus disguised he left the palace, uncertain which way to go, but resolved to keep searching till he had found his princess or perished in the attempt.

Meanwhile the Hindu, mounted on his enchanted horse with the princess behind him, arrived early next morning in the vicinity of the capital of the kingdom of Cashmere. He brought his steed down to earth in a wood, and left the princess on a grassy spot close to a rivulet of clear water, while he went to seek for food. When he came back, and he and the princess had eaten, he began to maltreat her because she refused to become

---

*An oriental monk of extreme poverty and austere life. The costume consists of a shirt of coarse linen, a white mantle about the shoulders, a leather girdle, and an enormous brimless hat. The legs of the dervish are always bare, and the breast exposed.

his wife. She called loudly for help, and luckily her cries were heard by the Sultan of Cashmere and his attendants, who were returning from hunting.

They at once came to her rescue, and the sultan, addressing the Hindu, demanded who he was, and wherefore he ill-treated the lady. The Hindu, with great impudence, replied: "She is my wife, and what has anyone else to do with our quarrel, I would like to know?"

"My lord," cried the princess, "whoever you are that Heaven has sent to my assistance, have compassion on me. Put no faith in this abominable magician. He has this day torn me away from the Prince of Persia, my destined husband, and has brought me hither on the enchanted horse you behold there."

She would have said more, but her tears choked her. The Sultan of Cashmere, however, was convinced by her beauty and majestic air that she spoke the truth, and he ordered his followers to cut off the Hindu's head, which was done immediately. Then he conducted the princess to his palace, where he lodged her in a beautiful apartment, next his own, and selected some women slaves to attend her.

The joy of the princess was boundless at finding herself delivered from the Hindu, of whom she could not think without horror. She flattered herself that the sultan would complete his generosity by sending her back to the Prince of Persia; but in this hope she was

much deceived. When her deliverer quitted her presence that evening, it was with the resolve that the sun
should not set again without the princess becoming his
wife. He therefore issued a proclamation, commanding a general rejoicing of the inhabitants of the capital
on the morrow. At the break of day drums were beaten,
and there was blowing of trumpets and the clash of
cymbals, and sounds of joy echoed throughout the city.

The Princess of Bengal was early awakened by the
noise, but she did not for a moment imagine it had anything to do with her. When the sultan came to wait on
her, and had inquired after her health, he told her that
the trumpet blasts she heard were part of the solemn
marriage ceremonies for which he begged her to prepare.
This unexpected announcement put her into such a
state of agitation that she fainted away.

The women slaves who were present ran to her
assistance, but it was a long time before they succeeded
in bringing her to herself. At length her senses began
slowly to return, and then, rather than break faith with
the Prince of Persia by consenting to such a marriage,
she resolved to feign madness. She therefore uttered
all sorts of absurdities, and even rose to her feet as if to
attack the sultan, insomuch that he was greatly alarmed
and regretted that he had made his proposal so unsea-
sonably.

When he found that her frenzy increased rather than
abated, he left her with her women, charging them to

take the greatest care of her. He sent often that day to inquire how she was, but her attendants could report no improvement. The next day she continued to talk wildly and show other marks of a disordered mind, and the sultan summoned all the doctors belonging to his court to consult together over her sad state. One at a time they entered her apartment to make an examination, but as each man approached she gave way to such violent paroxysms that not one dared to lay a finger on her.

It was evident to the sultan that his court physicians could do nothing toward curing her, and he sent for various other doctors, the most celebrated in the kingdom; but they had no better success. Afterward he despatched messengers to the courts of neighboring rulers promising magnificent rewards to whoever could devise a cure for her malady. This proclamation brought many foreign physicians to Cashmere, and all were given an opportunity to try their skill, but they accomplished nothing.

During this interval Prince Ferozeshah, disguised in the costume of a dervish, wandered sadly from place to place, making diligent inquiry everywhere after his lost princess. At last he arrived in a large city of India where he heard a great deal of talk about a Princess of Bengal who had gone crazy on the very day she was to have been married to the Sultan of Cashmere. This was enough to induce him to hasten toward the kingdom of that monarch. On arriving at the capital he secured lodging at an inn, where he soon heard the full particulars of the fate of the Hindu magician, and of the sultan's frustrated intention to marry the princess he had rescued.

Ferozeshah then provided himself with a doctor's robe, and as his beard had grown long during his travels, he felt sure he would easily pass for the character he assumed. He went boldly to the palace, and announced to the chief of the officers his wish to be allowed to undertake the cure of the princess.

Some time had elapsed since any physician had presented himself, and the sultan had begun to lose all hope of ever seeing the princess restored to health. But as soon as he was informed that another doctor had arrived his hope revived and he had him at once admitted to his presence. After telling him that the mere sight of a physician threw the princess into transports of rage he conducted him into a closet, whence, through a lattice, he might see her without being observed.

Ferozeshah looked and beheld his beautiful princess reclining on a sofa, with tears in her eyes, singing softly to herself a song bewailing her sad destiny, which had deprived her, perhaps forever, of the being she loved so tenderly. The young man's heart beat fast as he listened; for he needed no further proof that her madness was feigned, and that her affection for him was unshaken. On leaving the closet, he told the sultan that certain signs made him sure the princess's malady was not incurable; "But," said he, "I must see her and speak with her alone, and I hope she will receive me favorably, in spite of the violent manner she has shown toward other physicians."

The sultan readily consented that the doctor should attempt the cure in his own way, and the prince was ushered into the apartment of the princess. As soon as she caught sight of his doctor's robe, she sprang from her seat in a fury and heaped insults on him. The prince, however, went directly toward her, and when he was near enough so that his words would be heard by her and no one else, he said in a low voice: "Look at me, princess, and you will see that I am no doctor, but the Prince of Persia, who has come to set you free."

At the sound of his voice the princess suddenly grew calm, and an expression of joy overspread her face. For some minutes she was too delighted to speak, and Prince Ferozeshah took advantage of her silence to tell her as briefly as possible of his long search for her, and his rapture at finally discovering her. He then asked her to inform him of all that had happened to her since the Hindu carried her away, so that he might the better devise some means of rescuing her from the tyranny of the sultan.

It needed but a few words from the princess to make him acquainted with the whole situation, and in conclusion she declared she had made up her mind to die rather than permit herself to be forced into a union with the Sultan of Cashmere.

The prince then inquired if she knew what became of the enchanted horse, after the death of the Hindu magician. She answered that she did not know with certainty, but supposed the sultan had taken care of it as a curiosity. Ferozeshah did not doubt that the sultan had the horse, and he and the princess consulted over a plan for making use of it in escaping to Persia. But first it was necessary that she should receive the sultan with civility the next day, in order to make him believe that her malady was being overcome and thus win his entire confidence in the pretended physician.

The sultan was much pleased when the prince told him the effect of his first visit, and he was still more pleased on the following day when the princess received him without any of her usual frenzied violence. He was persuaded that her cure was far advanced, and he affirmed to her that he regarded the prince as the greatest physician in the world and exhorted her to carefully follow the directions of so skilful a doctor. After he retired from her apartment the prince asked him how the Princess of Bengal had reached Cashmere, which was so distant from her own country.

The sultan at once informed him of the Hindu and the enchanted horse, and added that the horse was now kept in his treasury as a curiosity, though he was quite ignorant of how it could be used.

"Sir," said the pretended physician, "the tale you tell supplies me with the clue I needed to complete the recovery of the princess. During her journey hither on the enchanted horse, something of its enchantment has been communicated to her person. This can only be dissipated by a certain incense of which I possess the secret. If your Highness would entertain yourself, your court, and the people of your capital, with the most surprising sight that ever was beheld, let the horse be brought tomorrow into the great square before the palace and leave the rest to me. I promise to show you and all the assembly the Princess of Bengal completely restored in body and mind. In order to make the spectacle as impressive as possible, I suggest that she be richly dressed, and adorned with valuable jewels."

The sultan agreed to do all that the prince proposed, and the following morning he had the horse taken from the treasury and placed in the great square before the palace. Soon a rumor had spread through the town that something extraordinary was about to happen, and such a crowd collected that the sultan's guards had to be called out to prevent disorder, and to keep an open space around the horse.

When all was ready, the sultan appeared, and took his place on a platform with the chief nobles and officers of his court. The Princess of Bengal, attended by a number of ladies, approached the enchanted horse and the women helped her to mount. As soon as she was in the saddle with the bridle rein in her hand, the physician placed about the horse some large braziers full of lighted charcoal, into each of which he threw a delicious perfume. Then with downcast eyes, and hands crossed over his breast he walked three times around the horse, muttering the while what the onlookers supposed to be words of magic. Soon there arose from the burning braziers a thick smoke which almost concealed the horse and princess. This was the time for which he had been waiting. He sprang lightly up behind the lady, leaned forward and turned the peg, and as the horse darted up into the air, he shouted: "Sultan of Cashmere, when you would marry a princess who implores your protection, first learn to obtain her consent."

Thus the prince rescued the Princess of Bengal, and returned with her to Persia. He alighted in the public square before the palace of the emperor, his father; and the wedding was only delayed long enough to make the preparations necessary to render the ceremony as magnificent as possible. After the rejoicings were over the emperor sent an ambassador to the King of Bengal with an account of what had passed, and asked his approbation of his daughter's alliance with the Prince of Persia. The King of Bengal considered this alliance an honor, and he granted his approval with great pleasure and satisfaction.

IX

KING BEDER AND THE PRINCESS JEHAUNARA

AN ancient king of Persia, who had distinguished himself in peace and war, one day bought a slave maiden of more than ordinary beauty, for whom he gave ten thousand pieces of gold. So attractive was she that he loved her at first sight, and he did everything he could to make her comfortable and happy. A portion of the palace was set apart for her use, and she had servants to wait on her; yet for almost a year she she was never seen to laugh; and she never spoke a single word to the king, nor to any of her attendants.

At last, near the end of the year, while the king was expressing to her, in endearing terms, his love and admiration, she suddenly smiled, and commenced to speak. "Sir," she said, "my name is Gulnare of the Sea. My father was one of the most powerful monarchs of the ocean; and when he died my brother Saleh reigned in his stead. At length a neighboring prince invaded our kingdom, and for the sake of safety we left our palace and took refuge in a strong fortress. My brother wished me to marry. 'In the present condition of our affairs,' said he, 'I see no probability of matching you to any of the rulers of the sea; and therefore it seems to me best that you should think of marrying one of the rulers of the land. Believe me, there are kings of the land who are in no way inferior to those of the sea.'

"At this discourse I was much grieved. 'Brother,' said I, 'you know that we are descended from the kings and queens of the sea without any mixture with those of the land. Therefore I will not marry anyone but some noble sea prince whose ancestry is as exalted as my own; and I have taken an oath to that effect.'

"We talked further, and as he continued to urge his view I became angry. After he left me, so peevish was my mood, that I determined not to stay in my brother's household any longer. I therefore went out from the fortress and came up to the surface of the sea. There I found myself near an island, and I left the water and sat on the shore in the moonlight. By and by a man came along. He seized me, carried me to his abode, and wanted to make me his wife. When I persisted in refusing to marry him he sold me to the merchant of whom you purchased me.

"As for you, sir, if you had not shown me all the respect you have hitherto shown, and given me such undeniable marks of your affection I would not have remained with you. The portion of your palace that you have assigned to me faces the sea, and the salt waves wash its base. I would have thrown myself into the water out of this window and gone back to my mother, my brother, and the rest of my relations."

"My dearest princess," cried the king, "what wonders have I heard! You are henceforth my wife, the Queen of Persia; and by that title you shall be proclaimed throughout my whole realm. Tomorrow you shall be crowned with the utmost pomp and splendor. But I beseech you, madam, to inform me more particularly of the kingdom and people of the sea. I cannot comprehend how it is possible for you to dwell under the water without being drowned."

"Sir," responded Gulnare, "we walk at the bottom of the sea with as much ease as you do on land. It does not trouble us to breathe, and, what is yet more remarkable, the water never wets our clothes; so that when we visit the land, we have no occasion to dry them. I must inform you also, that the water does not in the least hinder us from seeing, and as we have quick, piercing sight, we can discern any object as clearly in the deepest part of the sea as you do on land. The palaces of our rulers and nobles are magnificent. Some of them are constructed of marble of various colors, and others of rock crystal, or mother-of-pearl, or coral.

"As we have a marvelous ability to transport ourselves whither we please in the twinkling of an eye, we have no occasion for carriages or horses. To be sure the king has his stables, and his sea-horses, but the horses are seldom used except on days of public rejoicing. I pass over a thousand other curious particulars relating to our countries, in order to speak of something of greater importance. It is my earnest desire that you grant me leave to send for my mother and sisters, and for the king my brother, to whom I have a great desire to be reconciled. They will be very glad to find me the wife of the mighty King of Persia, and I think you would be pleased to see them."

"Madam," said the monarch, "you are queen; do whatever you please. I will endeavor to receive them with the honor that they merit. But I would fain know when they will arrive, that I may give orders to prepare for their reception."

"There is no need of any preparation," said the queen. "I intend that they shall be here in a few minutes, and if your Majesty will step into the next room, and look through the lattice toward the sea, you will witness the manner of their arrival."

The king went to the next room, and Queen Gulnare had one of her women bring her a fire-pan with a little fire in it. After that she bade the servant retire, and shut the door. When she was alone, she took a piece of aloes-wood and put it into the fire-pan, and while the smoke was ascending repeated some mysterious words and gave a loud whistle. She continued to feed the fire and repeat spells until the sea foamed and there came forth from it a young man of comely form, and of beautiful countenance, having red cheeks, and whiskers of a light green color. A little behind him was a lady, advanced in years, but with a majestic air, attended by five young maidens who were scarcely less beautiful than Queen Gulnare.

They walked with wonderful swiftness along the wave-tops, and when they came to the palace leaped nimbly up, one after another, through the window into the apartment of the queen. They were King Saleh, his mother, the Queen Fareshah, and his sisters. After they had embraced Gulnare, with tears of joy, the King of Persia came in and welcomed them with great warmth and heartiness. During their stay he treated his illustrious guests to continual feasts, in which he omitted nothing that might show his grandeur and magnificence. King Saleh had made peace with the enemy that had invaded his realm, and his kingdom was now so quiet and orderly that he and his relatives felt there was no need of hastening their return, and they stayed at the palace of the King of Persia for several months.

After they were gone Queen Gulnare, though she missed their companionship, was on the whole cheerful and contented. At length, she gave birth to a son, and as the young prince was beautiful of countenance, his parents thought no name so proper for him as Beder, which in the Persian language signifies the *Full Moon*. In token of gratitude to heaven for sending him a son, the king was very liberal in his alms to the poor, caused the prison doors to be set open, and gave all his slaves their liberty. He distributed vast sums among the ministers and holy men of his religion, he gave large presents to his courtiers, and had a considerable sum thrown amongst the people; and he ordered rejoicings to be kept up for an entire week in his capital.

Not long afterward the queen's mother and brother and sisters came to see her. While they were talking with Gulnare in her Majesty's chamber, the nurse brought in the young Prince Beder from an adjoining room. King Saleh ran to embrace him, received him in his arms and kissed and caressed him with the greatest tenderness. He took several turns around the room, dancing and tossing the baby about, and then suddenly sprang out of an open window and plunged into the sea with him. The King of Persia, who had entered the queen's room just in time to see this occurrence was overwhelmed with affliction. He began to weep and wail and declared he should see his son no more.

"Sir," said Queen Gulnare with a quiet and undisturbed countenance, "grieve not. The young prince is my son as well as yours, and he will have the advantage his uncle and I possess of living equally well in the sea and on the land."

Queen Fareshah affirmed the same thing; yet all they said had no effect on the king, who could not recover from his alarm until Prince Beder should return. Only a short time had elapsed when the sea became agitated and King Saleh rose from it with the young prince in his arms. He held him up so those in the

palace could see that the baby was safe and sound, and
came in at the window from which he had leaped.
After restoring Prince Beder to his nurse, King Saleh
opened a box he had fetched from his palace. It contained three hundred diamonds as large as pigeons'
eggs, a like number of rubies and emeralds of extraordinary size, and thirty necklaces of the finest pearls.

"Sir," said he to the King of Persia, presenting him
with the box, "I beg you to accept this small token of
gratitude in acknowledgement of the many favors you
have been pleased to confer on my sister."

Then he said that he and his mother and the five
princesses must depart; and the King of Persia assured
them that he was sorry it was not in his power to return
their visit in their own dominions. Many tears were
shed on both sides when they separated. After this
royal company of the sea had gone the King of Persia
said to Gulnare: "O queen, I shall honor your relatives
as long as I live, and I shall never cease to bless heaven
for directing you to me."

Prince Beder was brought up and educated with the
utmost care. As he advanced in years his continual
sprightliness, agreeable manners, and ready wit gave
the liveliest pleasure to his parents; and this pleasure
was increased because King Saleh, the Queen Fareshah,
and the princesses came from time to time to partake
of it. He was taught to read and write, and at the age
of twenty was perfect master of all that it became a

prince of his rank to know. Moreover, he was wise and prudent, so that the king, who began to perceive the infirmities of age coming on, decided to resign to him the possession of his throne.

A day for the coronation was appointed, and, in the midst of the whole assembly of viziers and great men of the realm, the King of Persia came down from his throne, took the crown from his head and put it on that of Prince Beder. Then he seated his son on the throne and prostrated himself before him, as a token that he transferred to him his authority.

King Beder's reign began most happily. He addressed himself to the reformation of abuses and to the promotion of the happiness of his people. At length his father died, and Beder, in accordance with ancient custom, mourned a whole month and was not seen by anyone during that time. When the month had passed, he laid aside his mourning and resumed his task of governing the kingdom. About this time, his uncle, King Saleh, came to visit him, and one evening while they were talking of various matters King Saleh spoke in such glowing terms of the graces and beauties of the fairest of the sea-princesses, the lovely Jehaunara, that King Beder desired to have her for his wife. In vain, his mother and his uncle explained the difficulties in the way of the fulfilment of his wish, on account of the pride of her father, the King of Samandal, who would refuse the hand of his daughter to any earth-born monarch, however illustrious and powerful he might be. King Beder had set his mind on winning this fair maiden, and he never ceased to weary his uncle with complaints, till he promised to take him to his own dominions and give him a chance to obtain the object of his wishes.

King Saleh then handed his nephew a ring and said: "Here, take this, put it on your finger, and fear neither the water of the sea nor any of the great fishes and monsters that inhabit the ocean depths."

The King of Persia put on the ring, and King Saleh said: "Do as I do."

Immediately they mounted lightly into the air, and soon had plunged into the sea, where they continued on their course until they arrived at King Saleh's palace. The young King of Persia was conducted to the apartments of Queen Fareshah, who presented him to the princesses; and while he was talking with them, she left him and went with her son into another room. There King Saleh told how his nephew had fallen in love with the Princess Jehaunara, and wanted them to contrive measures to procure her for him in marriage.

"I much wish that we did not need to make this demand," said the queen; "but as my grandson's peace and happiness depend on it, we will do what we can. You well know that the King of Samandal has refused to wed his daughter to any of the monarchs of the sea who have asked her of him, saying that they were not her equal in beauty or any other desirable quality. I fear we shall be likewise rebuffed; but we will try to propitiate him with a gift worthy a king to give, and a king to receive."

The queen prepared the present herself. It consisted of diamonds, rubies, emeralds and pearls, all of which she put into a rich box. Next morning King Saleh took the box of jewels and departed with a chosen troop of officers and attendants. He soon arrived at the palace of the King of Samandal, who delayed not to give him audience. King Saleh, after prostrating himself at the foot of the throne, took the box of jewels from one of his servants and opened and presented it.

"You would not make me such a gift," said the King of Samandal, "unless you had a request to propose. If there be anything in my power to grant, you may freely command me, and I shall take the greatest pleasure in complying with your wishes. Speak, and tell me frankly wherein I can serve you."

"I must own," responded King Saleh, "that I have a boon to ask of your Majesty. The thing that I desire is to have you allow your daughter to marry into our family, and thus strengthen the alliance that has long existed between our two kingdoms."

At these words the King of Samandal burst into a loud laugh and fell back on his throne against a cushion. Then with a proud air he said: "King Saleh, I have always thought you were a man of sense and prudence; but now I am convinced that I was mistaken. Tell me,

I beseech you, where was your discretion that you should think of aspiring to marry the daughter of so powerful a monarch as I am. You ought to have considered the great distance between us, and not run the risk of losing in a moment the esteem I have had for you."

King Saleh was hurt by this affronting answer, and could scarcely restrain his anger. However, he replied with all possible self-control: "O king, may your life be preserved! I do not demand your daughter for myself, but for the young King of Persia, my nephew, whose power and grandeur cannot be unknown to you. Everybody acknowledges the Princess Jehaunara to be the most beautiful maiden of the sea; but it is also true that the King of Persia is the handsomest and most accomplished ruler on the land. The princess is worthy of the King of Persia, and the King of Persia is no less worthy of her."

The King of Samandal on hearing this speech was violently enraged, and his response was both loud voiced and insulting. "Dog," cried he, "dare you talk to me in this manner? Can you think that the son of your sister Gulnare is worthy of my daughter? Guards, seize the insolent wretch, and strike off his head!"

The guards were about to obey his commands, but while they were drawing their cimeters, King Saleh, who was remarkably nimble and vigorous, escaped from the room. At the palace gate he was surprised to find a thousand of his own men, well armed and equipped, whom the queen, his mother, anxious about the reception he was likely to meet at the court of the King of Samandal, had sent to his aid. He told them in a few words how matters stood, and putting himself at their head again entered the palace. They soon dispersed the guards of the King of Samandal and secured the king himself. Then they went from apartment to apartment searching after the Princess Jehaunara. But on the first alarm, she and her attendants had sprung up to the surface of the sea and escaped to an uninhabited island.

While the unsuccessful search for the princess was taking place in the palace of the King of Samandal, some of King Saleh's attendants hastened to the queen-mother and related what had happened. King Beder, who was present at the time they made their report, was much concerned, for he looked on himself as the principal cause of all the trouble. Therefore, not caring to remain at King Saleh's court any longer, he left the palace and darted up to the surface of the sea. He did not know the way to his own kingdom, and he chanced to land on the very island to which the Princess Jehaunara had escaped.

Greatly disturbed in mind, he had seated himself in the shade of a pleasant grove, when he heard sounds of the human voice, but was too far off to understand what was said. He arose and advanced softly toward the place whence the sounds proceeded, and presently perceived a fair maiden, whose beauty dazzled him. "This must be the Princess Jehaunara," said he to himself, stopping and considering her with great attention. "Doubtless fear has obliged her to abandon her father's palace."

Then he came forward, and showing himself, approached the lady with profound reverence. "Princess," said he, "a greater happiness could not have befallen me than the opportunity to offer you my services. I beseech you, therefore, fair lady, to accept them; for it is impossible that a lady in this solitude should not want assistance."

"True, sir," responded Jehaunara sorrowfully, "I am a princess, daughter of the King of Samandal, and I was happy in my own apartment of my father's palace, when suddenly I heard a dreadful noise. Tidings were brought me that King Saleh, I know not for what reason, had forced the palace gates, seized the king, my father, and slain all the guards who made any resistance. I had barely time to escape, and I made my way hither."

"Fair princess," said King Beder, "your anxiety is most natural; but it is easy to put an end both to it and to your father's captivity. I am Beder, King of Persia. King Saleh is my uncle. He has no design to seize your father's dominions. His only wish is to obtain the consent of your father that you should be my wife. I had already given my heart to you simply from the account he gave me of your beauty, and now I beg you to be assured that I will love you as long as I live."

This explanation did not produce the effect King Beder expected. When she heard that he had been the occasion of all the ill-treatment of her father and of the grief and fright she had herself endured, she considered him an enemy. However, she resolved not to let King Beder know of her antipathy, but to devise some stratagem whereby she might deliver herself out of his hands. Then she beguiled him with soft discourse, and he never suspected her artifices.

"O my master, and light of my eyes!" said she, "you must be the son of the Queen Gulnare, who is so famous for her wit and beauty. I rejoice that you are the son of such a worthy mother. My father was much in the wrong to oppose our union. Had he but seen how comely you are, he must have consented to make us happy."

So saying, she reached forth her hand to him as if in token of friendship. King Beder believed himself arrived at the very pinnacle of happiness, and he was stooping to kiss the hand he held when she pushed him back saying: "King, quit the form of a man, and take that of a white bird with a red bill and red claws."

Immediately King Beder was changed into such a bird as she described, to his great surprise and mortification. The princess called one of her women and said: "Take him to Dry Island and leave him there."

This Dry Island was a barren rock without a single green thing on it or a drop of fresh water. The attendant conveyed the bird to the island, but when she got there she said to herself: "It would be a great pity to let so worthy a monarch perish in this desolation of hunger and thirst. The princess, who is naturally good and gentle, will very likely later repent of her cruel order."

She accordingly conveyed him to an island abounding with trees and fruits and streams, and then returned to her mistress.

Meanwhile King Saleh, after seeking everywhere in vain for the Princess Jehaunara, shut up the King of Samandal in his own palace under a strong guard; and having issued the necessary orders for governing the kingdom, returned to give the Queen Fareshah an account of what he had accomplished. The first thing he did on his arrival was to ask for his nephew; and he learned with great surprise and vexation that he could not be found. "When word was brought that you had fought with the King of Samandal," said the queen, "he fled; but whether because he was terrified or for some other reason I do not know."

This news greatly afflicted King Saleh. He sent search parties everywhere, but in vain. Presently he left his kingdom in the control of his mother and went to govern that of the King of Samandal, whom he continued to keep a prisoner with great vigilance, though with all due respect to his kingly character.

Queen Gulnare had long been expecting the return of her son, and after receiving no tidings from him for many days, she descended into the sea and went to her mother. She was affectionately welcomed, and then Queen Fareshah told with what zeal King Saleh went to demand the Princess Jehaunara in marriage for King Beder, and of all else that had occurred, including the young king's disappearance. "We have sought diligently after him," added she, "and my son, who has gone to govern the kingdom of Samandal, has done all that lay in his power. I have not lost hope of seeing King Beder again, and shall not be surprised if he appears when we least expect it."

Queen Gulnare was not satisfied with this hope. She felt certain that her son had perished, and lamented bitterly, laying all the blame on King Saleh. Her mother made her consider the necessity of not yielding too much to grief. "Since it is not certain," said she, "that the King of Persia is absolutely lost, you ought to neglect nothing to take care of his kingdom for him. Return therefore to your capital and preserve the public peace."

So Queen Gulnare went back to the capital of Persia, and, aided by the prime minister and council, governed with the same tranquility as if the king had been present.

Poor King Beder was not a little surprised when he found himself alone and in the form of a bird. He was the more unhappy because he knew not where he was, or in what direction the kingdom of Persia lay. But if he had known and had tried the power of his wings to traverse the seas, and had reached his own dominions, what could he have gained? He would have the mortification to continue in the same form, and not be accounted even a man, much less acknowledged the King of Persia. There was nothing to do but remain where he was, live on such food as birds are accustomed to eat, and to pass the night in a tree.

After a while a peasant, skilled in taking birds with nets, came to the island. He saw King Beder with his white feathers and red bill and feet, and began greatly to rejoice; for he had never before seen so fine a bird. Then he employed all his art and cast his net so cleverly that he took the bird captive. Delighted with his prize, which he believed to be of far more value than any of the birds he commonly ensnared, he shut it up in a cage, and carried it away to the capital of the country in which he lived. He believed the king would like to possess such a bird, and he went directly to the palace and placed himself before the monarch's apartment. His Majesty presently looked out of a window, and no sooner did he observe the beautiful bird, than he sent an officer of his household to buy it for him. The officer went to the peasant and asked the price of the bird.

"If it be for his Majesty," answered the peasant, "I humbly beg him to accept it from me as a gift, and I desire you to carry it to him."

The officer took the bird to the king, who thought it so great a rarity that he sent the peasant ten pieces of gold. When the peasant received the money he departed very well satisfied. The king ordered that the bird should be put in a handsome cage and be given grain to eat and water to drink. After a time the officer brought the cage into the royal chamber, and the king, that he might better view the bird, took it out and perched it on his hand. "How beautiful!" said he.

Dinner was served just then, and the bird flapped its wings, leaped off the king's hand and flew to the table. There it began to peck at the bread and meat and other victuals, going from plate to plate. The king was much surprised, and he immediately sent the captain of the guards to ask the queen to come and see this wonder. When the officer related to her Majesty what had occurred, she came forthwith; but she no sooner saw the bird than she covered her face with her veil* and started to leave the room. The king, surprised at her actions, as there was no man present in the chamber but himself, asked the reason of her conduct.

"Sir," answered the queen, "this is not, as you sup-

---

*The Mohammedan women all wear veils when they go out on the street or when they are in the presence of men not of their own household.

pose, a bird, but King Beder of Persia. He has been changed into this form by the Princess Jehaunara, daughter of the King of Samandal. She took this method of revenging herself for the ill-treatment of her father by King Saleh."

The king knew his queen to be a skilful magician, and he earnestly besought her to break the enchantment, that King Beder might resume his own form.

"O king," said she, "be pleased to take the bird into your private room, and I will present to you a monarch worthy of your royal consideration."

The bird had stopped eating. It understood what was said, and of its own accord hopped into the room the queen had indicated. She came in soon afterward carrying in her hand a cup full of water; and when she had uttered some mystical words over the water it began to bubble, and she sprinkled a little on the bird. "By virtue of those magic words I have just pronounced," said she, "quit the form of a bird and return to the form in which you were created."

Scarcely was this command spoken when the bird shook violently and was transformed into a young man of right royal demeanor. King Beder immediately fell on his knees, and thanked God for the favor that had been bestowed on him. He then prostrated himself before the king, his benefactor, and would also have made his acknowledgements to the queen, but she had gone to her own apartment. The king invited Beder to sit at the table with him, and heard from his own lips the wonders of his history. When he ended, the king said: "Tell me, I beseech you, in what I can further serve you."

"Sir," responded King Beder, "I entreat you to grant me one of your ships to transport me to Persia, where I fear my absence may have occasioned some disorder, and where my mother may be distracted because of the uncertainty whether I am alive or dead."

The king gladly granted his request, and as soon as there was a fair wind King Beder embarked. For ten days he had a favorable voyage, but on the eleventh day there arose a furious tempest. The ship was not only driven out of its course, but so violently tossed that all its masts were broken off, and it was hurried along at the pleasure of the gale until it struck a rock and sank. All who were on the ship were drowned except King Beder. He succeeded in grasping a piece of the wreck, and after being dashed about for some time by the waves in great uncertainty of his fate, he perceived that he was near the shore, and in the distance he could see a large city. By exerting all his remaining strength he contrived to swim to the land. Scarcely was he out of the water when, to his great surprise, numerous horses, camels, mules, oxen, cows and other animals crowded to the shore and put themselves in a posture to oppose his going toward the city. He sheltered himself among the rocks till he had recovered his strength, and then forced a way through the crowd of animals. It was with the utmost difficulty that he conquered their obstinacy. They seemed to be trying to make him understand that it was dangerous to proceed.

Nevertheless he went on and entered the city. Presently he stopped at one of the shops, where various sorts of fruit were exposed for sale, and saluted an old man who was sitting within. The old man lifted his head, and when he observed the comeliness and dignity of the youth, he asked him with evident anxiety whence he came, and what business had brought him there.

King Beder in a few words told of the shipwreck, and the old man said: "Come in, sir. Stay no longer on the threshold lest some misfortune may happen to you. I will tell you at leisure why it is necessary you should take this precaution."

The young king entered the shop and sat down, and the old man gave him food. Although King Beder was very eager to hear what he had to tell, the old man could not be prevailed on to talk till his visitor had done eating. Then he said: "You have great reason to thank God that you got hither without any accident."

"Alas! why?" demanded King Beder, much amazed and alarmed.

"Because this is the City of Enchantments," answered the old man; "and it is governed by Queen Labe, who is a beautiful woman and also a most dangerous sorceress. The horses, mules, and other animals which you have seen are all men, whom she has transformed by her magic art. She receives every stranger who enters the city in the most obliging manner, caresses, regales, and lodges him magnificently and gives him many reasons to believe she loves him. But she does not allow her victims long to enjoy this happiness. There is not one whom she has not changed into some animal at the end of forty days. The creatures who opposed your coming to the city did all they could to make you comprehend the danger to which you were exposing yourself."

This account exceedingly afflicted the young King of Persia, and he trembled like a reed shaken by the wind. "To what extremities has my ill-fortune reduced me!" he exclaimed. "I am hardly freed from one enchantment, which I look back on with horror, but I find myself exposed to another no less terrible."

He then related his entire story to the old man, and in particular told of his love for the Princess of Samandal and her cruelty in transforming him into a bird the very moment he had seen her and declared his love to her.

When he finished speaking, the old man tried to encourage him by saying: "Notwithstanding all I have told you of the magic queen, you need not fear her. My name is Abdallah, and I am generally beloved throughout the city, and am not unknown to the queen herself, who has much respect for me. It was well that you addressed yourself to me rather than to anyone else, for you are secure in my house. I advise you to dwell with me, and, provided you do not stray hence, you will have no cause to complain of my bad faith."

King Beder thanked the old man for the kind protection he was pleased to afford him, and he sat down at the entrance to the shop, where his handsome features and graceful bearing attracted the eyes of all who passed. The old man was glad to hear the praise that was bestowed on the young king. He was as much affected by it as if the king had been his own son, and he conceived a fondness for him, which augmented every day.

They had lived about a month together, when Queen Labe passed by. The queen's guards, a thousand in number, well armed and mounted, marched first with their cimeters drawn. Then followed a thousand servants of the household clothed in brocaded silk, also handsomely mounted. Lastly came as many young ladies on foot, richly dressed, and adorned with precious stones, marching gravely, and carrying short spears in their hands. In the midst of them appeared Queen Labe, on a horse glittering with diamonds and having a golden saddle. As soon as the queen came opposite the shop she saw King Beder sitting in front of it and was much impressed by his good looks. She stopped and called to Abdallah. "Tell me," said she, "who is this beautiful and charming young man?"

Abdallah prostrated himself to the ground, and rising

replied: "This is my adopted son. I have no children of my own, and he dwells here to be comfort and company for me."

"Will you not oblige me," said Queen Labe, "by letting this young man come to my palace? Do not refuse, and I will make him great and powerful. Although it is usually my purpose to do evil to mankind, he shall be an exception. I promise you shall never have occasion to repent having obliged me in this manner."

Old Abdallah was exceedingly grieved, both on his own account and King Beder's that the queen's request was so urgent. He could not well refuse to grant it, and he said: "Madam, I rely on your royal word and only beg you to delay this great honor to my adopted son till you again pass this way."

"That shall be tomorrow," responded the queen; and she inclined her head as a token of being pleased and went forward with her troop of attendants.

She did not fail to appear at the old man's shop on the next day, travelling in the same pomp as she did the day previous. "Abdallah," said she, "you may judge of my impatience to have your adopted son with me, by my punctuality in coming to get him at the time you appointed."

The old man, who had prostrated himself as soon as he saw the queen approaching, rose when she had done speaking and advanced as far as her horse's head.

King Beder and the magic queen

"Mighty queen!" he said, "I hope you will not be offended at any unwillingness you may suspect I have to trust my adopted son with you. The reasons I have for hesitation you well know, and you would reduce me to despair, were you to deal with him as you have with others."

"I swear that I will not," responded the queen, "and I once more repeat the oath I made yesterday."

Then the old man turned toward King Beder, and taking him by the arm presented him to the queen. "Madam," said he, "I beg of you to let him come to see me sometimes."

The queen agreed that he should, and she ordered a purse of a thousand pieces of gold to be given to Abdallah in token of her gratitude. She had caused a horse to be brought, as richly caparisoned as her own, for the King of Persia, and while he was mounting, she said to Abdallah: "I forgot to ask you your son's name."

"His name is Beder," said the old man.

The queen had the young king ride beside her, and when they arrived at the palace they alighted and went in together, followed by the queen's women and chief officers. She herself showed him through the palace, where there was nothing to be seen but gold, precious stones, and furniture of wonderful magnificence. After a time a banquet was served, and this banquet included every luxury that could be prepared for a royal table.

In the evening there was a concert and other amusements to add to the gratification of the guest whom the queen desired to honor.

In the days that followed, Queen Labe did everything she could for King Beder's enjoyment. At length, however, the period in which she was accustomed to treat her guests in this fashion came to an end. That night she entered the king's chamber when she believed he was asleep; but though he had closed his eyes he was sufficiently awake to have his suspicions aroused by her evident care to avoid making any noise. So he cautiously began to watch her motions. The first thing she did was to open a chest, and take out various cooking utensils and a number of small boxes, which she arranged on a table. From one of the boxes she sprinkled some yellow powder in a trail across the chamber floor. Then she uttered a few magic words that made the trail of powder change to a rivulet of water.

Great was the astonishment of King Beder, who trembled with fear; but he still pretended to sleep. She next dipped up some of the water in a vessel, poured it into a basin that contained flour and made a dough. After kneading the dough with her hands for a long time and mixing it with several drugs which she took from different boxes, she made a cake. A little fire was burning in the fireplace, and she placed a covered baking-pan on the coals with the cake inside of it. While the cake was baking she restored the utensils and boxes to the chest, and pronounced certain words that made the rivulet vanish. As soon as the cake was baked, she took it off the coals, set it and the baking-pan into the chest, and left the room.

Up to this time the pleasures and amusements of the court had made King Beder forget the good old man who had befriended him; but the next morning, because of what he had witnessed in his chamber, he expressed a great desire to visit Abdallah.

"You have my permission to go," said the queen; "but return soon, for I cannot possibly live without you."

She ordered a horse to be brought for him, and he mounted it and departed. Old Abdallah was overjoyed to see King Beder, and he embraced him tenderly. "Well, and how have you passed your time with that abominable sorceress?" he asked, after they had seated themselves.

"The queen has been extraordinarily kind to me," answered King Beder; "but I observed something last night which gives me reason to suspect that all her kindness is only deceit;" and he related what he had seen.

"This wicked enchantress has formed a mischievous scheme against you," responded the old man laughing. "But fear nothing. I know how to make the mischief she intends you fall on herself. It is high time she was treated as she deserves."

So saying, he got two cakes, which he put into King Beder's hands and instructed him carefully as to their use. These cakes looked exactly like that the queen had made. One of the two, however, was magic, and the other ordinary; and Abdallah cautioned the king to keep them separate and remember which was which.

King Beder thanked the old man in the warmest terms, and after some further conversation he returned to the palace. On his arrival he was told that the queen waited for him with great impatience in the garden. He went to her, and she no sooner perceived him than she came in haste to meet him. "My dear Beder!" exclaimed she, "it seems ages that I have been separated from you. If you had stayed ever so little longer I would have gone to fetch you."

"Madam," said Beder, "I can assure you that my absence was not without good reason. I could not make my stay any shorter with Abdallah, who loves me and had not seen me for so long a time. While I was there he gave me a cake, which I desire your Majesty to accept."

King Beder had wrapped up the magic cake in a handkerchief. This he took out and presented to the queen.

"I accept it with all my heart," she responded; "but I have made a similar cake for you during your absence. Before I taste of this I would like to have you eat a piece of mine."

"Fair queen," said King Beder, receiving her cake with great courtesy, "I cannot sufficiently acknowledge the favor you do me."

But in the place of the queen's cake he dexterously substituted the other which old Abdallah had given him, and breaking off a piece put it in his mouth. "Ah, queen!" he exclaimed, "I never before tasted anything so excellent in all my life"

They were near a cascade, and when the sorceress saw him swallow a bit of the cake, she took a little water in the palm of her hand and threw it in his face. "You young wretch, you villain!" cried she, "quit the form of a man and assume that of a one-eyed mule of hideous appearance."

The sorceress was strangely surprised to find that these words did not have the desired effect, and that he only gave a shudder of fear. Her cheeks reddened, and she said: "Dear Beder, I was only jesting with you. Let not your regard for me be diminished."

"Powerful queen," responded King Beder, "I could not help being a little alarmed at your strange exhortation. But we will say no more about it; and now, since I have eaten of your cake, will you do me the favor to taste mine?"

Queen Labe broke off a piece of the cake and ate it. She, however, had no sooner done so than she appeared much troubled and remained motionless. King Beder at once took water from the cascade, and throwing it in her face, said: "Abominable queen! quit the form of a woman, and be turned into a mare."

The same moment Queen Labe became a very beautiful mare; and so distressed was she to find herself thus transformed that she shed tears in great abundance. She bowed her head to the feet of King Beder, thinking to move him to compassion; but however much he may have pitied her, it was out of his power to repair the mischief he had done. He took her into the stable belonging to the palace, and ordered a groom to bridle and saddle her; yet of all the bridles which were in the stable, not one would fit. Then the king said to the groom: "Let two horses be saddled, one for you and the other for me. You can lead the mare and we will go to old Abdallah's."

King Beder alighted at Abdallah's door, and told him what had occurred, and how he could find no bridle that would fit the mare. "Only a magic bridle will fit her," said the old man; "but I have one, and I will bridle her myself."

After he had done so he said: "It is my advice that you stay no longer in this city. Let your groom go back to the palace with the horses you and he rode hither, and you can mount the mare and return to your kingdom. I have but one thing more to recommend to you; and that is, if you should ever happen to part with this mare, be sure not to give up the bridle."

The young king promised to remember this, and

after bidding Abdallah goodby, he departed. Three days later, as he was entering the suburbs of a great city, he met a venerable white-bearded man. "Sir," said the old man, stopping him, "may I ask from what part of the world you come?"

"From the City of Enchantments," he replied.

They were conversing together when an old woman joined them. She looked at the mare and began to sigh and weep. King Beder and the old man turned to her, and the king inquired what cause she had to be so much afflicted.

"Alas! sir," she answered, "it is because your mare resembles so perfectly one my son had, and which I still mourn the loss of on his account; for I fear he will die of sorrow. Sell her to me, I beseech you. I will give you what she is worth and thank you, too."

"Good woman," said King Beder, "I cannot comply with your request. My mare is not for sale; and even if she were, I believe you would hardly give a thousand pieces of gold for her, and I could not sell her for less."

"Why should I not give so much?" said the old woman. "If that be your lowest price, you need only say you will take it and I will produce the money."

The old woman was so poorly dressed that King Beder felt sure she could not possibly procure such a sum, and he carelessly responded: "Go fetch me the money and the mare is yours."

Immediately the old woman unloosened a purse she carried fastened to her girdle and took forth from it a thousand pieces of gold. At sight of all this money King Beder was vastly surprised and he said: "Do you not perceive that I spoke banteringly about the price of the mare. I assure you I cannot sell her."

The old man, however, looked frowningly at him and said: "Sir, it is necessary you should know that in this city no one is permitted, for any reason whatsoever, to deceive another, on pain of death. You cannot refuse to take this woman's money and deliver to her your mare, when she gives you the sum according to the agreement. I warn you also that you had better do this without any noise, if you would avoid serious trouble."

King Beder, mortified to find himself thus entrapped, regretfully alighted. He was so perturbed he did not even remember to safeguard himself by retaining the bridle as Abdallah had cautioned him to do. The old woman, who was really the mother of Queen Labe, and the person from whom the queen had learned all her magic art, quickly unbridled the mare, and taking some water in her hand from a stream that ran along by the roadside, threw it in the mare's face. "Daughter," she said, "reassume your own form."

The mare vanished, and there stood Queen Labe. King Beder would have fled, but the old woman uttered a weird call that summoned a genie of gigantic stature. This genie took King Beder on one shoulder, and the old woman and the magic queen on the other, and transported them to the palace of Queen Labe in the City of Enchantments.

Now the magic queen began to reproach King Beder. "Is it thus," said she, "that Abdallah and you repay all my kindnesses? I shall soon make you both feel my revenge."

Then, taking water in her hand she threw it in his face saying: "Quit the form of a man and take that of an owl."

These words effected her purpose, and she commanded one of her women to shut up the owl in a cage, and give it neither food nor drink. The woman took the cage, but she disregarded the queen's orders and fed the bird and gave it water. She and old Abdallah were friends, and she sent him word privately how the queen had treated his adopted son, and apprised him of the queen's design to destroy both him and King Beder.

As soon as the messenger was gone and Abdallah was alone he whistled in a peculiar manner, and a genie with four wings immediately presented himself before the old man and asked what he would have.

"Genie," said Abdallah, "I command you to preserve the life of King Beder, son of Queen Gulnare. Go to the palace of the magic queen, and find the compassionate attendant who has charge of the cage that contains King Beder in the form of an owl. Transport her to the capital of Persia that she may inform Queen Gulnare of the danger that threatens her son and the occasion he has for her assistance."

The genie disappeared, went to the palace and sought out the woman in charge of the cage. He told her why he had been sent to her, and then took her up and whisked her away to the capital of Persia. There he left her on the roof of Gulnare's palace. She descended into the queen's apartment and found Queen Gulnare and Queen Fareshah, her mother, lamenting their mutual misfortunes. After making them a profound reverence, she told them the great need King Beder had of their help.

Queen Gulnare, overjoyed at hearing of her son, embraced the good woman, declaring how much she was obliged for her information. Then she went immediately to command the trumpets to sound and the drums to beat, that the people of the city might know tidings had been received of King Beder. Next she consulted King Saleh, whom Fareshah had caused to come speedily thither.

"Brother," said she, "the king, my dear son, is in the City of Enchantments, in the power of Queen Labe. Both you and I must go to deliver him, and there is no time to be lost."

King Saleh forthwith assembled a body of his marine troops who soon rose out of the sea. He also called to his assistance his allies, the genies, who appeared with an army that outnumbered his own. When the two armies joined, he put himself at the head of them, with Queen Fareshah, Queen Gulnare, and the princesses, who all wished to have a share in the enterprise. They then ascended into the air, and presently arrived at the City of Enchantments where they instantly destroyed the magic queen, her mother, and all their followers.

Queen Gulnare had brought Queen Labe's attendant with her, and she now bade the woman fetch the cage in which her son was imprisoned. No sooner was it in her possession than she opened it, took out the owl and sprinkled a little water on him, saying: "My dear son, quit that strange form and resume your natural one of a man."

In a moment the hideous owl disappeared, and Queen Gulnare beheld King Beder, her son. She embraced him, so overcome with joy, that for some time she could only weep without uttering a word.

When she recovered herself she asked that old Abdallah be sent for. He soon arrived and she said: "My obligations to you have been so great, that there is nothing within my power I would not freely do for you as a token of my acknowledgement. Pray inform me how I can serve you."

"Noble queen," responded Abdallah, "If the lady I sent to you will consent to marry me, I ask only for your approval of our union, and for permission to spend the remainder of my days at the court of the King of Persia."

The queen then turned to the lady, and being assured by her blushes that she was not averse to the proposed match, she caused her to join hands with Abdallah, and King Beder promised them places of honor in his court.

This affair made the young king think of his love for Jehaunara, and he said to his mother: "Madam, there is one more person here whom I desire you to see happily mated."

She did not at first comprehend his meaning; but after a little considering, she said: "You doubtless allude to yourself, my son. I will do what I can."

Then she glanced toward her brother's sea-attendants and the genies who were still present. "Go and traverse both sea and land," said she, "and seek for the most lovely and amiable princess in existence. When you have found her, come and tell us."

"It is to no purpose for them to take all that trouble," said King Beder. "I have already given my heart to the Princess Jehaunara. Neither land nor sea can, in my opinion, furnish her equal. It is true that when I declared my love she treated me in a way that would have daunted an admirer less devoted than myself. But I feel that she was excusable. She could not treat me with less rigor, after my uncle had imprisoned the king her father, an act of which I was the innocent cause. But the King of Samandal can be restored to his kingdom, and he may consent to my union with his daughter."

"Son," responded Queen Gulnare, "if the Princess Jehaunara is the only person who can make you happy I will not oppose you. The king, your uncle, can have the King of Samandal brought, and we will see whether he has changed his mind."

King Saleh called for a chafing dish of coals, threw a certain powder into it and uttered some curious words. As soon as the smoke began to rise, the palace shook, and shortly afterward the King of Samandal accompanied by a guard of King Saleh's officers appeared. King Beder cast himself at the King of Samandal's feet, and said: "It is no longer King Saleh that demands the honor of your alliance for the King of Persia. It is the King of Persia himself who humbly begs that boon; and I persuade myself you will not persist in being the cause of the death of a king who can no longer live if he does not share life with the amiable Princess Jehaunara."

The King of Samandal did not allow the King of Persia to remain at his feet. He obliged him to rise and embraced him, saying: "Live, sir; she is yours. My daughter has always been obedient to my will and I do not think she will oppose it now."

Then he ordered one of his officers, whom King Saleh had permitted to attend him, to go for the princess and bring her to him immediately. On her arrival the King of Samandal said: "Daughter, I have provided a husband for you. He is the handsomest and most accomplished monarch at present in the world. I mean the King of Persia. The preference he has given to you over all other princesses obliges us both to express our gratitude."

"Sir," said the princess, "you well know. that I am always ready to obey you; and I hope the King of Persia will forget my ill-treatment of him. It was duty, not inclination, that forced me to act as I did."

The wedding was celebrated in the palace of the City of Enchantments with the greatest solemnity, and was attended by all the princes and princesses whom the magic queen had changed into animals, and who now, on the cessation of her sorceries, had resumed their human form.

Afterward King Saleh conducted the King of Samandal to his dominions, and put him again in possession of his throne; and the King of Persia, now at the height of his wishes, returned to his capital with the beautiful Princess Jehaunara.

X

ALADDIN AND THE WONDERFUL LAMP

IN the large and rich capital city of China, there once
lived a tailor named Mustapha. He was very poor,
and it was with difficulty that he maintained himself
and his family, which consisted only of his wife and a son.

Aladdin, as the son was called, was careless and lazy.
He was disobedient to his father and mother, and spent
much of his time playing in the streets and public places
with idle children of his own age.

When he was old enough to learn a trade, his father
took him into his shop and taught him how to use a
needle; but all Mustapha's endeavors to keep his son
at work were in vain, for no sooner was his back turned
than the boy was gone for the day. Mustapha chastised
him again and again, yet Aladdin continued to cling to
the habits he had formed, and his father was forced to
the conclusion that his efforts to reform him were of no
avail. This so grieved Mustapha that he fell sick and
shortly afterward died.

Aladdin, now that all restraint was removed, gave
himself entirely over to his shiftless habits, and except
at mealtime was never out of the streets all day long.
This course he followed until he was fifteen years old,

without giving his mind to any useful pursuit, or ever considering what would become of him. One day, when he was playing in the street, as usual, a stranger who was passing stopped to observe him.

This stranger was a magician who had recently arrived from Africa, his native country. He needed the help of a youth in an enterprise he had undertaken, and Aladdin's countenance indicated that here was a boy suited to his purpose. By making inquiries of the boy's companions he learned Aladdin's name and something of his history, without the youth himself being aware of what the stranger was doing. Then the magician took Aladdin aside from his playmates and said: "Child, is not your father Mustapha the tailor?"

"Yes, sir," answered the boy; "but he has been dead for several years."

At these words the African magician threw his arms about Aladdin's neck, kissed him with tears in his eyes, and said: "I am your uncle. Your worthy father was my own brother, and I knew you at first sight, you are so like him."

Then he gave the boy a handful of small coins, saying: "Go to your mother, give her my love, and tell her I will visit her tomorrow, that I may see where my good brother lived so long and ended his days."

Aladdin ran home, overjoyed with the money that had been given him. "Mother," said he, "I am just now come from a man who says he is my father's brother. He cried and kissed me when I told him my father was dead, and he gave me money and sent his love to you. He intends to visit you tomorrow."

"Indeed, child," she said, "I never knew that your father had a brother."

Nevertheless she busied herself the next day making the house ready to receive the stranger. Toward night, after she had prepared supper, the magician knocked at the door and came in laden with a present of wine and fruits. He gave what he had brought into the hands of Aladdin and saluted the boy's mother. "My good sister," said he, "do not be surprised at your never having seen me all the time you have been married to my brother Mustapha of happy memory. I have been forty years out of the country, and for much of the time have dwelt in Africa. At last, as is natural, I desired to see my dear brother and my native land again. So I made the necessary preparations and set out on the long journey. Nothing ever afflicted me so much as to hear of my brother's death. But God be praised for all things!—it is a comfort for me to find, as it were, my brother in the son who has almost the same features."

The African magician, perceiving that the widow wept at the remembrance of her husband, changed the topic of conversation, and turning toward Aladdin, asked: "What business do you follow? Are you in any trade?"

At this question the youth hung his head, and was

not a little abashed when his mother said: "Aladdin is a lazy fellow. His father, when alive, strove to teach him his trade, but could not succeed; and since my husband's death, notwithstanding all I can say to the boy, he does nothing but idle away his time in the streets. I hope you can make him ashamed of his ways. Otherwise, I despair of his ever coming to any good. For my part, I am resolved, one of these days, to turn him out of doors and let him provide for himself."

"This is not well, nephew," said the magician. "You must think of working and getting your livelihood. There are many sorts of trades. Perhaps you do not like your father's, and would prefer another. I will try to help you; and if you have no mind to learn any handicraft, I will rent a shop for you, and stock it with merchandise."

To have a shop just suited Aladdin's fancy, and he told the magician that he would gladly accept this offer and was much obliged to him for his kindness.

"Well, then," said the African magician, "I will take you with me tomorrow, clothe you as handsomely as the best merchants in the city, and presently you shall open a shop."

This generosity made it impossible for the widow to doubt that the magician was her husband's brother. She thanked him heartily for his good intentions, and exhorted Aladdin to render himself worthy of his uncle's favor. Then she served the supper, and the three ate together with much cheerfulness and pleasant conversation. A little later the magician went away.

He came again the next day, and took Aladdin with him to a clothier who sold all sorts of ready-made garments. Aladdin chose those he preferred, and the magician paid for them. "Now," said the pretended uncle, "as you are soon to be a merchant it is proper you should become well acquainted with the fine shops and public buildings of the city."

He then showed him the largest mosques and the best places of business, went with him to the inns where the travellers lodged, and afterward to the sultan's palace. Lastly he took him to his own inn, introduced him to some of the merchants who frequented it and gave a feast to make them and his pretended nephew acquainted.

This entertainment did not end until night and then the magician conducted Aladdin to his mother. She was greatly delighted to see him so well dressed and bestowed a thousand blessings on his benefactor.

Early the next morning the magician called again for Aladdin and said he would take him for a stroll in the country, and that on the day following he would purchase the shop. They went together out of the city past some magnificent palaces, to each of which belonged beautiful gardens, that the public was free to enter.

Presently the magician declared he was tired, and he

and his nephew sat down in one of the gardens on the brink of a fountain of clear water, which discharged itself by the mouth of a bronze lion into a basin. "Come nephew," said he, "you must be weary as well as I. Let us rest ourselves, and we shall be better able to pursue our walk."

He pulled from his girdle a handkerchief in which were cakes and fruit, and while they ate he exhorted his nephew to stop going with bad company, and to seek that of wise and prudent men in order to improve by their conversation: "For," said he, "you will soon be a man yourself, and you cannot too early begin to imitate those who set a good example."

When they had eaten as much as they wanted, they got up and pursued their walk until they left the gardens and palaces behind. At length they entered a narrow lonely valley between two mountains. This was the place where the magician intended to execute the design that had brought him from Africa to China. "We will go no further," said he to Aladdin. "I will show you something wonderful, but first gather up all the loose dry sticks you can find that we may kindle a fire."

Aladdin soon collected a great heap, and the magician set fire to it. When the flames had begun to burn brightly the magician threw some incense on them and pronounced certain magical words. At once the earth opened just in front of him, disclosing a square flat stone with a brass ring fixed in it. Aladdin was so frightened he started to run away, but his false uncle caught hold of him and gave him such a box on the ear that he knocked him down. The boy got up trembling, and with tears in his eyes asked: "What have I done, uncle, to be treated in this severe manner?"

"Child," said the magician, softening, "do not be afraid. Simply obey me. Only thus can you reap the advantage I intend for you. Beneath this stone is hidden a treasure destined to be yours, which will make you richer than the greatest monarch in the world. No person but yourself is permitted to lift this stone or to descend into the cave to which it gives entrance. You must, however, do exactly what I command."

Aladdin, amazed at what he saw and heard, forgot his fears and his uncle's rough treatment of him. "Well," said he, "tell me what is to be done. I am ready to obey you."

"Take hold of the ring and lift up the stone," ordered the magician.

"Indeed, uncle," responded Aladdin, "I am not strong enough. You must help me."

"There is no occasion for my assistance," affirmed the magician. "If I help you we shall not be able to get the treasure. Take hold of the ring and lift up the stone. The weight will not trouble you."

Aladdin did as the magician bade him, raised the stone with ease, and laid it at one side. Then he saw that a flight of steps led downward into the earth and ended at a closed door.

"Descend those steps," said the African magician, "and open that door. It will let you into a palace divided into three great halls, one beyond the other. In each of the halls you will see four large brass cisterns full of gold and silver, but you must not meddle with any of this wealth. Before you enter the palace be sure to tuck up your robe and pass through the three halls without stopping. Have a care not to touch the walls even with your clothes; for if you do you will die instantly. Beyond the third hall is a garden planted with fine trees that are loaded with fruit. Walk directly across the garden to a terrace, where you will see a niche in which is a lighted lamp. Take the lamp and blow out the light. Then throw away the wick, pour out the liquid the lamp contains and put the lamp itself in your waistband and hasten back with it to me. You need have no fear that the liquid will soil your clothing, for it is not oil."

After these words the magician drew a ring from his finger and put it on one of Aladdin's, saying: "This is a talisman against all evil so long as you obey me. Go, therefore, boldly, and we shall both be rich for the rest of our lives."

Aladdin descended the steps, and, opening the door, found the three halls just as the magician had described them. He hastened on through them into the garden and crossed it to the terrace on the farther side. There he saw the lamp and took it from its niche, blew out the light, threw away the wick and the liquid, and put the lamp in his waistband. But as he came down from the terrace he stopped to observe the trees, which were loaded with wonderful fruit of different colors. On some of the trees the fruit was entirely white, and on others it was clear and transparent as crystal, while on still others it was red, green, blue, purple or yellow. In short, there was fruit of all colors. It was not fruit that could be eaten, for that which was white was pearls; the clear and transparent, diamonds; the red, rubies; the green, emeralds; the blue, turquoises; the purple, amethysts; and the yellow, sapphires. Aladdin, ignorant of the value of the fruit, would have preferred figs, or grapes, or pomegranates; but he resolved to gather some of every sort. After filling two new purses his uncle had bought for him, he wrapped some up in his robe and crammed his bosom as full as it could hold.

Thus loaded, he returned through the three halls and soon arrived at the mouth of the cave, where the African magician awaited him with the utmost impatience. "Make haste and give me the lamp!" cried the magician.

The last step up to the surface of the ground was a high one and Aladdin was so burdened he could not well clamber up alone. "I cannot get at the lamp now," said he; "but lend me your hand and help me out, and then I will give it to you."

The African magician knew that to assist the boy would destroy the charm. He therefore refused to aid him, though this only made Aladdin the more stubborn in declining to surrender the lamp. In despair of making the youth do his will the magician flew into a terrible passion, threw some more incense into the fire and pronounced two magical words. Immediately the stone which had closed the entrance to the staircase moved into its place, and the earth was restored over it just as if it had never been disturbed.

To avoid being hit by the stone Aladdin had shrank back down the stairway. The closing of the opening left him in dense darkness, and he cried with fear, and called out to the magician that he was ready to give up the lamp, But his tears and appeals were of no avail. The magician could neither see nor hear him. Of one thing Aladdin was now certain—the magician was no uncle of his, but a deceiver whose designs were evil. As a matter of fact, all that the magician cared for was to get possession of the lamp, which, though it looked very commonplace was capable of bestowing almost unlimited power and wealth on the person who had it. He had learned from his books of magic the secret of its value, and where to find it; but his art also revealed to him that he would not be permitted to take it himself, but must receive it as a voluntary gift from the hands of another person. Hence he employed young Aladdin, and hoped by a mixture of kindness and authority to make him obedient to his word and will. When he found that his attempt had failed he set out to return to Africa.

Aladdin descended to the bottom of the steps, intending to get into the palace where there was both space and light, but the door which was opened before by enchantment, was now shut by the same means. He then redoubled his cries and tears and sat down on the steps with the thought that he was destined to die a lingering death there in the darkness. At last he clasped his hands in prayer and in so doing rubbed the ring which the magician had put on his finger.

Instantly the darkness was dispelled and a genie of frightful aspect appeared and said: "What do you want? I am ready to obey whoever has that ring on his finger, I and the other slaves of that ring."

At another time Aladdin would have been frightened at the sight of so extraordinary a figure, but the possibility of being rescued from his apparently hopeless situation gave him courage. Without hesitation he answered: "Deliver me from this place."

No sooner had he spoken these words than he found himself on the very spot where the magician had last left him, and he lost no time in making the best of his way home. He told his mother all that had happened to him, and they were both very vehement in denouncing the cruel magician. After Aladdin had eaten a hearty meal he went to bed and slept soundly until late the next morning. When he awoke and dressed he went to his mother and asked her to give him his breakfast.

"Alas! child," said she, "I have nothing for you. Yesterday you returned so hungry that you ate all the provisions I had in the house. But I have spun a little cotton, and I will go and sell that and buy some food."

"Mother," said Aladdin, "keep your cotton for another time, and give me the lamp I brought home. That ought to sell for enough to supply us with both breakfast and dinner, and perhaps supper too."

Aladdin's mother got the lamp and said to her son: "Here it is, but it is very dirty. I believe it would fetch a higher price if it was cleaner."

She took some fine sand and water to scour it; but at the first rub a hideous genie of gigantic size appeared before her and said in a voice of thunder: "What do you want? I am ready to obey you. I serve whoever possesses that lamp, I and the other slaves of the lamp."

Aladdin's mother, terrified at the sight of the genie, fainted; but her son, who had already encountered a similar phantom in the cavern, was not alarmed in the least. He snatched up the lamp and said boldly: "I am hungry. Bring me something to eat."

The genie disappeared, but promptly returned with a large silver tray, on which were twelve covered dishes of the same metal, containing the most delicious viands. He set down the tray and vanished.

Aladdin fetched some water to sprinkle on his mother's face and revive her from her swoon. Whether it was the water or the smell of the food that effected her cure, she soon came to herself. "Mother," said Aladdin, "be not afraid. Get up and eat. Here is what will satisfy our hunger and give us strength."

His mother was much surprised to see the great tray and twelve dishes and to smell the savory odor which exhaled from the food. "Child," said she, "to whom are we indebted for this great plenty and liberality? Has the sultan been made acquainted with our poverty and had compassion on us?"

"Ask not now," responded Aladdin, "but sit down and eat. When we have done I will answer your questions."

The mother and son sat at breakfast until it was noon, and then they thought it would be best to eat dinner. Even after that was disposed of, enough was left for supper and two meals the next day. When Aladdin's mother had put away what remained, she said to her son: "I expect now that you will tell me what passed between you and that genie while I lay unconscious."

This he did, and she was greatly amazed. "But what have we to do with genies?" she said. "I never heard that any of my acquaintances had ever seen one.

How came that vile genie to address himself to me, and not to you, whom he had before met in the cave?"

"The genie you saw is not the one who appeared to me," answered Aladdin. "If you remember, the one that I first saw called himself the slave of the ring on my finger; and this you saw called himself the slave of the lamp you had in your hand. But I believe you did not hear him, for I think you fainted as soon as he began to speak."

"What!" cried the mother, "was your lamp the occasion of that cursed genie's addressing himself rather to me than to you? Ah! my son, take it where I shall never see it again. I had rather you would sell it than that I should run the hazard of being frightened to death by touching it again. It is my advice that you also part with the ring, and avoid having any dealings with genies in future."

"No," said Aladdin, "I shall take care not to dispose of a lamp or a ring that is so serviceable. That false and wicked magician would not have undertaken so long a journey to secure this wonderful lamp, if he had not known it was extremely valuable. Since we have come honestly by it, let us make a profitable use of it, though without any great show to excite the envy and jealousy of our neighbors. However, since you are so afraid of genies, I will take it out of your sight, and put it where I can find it when I want it. As for the ring I hope you will give me leave to continue to wear it on my finger."

His mother told him he might do as he pleased, but for her part she would have nothing to do with genies and ordered him never to speak of them again in her presence.

The next day when they had eaten all the provisions the genie had brought, Aladdin put one of the silver dishes under his vest, and went out early to sell it. He spoke to a peddler he met on the street, took him aside, and pulling out the dish showed it to him. The cunning peddler examined the dish carefully, and as soon as he had assured himself that it was good silver, wanted to know at how much Aladdin valued it. As the youth had never been used to such traffic he replied that he would trust to the peddler's judgment and honor. The peddler was somewhat confounded at this plain dealing, and as he doubted whether Aladdin understood the material or the full value of what he offered to sell, took a piece of gold out of his purse and gave it to him, though it was but the sixtieth part of the worth of the dish. Aladdin received the money very eagerly and retired with so much haste that the peddler was convinced that the youth would have willingly accepted an even smaller sum than that he had paid him. He started in pursuit of him to endeavor to get some change out of the piece of gold; but Aladdin had a good start, and he ran so fast it was impossible for the peddler to overtake him.

Before Aladdin went home, he called at a baker's, and bought some bread to carry back with him. What money was left he gave to his mother and this enabled her to purchase provisions enough to last them for some time. As soon as the food was gone Aladdin sold another dish, and thus they lived until he had disposed of all the twelve dishes. The peddler bought them and paid each time the same money as for the first, because he durst not offer less, in fear of arousing suspicion and losing so good a bargain. When Aladdin had sold the last dish, he still had the tray, which weighed as much as all the dishes put together. He would have carried it to his old purchaser, but it was too large and cumbersome, and he therefore was obliged to bring him home to his mother's house. After the peddler had estimated the weight of the tray, he laid down two pieces of gold, with which Aladdin was very well satisfied.

When all the money was spent, Aladdin had recourse again to the lamp. He took it in his hand and looked for the part where his mother had rubbed it with the sand and water. There he rubbed it also, and the genie immediately appeared and said: "What do you want? I am ready to obey whoever has that lamp in his hands, I and the other slaves of the lamp."

"I am hungry," said Aladdin. "Bring me something to eat."

The genie disappeared, and presently returned with
a tray containing the same number of covered dishes
as before, set it down, and vanished.

A day or two later, when the provisions were gone,
Aladdin took one of the dishes and went to look for the
peddler. But as he was passing by a goldsmith's shop,
the goldsmith called to him and said: "My lad, I
imagine that you have something to sell to the peddler
with whom I have several times seen you bargaining.
Perhaps you do not know that he is a great rogue. If
you choose to deal with me I will give you the full
worth of what you have to sell, or I will direct you to
other merchants who will not cheat you."

This offer induced Aladdin to pull the dish from under
his vest and show it to the goldsmith. The latter realized at first sight that it was made of the finest silver,
and asked him if he had sold such as that to the peddler.
Aladdin told him he had sold the peddler twelve such,
for a piece of gold each.

"What a villian!" exclaimed the goldsmith. "I will
soon let you see how much the peddler defrauded you."

He took a pair of scales, weighed the dish, and assured Aladdin that it was worth sixty pieces of gold,
which he offered to pay immediately.

"Sir," said Aladdin, "keep the dish and pay me the
money. I thank you for your fairness, and in future,
when I have silverware to sell, I will deal with you and
no one else."

Though Aladdin and his mother possessed a boundless treasure in their lamp, and might have had whatever they wished for, yet they lived with almost the same frugality as before, and it may easily be understood that the money for which Aladdin sold the second lot of dishes and tray was sufficient to maintain them for several years.

During this interval, Aladdin frequented the shops of the principal merchants, who sold linens, silk stuffs and jewelry, and oftentimes conversed with the tradesmen. Thus he acquired a knowledge of the world and a desire to improve himself. His acquaintance among the jewelers led him to comprehend that the fruits which he had gathered when he took the lamp were gems of immense value, instead of colored glass as he had fancied; but he prudently refrained from mentioning this to anyone, and did not even tell his mother.

One day, as Aladdin was walking about the town, he heard an order proclaimed, commanding the people to shut up their shops and houses, and keep within doors while the sultan's daughter went to the bath and returned. Aladdin was seized by a desire to see her face. As she always went veiled in the streets it was far from easy to gratify this wish. He, however, hid near the entrance to the bath hoping to see her countenance as she went in. Shortly after he had concealed himself, the princess came, attended by a crowd of ladies and slaves, and when she was within three or four paces of the door of the bath she removed her veil, and gave Aladdin a full view of her features. The princess was a noted beauty, and Aladdin was so enchanted by the glimpse he had of her that he determined he would try to win her for his wife.

After she reappeared and returned to the palace, Aladdin quitted his hiding-place and went home. His mother observed that he was inclined to be melancholy and silent, and she asked if he was ill. He then told her of what had occurred, and said in conclusion: "I love the princess more than I can express, and I intend to ask her in marriage of the sultan."

Aladdin's mother, on hearing this, burst out laughing, but she quickly checked her merriment and said: "Alas! child, what are you thinking of? You must be crazy to talk thus."

"I assure you, mother," responded Aladdin, "that I am in my right senses. I foresaw that you would reproach me with folly; but I tell you once more that I am resolved to demand the princess of the sultan in marriage; nor do I despair of success. I have the slaves of the lamp and of the ring to help me, and you know how powerful their aid is. Another thing that will greatly assist me is the fact that those pieces of glass, as we supposed them to be, which I got from the trees in the garden of the underground palace, are jewels of fabulous value, and fit for the greatest monarch. All the precious stones the jewelers have in

Bagdad are not to be compared with mine for size or beauty; and I am sure that the offer of them will secure the favor of the sultan. You have a large porcelain dish suitable to hold them. Fetch it and let us see how they will look, when we have arranged them according to their different colors."

Aladdin's mother brought the porcelain dish and he placed the jewels in it in such a way as to make them show off most effectively. His mother was so pleased by their brilliance and the variety of colors that she promised to carry them the next morning to the sultan. She was up before daybreak, took the porcelain dish that contained the jewels, wrapped it in a fine napkin, and set off for the sultan's palace. When she arrived at the gates, the grand vizier and the most distinguished lords of the court had just gone in to the council of state, and a crowd of the common people were following. She went with the rest into the spacious hall where the council was held and placed herself just before the sultan, who sat with the grand vizier and other officials on either side of him. Several cases were heard and adjudged; but at length the time came when the council generally broke up, and the sultan rose and returned to his apartment attended by the grand vizier. The other viziers and ministers of state then retired, and everyone else whose business or curiosity had called them thither did likewise.

When Aladdin's mother reached home she said:

"Son, I have seen the sultan, and am quite certain that he saw me, for I placed myself directly in front of him; but he did not find time to speak to me. Indeed, he was so much taken up with those who appealed to him for one reason or another that I pitied him and wondered at his patience. At last I believe he was heartily tired; for he rose suddenly and would not hear a great many who were ready to address him, but went away; and as I had begun to lose all patience and was extremely fatigued with staying so long, his action pleased me very well. I will go again tomorrow. Perhaps the sultan may not be so busy."

The following day she was again at the sultan's palace, but the monarch did not say a word to her any more than he had on the previous occasion. For several days she continued to be present at the council and always placed herself right in front of the sultan. Finally, on the sixth day, after the council had broken up and the sultan had returned to his private apartment, he said to the grand vizier: "I have for some time observed a certain woman, who is present every day in the audience-chamber carrying something covered over with a napkin. She places herself just before me and always stands from the beginning to the end of the council. If she comes again call her, that I may find out what she wants."

On the next audience day, when Aladdin's mother went to the palace as usual, the grand vizier pointed her out to an officer and bade him bring her to the sultan. She advanced with the officer to the foot of the throne and bowed her head to the floor.

"Rise, good woman," said the sultan, "and tell me what business brings you here."

"Monarch of monarchs," said she, "I beg you to assure me that you will pardon the boldness of my petition."

"Well," responded the sultan, "I will forgive you, be your request what it may. No hurt shall come to you. Speak freely."

When Aladdin's mother had taken these precautions, for fear of the sultan's wrath, she told him faithfully the errand on which her son had sent her. The sultan listened to her very calmly and, without making any comment on her extraordinary petition, asked her what she had brought tied up in the napkin. She took up the porcelain dish which she had set down at the foot of the throne, and after removing the cloth, presented the dish to the sultan.

His amazement was inexpressible at sight of the beautiful and valuable jewels, and he remained for some time lost in admiration. "How rich in color! how dazzling in brilliance!" he exclaimed at last.

When he had taken up and examined all the jewels, one after another, he handed the dish to his grand vizier and said: "Behold, admire, wonder! and confess that your eyes never saw jewels of such rare beauty before. What say you to such a present? Is it not worthy of the princess my daughter, and ought I not to bestow her on one who values her at such a price?"

The vizier, who wanted her to marry his own son, begged him to withhold her from this new applicant for three months, hoping that meanwhile he could persuade the monarch to accept his son as the husband of the princess.

The sultan granted his request, and said to the old woman: "You can tell your son that his proposal to marry the princess is not distasteful to me; but he must wait for three months. At the expiration of that time come again, and we will arrange for the wedding."

Aladdin's mother returned home much more gratified than she had expected, and related to her son the condescending answer she had received from the sultan. He thought himself the most happy of men at hearing this news, and so eagerly did he look forward to the end of the period the monarch had named that he counted every week, day, and even hour as it passed. When two of the three months had gone by, his mother went to a shop in the heart of the city one evening to buy oil and found there was a general rejoicing. The houses were decorated with flowers and banners and drapings of silk, and on the streets were many officers in costumes of ceremony riding on richly caparisoned horses. Aladdin's mother asked the oil merchant what was the meaning of all this festivity.

"Whence come you, good woman," said he, "that you do not know that the son of the grand vizier is to marry the sultan's daughter tonight?"

She did not wait to get her oil, but hurried out of the shop and ran home in breathless haste. "My son!" cried she, "you have been deceived. The sultan's fine promises will come to naught. This night the grand vizier's son is to marry the princess."

At this account Aladdin was thunderstruck, but he presently bethought himself of his magic lamp and determined to try to win the princess for himself in spite of the sultan's intentions. He went to his chamber, took the lamp and rubbed it. Immediately the genie appeared and said: "What do you want? I am ready to obey whoever has that lamp in his hands, I and the other slaves of the lamp."

"You have hitherto done everything I ordered," said Aladdin; "but now I am about to impose on you a harder task than any you have thus far undertaken. The sultan's daughter who was promised me as my bride, is this night to marry the son of the grand vizier. Bring them both hither to me as soon after the ceremony as they are alone."

"Master, you shall be obeyed," responded the genie.

Aladdin supped with his mother as usual and then went to his own apartment to await the return of the genie.

In the meantime the festivities in honor of the princess's marriage were conducted in the sultan's palace with great magnificence. The ceremonies were at last brought to a conclusion, and the princess and the son of the vizier retired to the room prepared for them; but no sooner had they entered it than the genie appeared. Without heeding in the least their amazement and alarm he took them up and instantly transported them to Aladdin's chamber.

"Remove the bridegroom," said Aladdin to the genie, "and keep him a prisoner till tomorrow at dawn. Then bring him back here."

As soon as Aladdin was left alone with the princess he endeavored to calm her fears, but with little success, and he soon left her. He, however, lay down just outside of the door, in order to guard her safety, and there stayed till morning.

At break of day, the genie brought back the vizier's son, and by Aladdin's command transported both bride and bridegroom to the palace of the sultan. Scarcely had the genie set them down in their own apartment when the sultan came to wish his daughter good morning. He kissed her, but she appeared so melancholy and gave him a look so expressive of great affliction that he was much concerned. Thereupon he went immediately to the apartment of the sultana and told her in what a state he found the princess and of how sadly and silently she received him.

"Sir," said the sultana, "I will go to see her."

The princess greeted her mother with sighs and tears, and signs of deep dejection. "How comes it, child, that you will not speak to your father?" asked the sultana. "What has happened?"

After some urging, the princess gave her mother a precise account of all that had transpired during the night. The sultana, however, did not in the least believe this tale, and bade her consider it an idle dream. "Say nothing of this to anyone else," she advised, "lest it be thought that you have lost your wits."

The grand vizier's son, elated with the honor of being the sultan's son-in-law, kept silence on his part, and the events of the night were not allowed to cast gloom on the festivities of the following day, in continued celebration of the royal marriage.

When night came, the bride and bridegroom were again attended to their apartment with ceremonies similar to those on the preceding evening. Aladdin had repeated his orders to the genie of the lamp, and no sooner were the princess and the grand vizier's son alone than they were removed in the same mysterious manner as before. They passed another uncomfortable night in exactly the same way as on the previous occasion, and then were conveyed to the palace of the sultan. The monarch soon came into their apartment to pay his compliments to his daughter, and she, unable to conceal from him any longer the unhappy treatment she had suffered, told him all that had occurred. The vizier's son acknowledged the truth of what she said, and added that, dearly as he loved the princess, he had rather die than go through another such fearful experience. He therefore wished to be separated from her. On hearing these strange tidings the sultan consulted with the grand vizier; and determined to declare the marriage cancelled, and to end the festivities, which were yet to last for several days.

This sudden change of mind on the part of the sultan gave rise to various reports. Nobody but Aladdin knew the secret, and neither the sultan nor the grand vizier had the least idea of who was responsible for the strange adventures that had befallen the bride and bridegroom.

On the very day that the three months named in the sultan's promise to Aladdin's mother expired she again went to the palace and stood in the audience-chamber just where she had before. The sultan knew her and directed his vizier to have her brought to him.

After prostrating herself she said: "Sir, I come at the time you appointed to ask you to fulfill the promise you made to my son."

The sultan observed closely her appearance of poverty and was less inclined than ever to keep his word. So he took council with his vizier who suggested that the sultan should attach such conditions to the marriage that no one could possibly fulfill them. In accordance with this advice the sultan turned to Aladdin's

mother saying: "I am ready to make your son happy
in marriage with the princess my daughter; but I cannot let her marry without some further proof of his
ability to support her in royal state. Tell him I will
fulfill my promise as soon as he shall send forty golden
trays full of the same sort of jewels you have already
presented to me. I require that the trays shall be carried by forty black slaves, who shall be led by as many
young and handsome white slaves, all dressed magnificently. On these conditions I am ready to bestow
the princess on him and I await his answer."

The mother of Aladdin bowed low and retired, thinking all her son's scheming had come to naught. "Where
can he get so many golden trays and such quantities
of precious stones to fill them?" said she. "It is alto-
gether out of his power, and I believe he will not be
much pleased with the result of my visit this time."

When she reached home she gave Aladdin an account
of her interview with the sultan and the conditions on
which he consented to the marriage. "The sultan
expects your answer immediately," said she; and then
added, laughing: "I believe he may wait a long time."

"Not so long as you think," responded Aladdin.
"This demand is a mere trifle. I will prepare at once
to satisfy him."

He retired to his apartment, summoned the genie of
the lamp, and asked him to immediately prepare and
present the gift. The genie disappeared, and within a

very short time a company of forty black slaves led by the same number of white slaves appeared opposite the house in which Aladdin lived. Each black slave carried on his head a golden basin full of pearls, diamonds, rubies and emeralds.

"Mother," said Aladdin, "pray lose no time. Before the sultan and his court rise, I would have you return to the palace with these slaves. They carry the present demanded as a dowry for the princess, and the sultan may judge by my diligence and exactness of the ardent desire I have to procure myself the honor of this alliance."

As soon as the splendid procession, with Aladdin's mother at its head, had begun its march, the people of the city all flocked to see the grand sight. The graceful bearing of the slaves, the richness of their apparel and the golden basins of gems they carried excited the greatest admiration. They entered the palace, and, after kneeling before the sultan, stood in a half-circle around the throne.

"Sir," said Aladdin's mother, addressing the sultan, "my son hopes this present will please you. He has tried to conform faithfully to the conditions you imposed."

The sultan hesitated no longer. Overpowered at the sight of this more than royal splendor he said: "Good woman, return and tell your son that I wait with open arms to embrace him. The more haste he makes to come and receive the princess from me, the greater will be my joy."

As soon as Aladdin's mother had gone, the sultan put an end to the audience. He rose from his throne and ordered the slaves to carry the trays of jewels into the apartment of the princess whither he went himself to examine them with her at his leisure.

Aladdin's mother hastened home. "My son," said she, "you may rejoice, for you have arrived at the height of your desire. The sultan has declared that you shall marry the princess, and would have you come at once to the palace."

Enraptured as he was with this news, Aladdin did not start immediately for the palace as his mother expected, but retired to his chamber. There he rubbed his lamp, and the obedient genie appeared. "Convey me at once to a bath," ordered Aladdin, "and supply me with as rich and magnificent a robe as ever was worn by a monarch."

No sooner were the words out of his mouth than the genie rendered Aladdin, as well as himself, invisible, and transported him into a bath of the finest marble. After Aladdin had bathed, the genie helped him to dress in a robe, the splendor of which astonished him, and then carried him back to his own chamber.

"Now," said Aladdin, "bring me a horse that surpasses the best in the sultan's stables. Furnish also twenty slaves, richly clothed, to attend me. Besides these, I want six women slaves to wait on my mother, each of whom must fetch her a complete dress fit for any sultana. Lastly I want ten purses, each containing a thousand pieces of gold."

The genie soon returned with the horse, the twenty slaves, ten of whom carried purses filled with gold-pieces, and six women slaves, each bearing on her head a dress for Aladdin's mother, wrapped up in a piece of silver tissue.

Aladdin presented the women slaves to his mother and gave her four of the purses to supply her with necessaries. The other six purses he left in the possession of the slaves who brought them and ordered that they should march before him as he went to the sultan's palace and throw the gold by handfuls among the people. Everything was now ready; Aladdin mounted his horse and the procession started. The innumerable concourse of people that gathered and watched him pass made the air echo with their acclamations, especially every time the six slaves who carried the purses threw handfuls of gold into the crowd.

On Aladdin's arrival at the palace, the sultan was surprised to find him more richly robed than he had ever been himself, and was impressed with his good looks and dignity of manner. He embraced him with demonstrations of joy, and led him amidst the sound of trumpets and all kinds of music to a hall where a feast was spread. The sultan and Aladdin ate by themselves, and at the other tables sat the great lords of the court arranged according to their rank. When the feast came to an end the sultan sent for a magistrate and commanded him to draw up a contract of marriage between the princess and Aladdin. The sultan then asked Aladdin if he would stay at the palace and complete the ceremonies of the marriage that day.

"Sir," replied Aladdin, "though great is my impatience to enter on the honor granted me by your majesty, yet I beg you to permit me first to build a palace worthy to receive the princess, your daughter. I pray you to give me sufficient ground near your palace, and I will have the new building completed as quickly as possible."

The sultan granted this request, and Aladdin took his leave, and returned home in the same manner as he had come. As soon as he dismounted he went to his chamber and summoned the genie. "I want you to build me a palace fit to receive the princess who is to be my wife," said Aladdin. "Its walls must be of gold and silver bricks laid alternately. In the middle above the rest of the structure I would like a large hall, and let each of its four walls contain six windows, the lattices of which, except one that I want left unfinished, are to be enriched with diamonds, rubies and emeralds, so that they shall exceed anything of the kind ever seen in the world. Do not fail to provide a safe treasure-house, containing plenty of gold and silver. There must also be stables full of the finest horses, and I shall want officers, attendants and slaves to form a retinue for the princess and myself."

When Aladdin gave these commands to the genie the sun had set. The next morning at daybreak the genie presented himself, and asked permission to carry Aladdin to the palace he had made. This exactly accorded with Aladdin's desire, and a moment later he was there, and saw that all his orders had been faithfully obeyed. He examined every portion of the palace, and particularly the hall with the four and twenty windows, and found it far exceeded his fondest expectations. "Genie," said he, "there is only one thing wanting, and that is a fine carpet for the princess to walk on from the sultan's palace to mine. Lay one down immediately."

The genie disappeared, but was back almost in the winking of an eye and reported the work done. Then he carried Aladdin home.

Not long afterward the sultan's porters came to open the palace gates. Great was their amazement to find what had been an unoccupied garden filled up with a magnificent palace. They told the strange tidings to the grand vizier, and he informed the sultan, who exclaimed: "This must be the palace which I gave Aladdin leave to build for my daughter. He has wished to surprise us and let us see what wonders can be done in a single night."

Aladdin, when the genie left him, requested his

mother to go to the princess and tell her that the palace would be ready for her reception in the evening. She dressed herself carefully and went accompanied by her slaves. The princess had her ushered into her own apartment, gave her a hearty welcome and treated her with great honor. Shortly after her arrival the sultan himself came in and was surprised to find her, whom he had before seen as a suppliant in humble guise, now more sumptuously attired than his own daughter.

Meanwhile Aladdin mounted his horse, and, attended by a retinue of servants, left his old home forever, and rode to the sultan's palace in the same pomp as on the day previous. He took with him the wonderful lamp, to which he owed all his good fortune, and wore the ring the African magician had given him. The sultan sent musicians with trumpets and cymbals to meet him, and he entertained him with the utmost magnificence.

At night, on the conclusion of the marriage cere-monies, the princess look leave of the sultan and made ready to go to the palace Aladdin had built for her. Bands of music led the procession, and four hundred of the sultan's young pages walked along side carrying torches, which, together with the illuminations of the two palaces made the vicinity as light as day. The princess, conveyed in a superb litter and attended by her women slaves, went from one palace to the other on the carpet the genie had put down for the purpose. Aladdin, who had gone on ahead, received her at the entrance and led her to the hall of four and twenty windows which was lighted by an infinite number of wax candles. There a noble feast was served. The furniture of the hall and all its ornaments were of such exquisite workmanship and rich materials that the princess, dazzled to see so much wealth in a single room, said to Aladdin: "I thought nothing in the world was so beautiful as my father's palace; but the sight of this hall shows me that I was deceived."

When the supper was ended, there entered a company of female dancers, who performed according to the custom of the country, at the same time singing verses in praise of the bride and bridegroom. Not until after midnight did the festivities cease.

The next morning Aladdin called on the sultan and entreated him to come and enjoy a repast with the princess. To this proposal the monarch gladly assented, and he and Aladdin returned together. They made a tour of the palace, and when, last of all the sultan entered the hall with the windows that were enriched with diamonds, rubies and emeralds, he exclaimed: "This palace is unequalled in its beauty and splendor the world over. It has only a single fault. Was it by accident that one of these windows was left incomplete?"

"Sir," answered Aladdin, "the omission was by design. I wished your Majesty to have the glory of finishing this hall."

"Your intention pleases me," said the sultan, "and I will give orders about the work immediately."

He sent for the best jewelers and goldsmiths in the city, and by the time the repast Aladdin had provided was eaten, they had arrived. The sultan showed them the unfinished window, and said: "I want you to fit up this window to match the others. Examine them well, and do the work as quickly as you can."

The jewelers and goldsmiths examined the three-and-twenty windows with great attention, and after they had consulted together to know what materials each could furnish they again presented themselves before the sultan. "Sir," said the principal jeweler, "we are willing to exert our utmost care and industry to obey you; but among us all we have not jewels enough for so great a work."

"I have more than are necessary," responded the sultan. "Come to my palace, and you shall choose what may answer your purpose."

When the sultan returned to his palace, he ordered his jewels to be brought out, and the jewelers took a great quantity, particularly of those Aladdin had presented to him. Yet they used them without making any great advance in their work, and they came several times for more. At the end of a month all the jewels the sultan had, as well as their own, were exhausted and still their work was not half finished.

Aladdin, who knew that the sultan's endeavors to

make this window like the rest were in vain, bade the jewelers to desist from their attempt. "Undo what you have begun," said he, "and carry all the sultan's jewels back to him."

This task of pulling the window to pieces occupied them only a few hours, and when they had finished and were gone, Aladdin resorted to his lamp. No sooner had he rubbed it than the genie appeared, and Aladdin said: "I ordered you to leave one of the four-and-twenty windows of this hall imperfect; but now I would have it made like the others.

Immediately the genie vanished. Aladdin had occasion to leave the hall for a few minutes, and when he returned he found the window completed and as perfect and beautiful as any of the rest. Shortly afterward, the sultan, who had been greatly surprised by a visit from the jewelers and goldsmiths returning his jewels, came hurrying to his son-in-law's palace to inquire why he had ordered work on the window stopped.

Aladdin met him at the gate, and conducted him to the grand reception hall, where the sultan was amazed to find the window that was left imperfect now exactly like the others. He fancied at first he must be mistaken, and he examined the windows on each side of it, and afterward all the rest of the four-and-twenty. "My son," said he, convinced at last, "what a man you are to do such astonishing things in the twinkling of an eye! The more I know of you, the more I admire you."

As time went on and Aladdin became used to his new position in the world, he did not confine himself to his palace, but went with much state, sometimes to one mosque, and sometimes to another, to prayers, and he visited the grand vizier and the principal lords of the court. Every time he went out, he caused two slaves to walk by the side of his horse, to throw handfuls of money among the people as he passed through the streets and squares. This generosity and his affable behavior gained him the love and blessing of all the inhabitants of the city.

But far away in Africa the magician, who supposed he had destroyed Aladdin, one day determined to inform himself with certainty whether the youth had perished in the underground cave or not. After he had resorted to a long series of magic tests he was amazed to find that Aladdin, instead of dying in the cave, had made his escape, and was living in royal splendor by aid of the wonderful lamp.

On the very next day the magician started for the capital of China, where, on his arrival he engaged lodging at an inn. He quickly learned about the wealth, charities, happiness and splendid palace of Aladdin, and he went to see the wonderful building. At sight of its gold and silver walls and bejeweled windows, he knew that none but genies, the slaves of the lamp, could have erected it; and envious of Aladdin's high estate, he returned to the inn, determined to find out whether

Aladdin carried the lamp about with him, or where he left it. His magic art soon informed him, to his great joy, that the lamp was in the palace. "Well," said he, rubbing his hands gleefully, "I shall soon have that lamp, and I shall make Aladdin return to his original poverty."

Aladdin at this time was unluckily absent on a hunting trip and would not return for another week. This gave the magician the opportunity he wanted and he resolved on his plans at once. From a coppersmith he obtained a dozen handsome well-polished copper lamps and put them in a basket. With this basket hanging on his arm he went directly to Aladdin's palace, and as he approached it began crying: "Who will exchange old lamps for new ones?"

A crowd of children collected, who hooted at him and thought he was a madman or a fool, as did all who chanced to be passing by. But the magician regarded not the jeering crowd, and continued to shout: "Who will exchange old lamps for new ones?"

He repeated this as he walked back and forth in front of the palace until the princess heard the hubbub and sent a woman slave to inquire what it was about.

The slave returned laughing so heartily that the princess rebuked her. "Madam," said the slave, "who can help laughing to see an old man with a basket on his arm, full of fine new lamps offering to exchange them for old ones? The children and the rest of the mob crowd about him so that he can hardly stir and they make all the noise they can in derision of him."

Another slave, hearing this, said: "Now you speak of lamps, I know not whether the princess may have observed it, but there is an old one on a shelf of our master's dressing-room, and whoever owns it will not be sorry to find a new one in its stead. If the princess chooses, she may have the pleasure of finding out whether this old man is so silly as to give a new lamp for an old one, without requiring anything for the exchange."

The princess, who was not aware of the value of this lamp, and the importance of keeping it safe, entered into the pleasantry and commanded a slave to take it out to the old man. No sooner did the slave with the lamp in her hands get to the palace gate than she called to the African magician, showed him the lamp and said: "Give me a new one for this."

He was sure it was the lamp he wanted, for there could be no other such in the new palace where he doubted not all the rest of the utensils were of shining gold or silver. He snatched it eagerly out of the slave's hand and thrust it as far as he could into his bosom. Then he held out his basket and bade her select the lamp she liked best. The slave picked out one and turned to carry it to the princess, while the place rang with the shouts of the children scoffing at the old man's folly.

Little he cared, and he left off crying his lamps and

went away as fast as he could. He had succeeded in his purpose, and the lamps that were left in his basket were of no further use to him. As soon as he was out of sight of the palace and the mob, he betook himself to one of the least-frequented streets and set down basket and all in a vacant doorway. At length he came to a city gate, passed through and pursued his way until he reached a lonely spot out of view of all habitations. There he remained till nightfall, when he pulled out the lamp and rubbed it.

At this summons the genie appeared and said: "What do you want? I am ready to obey whoever has that lamp in his hands, I and the other slaves of the lamp."

"I command you," said the magician, "to transport me and the palace which you and the other slaves of the lamp have built in this city, to Africa. Wait until all the people in the palace are asleep and carry them with it."

The genie vanished without replying, and that night he and the other genies who were the slaves of the lamp carried the palace entire to Africa, and did this so gently as not to awaken any of its sleeping inmates.

Early the next morning, when the sultan looked out of his window toward Aladdin's palace, he rubbed his eyes in amazement, for the beautiful building was nowhere in sight. He could not comprehend how so large a structure, which he had seen plainly every day for some years, should vanish so soon and not leave the least sign behind. In his perplexity he ordered that the grand vizier be sent for in haste, and when he arrived asked him what had become of the palace.

The grand vizier, who in secret bore no good will to Aladdin, intimated his suspicion that the palace was built by magic, and that Aladdin had made his hunting excursion an excuse for its removal with the same suddenness that it had been erected. He induced the sultan to send a detachment of his guards to seize Aladdin and make him a prisoner. This was done and Aladdin was brought home in chains and dragged into the presence of the sultan, who at once ordered the executioner to cut off his head. The executioner had Aladdin kneel down, bandaged his eyes and raised his cimeter to strike. But the news of Aladdin's arrest had reached the city even before he and his captors did, and the people, whose affection Aladdin had secured by his largesses and charities, were soon swarming around the palace. Many of them were armed, and just as the executioner was about to strike the fatal blow they forced their way in at the gates. The tumult outside was so loud, and the sight of the angry leaders who came running into the council chamber was so alarming, that the sultan called to the executioner to stay his hand. Then, to avoid the danger of an insurrection, he ordered Aladdin to be unbound, and pardoned him in the sight of the crowd.

As soon as Aladdin found himself at liberty, he addressed the sultan, and said: "Sir, I beg you to tell me what crime I have committed which has caused me to lose your favor."

"Your crime, wretched man!" exclaimed the sultan. "Do you not know it. Follow me and I will show you."

He took him to a window and pointed out toward the spot where the palace had stood. "False wretch!" said he, "where is your palace and my daughter?"

Aladdin looked and was speechless with astonishment. At last he recovered himself and responded: "It is true, I do not see the palace, but I am not concerned in its removal. Grant me forty days, and if in that time I cannot restore it I will suffer death at your pleasure."

"I give you the time you ask," said the sultan, "but at the end of the forty days forget not to present yourself before me. My daughter I must have, or your life shall pay the penalty."

Aladdin went sadly forth from the sultan's palace. The lords who had courted him in the days of his splendor now declined to have any words with him, and for three days he wandered about the city, exciting the wonder and compassion of the multitude by asking everybody he met if they had seen his palace or could tell him anything of it. Late on the third day he rambled out into the country, and he was walking along near a river when he slipped and fell down its bank, and thus chanced to rub the ring on his finger which the magician had given him. Immediately the same genie whom he had seen in the cave appeared.

"What do you want?" asked the genie. "I am ready to obey whoever has that ring on his finger, I and the other slaves of the ring."

Aladdin, agreeably surprised at an offer of help so little expected, replied: "Genie, show me where the palace is that I caused to be built, and transport it back to its proper place."

"I have not the power to fulfil your command except in part," said the genie. "The slaves of the lamp carried the palace away and they alone can bring it back."

"Then I command you to take me to my palace, in whatsoever part of the world it may be," said Aladdin. "Leave me there under my dear wife's window."

These words were no sooner out of his mouth than the genie transported him to Africa, and left him close beside his palace, which stood in the midst of a large plain at no great distance from a city. Night was coming on, and the prince, who had sat down to devise a scheme for making his presence known to the princess, fell asleep out of sheer weariness.

The next morning the princess rose early, and she had just finished dressing when one of her attendants chanced to look out through the window and saw Aladdin. The servant instantly informed her mistress, who ran to the window, and opened it. Aladdin, awakened by the sound the window made, looked up, as she looked down, and great was their joy. "I will send a servant to unlock the private door a few steps to your right," said she. "Enter and come up."

The door was soon opened, and Aladdin was conducted up to the princess's apartment. In their happiness at meeting, after their cruel separation, they embraced and shed tears. Then they sat down and Aladdin said: "I beg of you, princess, before we speak of anything else, to tell me what has become of an old lamp which stood on a shelf in my dressing-chamber."

"Alas!" answered the princess, "I was afraid our misfortunes might be owing to that lamp; and what grieves me most is that I have been the cause of them. I was foolish enough to exchange the old lamp for a new one, and the next morning I found myself in this strange country, which I am told is Africa."

"Now that you have explained where we are," cried Aladdin, "I know that what has happened is due to the vile magician who pretended he was my uncle. Where is the lamp?"

"The magician carries it about with him carefully wrapped up in his bosom," replied the princess. "Of this I can assure you, because he pulled it out before me and showed it to me in triumph."

"Princess," said Aladdin, "I think I know how to deliver you and regain possession of the lamp on which all our prosperity depends. But it will be necessary that I first go to the town. I shall return by noon and will then tell you what must be done to insure success. Let the private door be opened at my first knock."

When Aladdin was out of the palace he hastened to the city. After going through several streets he came to the shop of a druggist and went in and bought a certain powder for which he paid a piece of gold. He then returned to the palace.

As soon as he had rejoined the princess he said: "You must help in the scheme I have devised. Assume a friendly manner toward the magician, and ask him to oblige you by partaking of a feast that you will prepare in his honor. Put this powder in the cup from which he will drink, and his death will follow. Then we will regain possession of the lamp."

The princess agreed to do as he wished, and when he left her she arrayed herself gaily for the first time since she left China. That evening, when the magician came in, she surprised him by assuming a look of pleasure and asked him to a feast in the hall of the four-and-twenty windows. He most willingly accepted, and toward the end of the repast, during which she had tried to be very agreeable, she handed him the drugged cup. He drank its contents, out of compliment to her, even to the very last drop, and then fell back lifeless.

Aladdin was waiting just outside of the door, and the princess ran and let him in. She flung her arms around his neck and kissed him, but he put her away saying:

The death of the African magician

"I have more to do. Retire to your apartment for a little while."

When the princess and her attendants were gone out of the hall, Aladdin went to the dead magician, took the lamp from under his vest and after removing its wrappings, rubbed it. The genie promptly appeared, and Aladdin said: "I command you to convey this palace instantly to the place whence it was brought hither."

The genie bowed his head in token of obedience and disappeared. A little later the palace was back in China, and the princess as she sat in her chamber only felt two little shocks, the one when the palace was lifted up and the other when it was put down, with a very short interval of time between.

On the morning after the restoration of Aladdin's palace the sultan was mourning over the fate of his daughter when he chanced to look out of the window and thought he saw that the vacancy created by the disappearance of the palace was filled. On looking more attentively he was convinced beyond the chance of doubt that he saw his son-in-law's palace. His sorrow and grief gave way to joy and gladness, and he hastened to visit the restored palace, anxious to know something of the fate of its former inmates.

Aladdin, who was on the watch and saw him coming, met him at the entrance and led him to the princess's apartment where the happy father embraced his daughter with tears of joy. After explanations of all that had happened were made, the sultan restored Aladdin to his favor and expressed regret for the apparent harshness of his treatment of him, which he declared was wholly due to his paternal love for the princess, his daughter.

A ten days' feast was proclaimed, and it seemed as if Aladdin might now live the rest of his life in peace; but that was not to be. The African magician had a younger brother, who was, if possible, more wicked and cunning than himself. As soon as this brother learned of the other's fate he departed for China vowing that he would be revenged. After crossing plains, rivers, mountains, and deserts and enduring much fatigue, he arrived at the Chinese capital, and took lodging at an inn. He had not been long in the city before he noticed that everyone was talking of a pious woman called Fatima, who wrought many miracles. As he fancied she might be of use to him in his plot for the destruction of Aladdin he requested to be informed more particularly about the holy woman and the sort of miracles she performed.

"What!" said the person whom he addressed, "have you never seen her? She is the admiration of the whole town for her fasting and her exemplary life. Except Mondays and Fridays she never stirs out of her little cell, but on those days she comes into the town and does an infinite deal of good; for there is not a sick person whom she does not put her hand on and cure."

One night the magician went to the hermitage of this good woman and killed her. In the morning he dyed his face the same hue as hers, arrayed himself in her gown and veil and girdle, took her staff in his hand and went straight to the palace of Aladdin. On the way thither the people, supposing he was the holy woman, crowded around him to beg his blessing; and those who were suffering from disease kneeled for him to lay his hands on them, which he did, muttering some words in form of a prayer. At last he came to the square before Aladdin's palace, and he had been there only a short time in the midst of the noisy crowd that had followed him when the princess observed him from her window.

She had long heard of Fatima, but had not hitherto seen her. So she sent four of her woman slaves to ask the holy woman to come into the palace. As soon as the crowd saw the attendants from the palace, it made way, and the magician advanced to meet them.

"Holy woman," said one of the slaves, "the princess would like to have a little conversation with you."

"She does me great honor," responded the false Fatima. "I am ready to accompany you to the palace."

When he was ushered into the presence of the princess she made him sit down beside her and said: "My good woman, I have one thing to request of you. It is that you stay with me always, so I may be edified by your way of living, and pattern after your good example."

"Princess," said the magician, "I beg you not to ask what would interfere with my prayers and devotions."

"Your staying here shall be no hindrance to you," declared the princess. "I have a great many apartments unoccupied. You can choose which you like best and have as much liberty to perform your devotions as if you were in your own cell."

The magician, who really desired nothing so much as to thus become an inmate of the palace, in order to more easily carry out his designs, did not long excuse himself from accepting the obliging offer made by the princess. "Madam," said he, "whatever resolution a poor wretched woman such as I am may have made to renounce the pomp and grandeur of this world, I dare not presume to oppose the will and commands of so pious and charitable a princess."

"Then come with me," said the princess, rising. "I will show you what vacant apartments I have, that you may select the one which in future will be yours."

The magician followed the princess, and of all the apartments she showed him, made choice of that which was the worst, saying it was too good for him, and he only accepted it to please her.

Afterward the princess would have brought him back into the great hall to dine with her. But in that case he would be obliged to show his face, which thus far he had kept concealed with Fatima's veil. He therefore begged earnestly to be excused, telling her that he never ate anything except bread and dried fruits, and he preferred to have that slight repast sent to his own apartment.

"Your wishes shall be respected," said the princess, "and I will order for you such a dinner as you desire. But remember I want to talk with you as soon as you have finished eating."

When the false Fatima rejoined the princess he was as warmly greeted as before. "I am delighted," said she, "to have as a guest so holy a person as yourself, who will confer a blessing on this palace. But now I am speaking of the palace, tell me how you like it. What do you think of this hall?"

The pretended Fatima surveyed the hall from one end to the other, and said: "The opinion of such a solitary being as I, who am unacquainted with what the world calls beautiful, is of little value in this matter. However, I will say that so far as I can judge, the hall is truly admirable except in one particular."

"What is that?" inquired the princess. "For my part I had believed it absolutely perfect, but if there is a lack it shall be supplied."

"Forgive me the liberty I have taken," said the magician; "but I think if a roc's egg was hung up in the middle of the dome, this hall would be the wonder of the world."

"My good woman," said the princess, "what is a roc, and where may one get an egg?"

"It is a bird of prodigious size, which inhabits the summit of Mount Caucasus," was the magician's reply. "The architect who built your palace can easily get you one of its eggs."

The princess thanked the magician for his advice, and conversed with him on other matters; but she could not forget the roc's egg and resolved to request it of Aladdin when he next visited her apartment. He came in toward evening and found her in a very ill-humor. "What is amiss?" he asked.

"All my pleasure in the hall of four-and-twenty windows is spoiled," she replied, "for want of a roc's egg hanging from the dome."

"If that is all," responded Aladdin, "you shall soon be happy."

He left her and went to the great hall. There he pulled out of his bosom the lamp, which he now always carried about with him. He rubbed it and the genie immediately appeared. "Genie," said Aladdin, "I command you to bring a roc's egg and hang it up in the dome of this hall."

"Wretch!" cried the genie in a loud and terrible voice, "have not I and the other slaves of the lamp done everything for you? and yet such is your unexampled ingratitude that you ask me to bring my master and hang him up in this dome. You and your wife and your palace deserve to be burnt to ashes; but I spare you because this request did not originate with you.

It's true author is the brother of the African magician. He is now in your palace disguised as the holy woman Fatima, whom he has murdered, and it is at his suggestion that your wife makes this wicked demand. His design is to kill you. Therefore take care of yourself."

So saying the genie disappeared, and Aladdin went back to the princess. Without mentioning a word of what had happened he sat down and complained that his head ached. On hearing this, the princess told him that the holy Fatima was in the palace. "I will have have her summoned," said the princess, "for doubtless she can cure you."

When the pretended holy woman entered the apartment, Aladdin said: "I am glad you are here at so fortunate a time. A violent pain in my head torments me, and I hope you will not refuse me that cure which you impart to afflicted persons."

He arose and held down his head, and the counterfeit Fatima advanced toward him with his hand on a dagger concealed in the girdle under his gown. Aladdin observed this, and he snatched the weapon from the magician's hand and pierced him to the heart.

"My dear husband, what have you done?" cried the princess. "You have killed the holy woman!"

"No," said Aladdin, "I have not killed Fatima, but a villain who would have assassinated me if I had not prevented him. This wicked man is the brother of the African magician who so recently attempted our ruin."

He drew aside the veil from the dead man's face and told her the fate of the true Fatima, and how narrowly she and the palace had escaped destruction through the treacherous suggestion which had led to her request.

After this Aladdin and his wife lived in peace, and when the sultan died Aladdin reigned in his stead.

XI

HOW BABA ABDALLAH BECAME POOR

THE Caliph Haroon Alrashid was accustomed to go about the city of Bagdad in disguise that he might see for himself the condition of the people and hear their comments on his court and government. On one occasion he and his grand vizier clothed themselves as foreign merchants and went their way through the different parts of the city. As they were crossing a bridge from the portion of the city which lies on one side of the river Euphrates to that which lies on the other, they met an old blind man who asked alms of them. The caliph put a piece of gold into his hand, and the blind man instantly caught hold of the caliph's arm and stopped him. "Sir," said he, "pray pardon me for detaining you, but I desire you to give me a box on the ear. Either do that or take your money back, for I cannot receive it except on the condition I have named without breaking a solemn oath I have sworn to God."

Having thus spoken, the blind man released the caliph's arm that he might strike, but for fear he should pass on without doing it, held him fast by his clothes.

The caliph, surprised both at the words and actions of the blind man, responded: "I cannot comply with your request. It would be unseemly that I should lessen the merit of my charity by treating you as you would have me."

But though he endeavored to get away, the blind man clung to him so persistently he could not free himself. Therefore, unwilling to be detained longer, he yielded to the blind man's request and gave him a slight blow. Then the blind man let the caliph go, and thanked and blessed him.

Later, the caliph, on his way to his palace, observed in a street, which he had not passed through for a long time, a newly built edifice, which seemed to be the residence of some great lord of the court. He asked the grand vizier if he knew to whom it belonged.

"I do not know," replied the vizier, "but I will go and inquire."

One of the dwellers on the street, whom he questioned, told him that the house belonged to Cogia Hassan, a man who had formerly worked at rope-making, but who evidently had acquired great wealth, as he defrayed honorably and generously the expenses he had been at in building.

The grand vizier rejoined the caliph, and gave him a full account of what he had heard. "I must see this fortunate rope-maker," said the caliph, "and also the blind beggar we met on the bridge. Go therefore, and ask them to come tomorrow to my palace."

Accordingly the vizier sought out the rope-maker

and the blind man, and the next day brought them into the presence of the caliph. They prostrated themselves before the throne, and when they rose the caliph asked the blind man his name.

"My name is Baba Abdallah," was the reply.

"Baba Abdallah," said the caliph,"I ordered you to come hither to know from yourself why you made the unwise oath of which you told me. Speak freely, and hold back nothing, for I will know the truth."

The blind man cast himself a second time at the foot of the caliph's throne, with his face to the floor, and then rising spoke as follows:

Commander of the Faithful, I most humbly ask your pardon for requiring you to box my ear. As to the extravagance of my action, I own that it must seem strange to mankind, but in the eyes of God it is a slight penance for an enormous crime of which I have been guilty, and for which, if all the people in the world were each to give me a box on the ear, it would not be a sufficient punishment.

I was born at Bagdad. My father and mother died while I was yet a youth, and I inherited from them an ample estate. Though I was young I did not squander away my fortune in idle luxury, but took advantage of every opportunity to increase it by my industry. I soon became rich enough to purchase fourscore camels. These I let out to merchants, who hired them at a considerable profit to me for carrying merchandise from place to place.

One day, as I was returning with my unloaded camels from Bussorah, whither I had carried some bales that were to be sent to the Indies, I stopped at a place where there was good pasturage, some distance from any habitation, to let my beasts graze. While I was sitting there a dervish, who was walking toward Bussorah, came and sat down beside me to rest himself. I asked him whence he came and where he was going. He put the same questions to me; and when we had satisfied each other's curiousity, we produced our provisions and ate together.

During our repast the dervish told me he knew of a spot not far away, where there were such immense riches, that even if all my fourscore camels were loaded with gold and jewels taken thence, the amount of treasure they could carry would not be missed.

This intelligence so charmed me that I could scarcely contain myself. "Good dervish," said I, "show me where the treasure is."

"I am ready to conduct you to it," said the dervish, "and we will load your camels with the jewels and gold on condition that when they are so loaded, you will let me have one half of them. Afterward we will separate and each take his camels where he pleases. You see there is nothing but what is strictly equitable in this division; for if you give me forty camels, you will procure by my means the wherewithal to purchase thousands."

I agreed to his proposal, and at once collected my camels and set out with the dervish. We travelled for some time and then came to the entrance of a valley. This entrance was so narrow that two camels could not go through it abreast, and the mountains on either side were very high and steep. When we had gone on into the valley, the dervish bade me stop the camels, and he proceeded to gather some sticks and light a fire. That done, he cast some incense onto the flames, pronounced certain words which I did not understand, and a thick smoke arose. The smoke soon drifted away, and the rock forming the side of the valley opened and exposed to view a magnificent palace in the hollow of the mountain.

We entered the palace and found ourselves surrounded by treasures on all sides. So eager was I to possess them, that, like an eagle seizing its prey, I fell on the first heap of golden coin that was near me. The dervish, however, paid more attention to the jewels than to the gold, and I soon followed his example. My sacks were large, but I was obliged to proportion my burden to the strength of my camels. As soon as the camels were loaded with all they could well carry the dervish used the same words to shut the treasury that he had used to open it, and after the doors had closed, the rock seemed as solid and entire as it was before.

We now divided our camels, came out of the valley, and went on until we arrived at the great road where we were to part, the dervish to go to Bussorah, and I to Bagdad. To thank him for his great kindness I made use of the most expressive terms, testifying my gratitude that he had let me have a share of such riches. We embraced each other and started on our different routes. But I had not gone far, following my camels, which paced quietly along, when the demon of envy took possession of my heart. I deplored the loss of the other forty camels, and much more the riches wherewith they were loaded. "The dervish has no occasion for all this wealth," said I to myself; "for he is master of the treasure and can have all he pleases."

So I stopped my camels, ran after the dervish, called to him as loud as I could and signalled to him to stop, which he did. When I came to him, I said: "Brother, I had no sooner parted from you than a thought came into my head which neither of us had reflected on before. You are a recluse, whose habit it is to live in quiet, free from all the anxieties of the world, and intent only on serving God. You probably know not what trouble you have taken on yourself to care for so many camels. It is my advice that you keep but thirty and let me relieve you of the other ten. You will find them awkward creatures to manage. I have had experience, and I know whereof I speak."

"I believe you are right," responded the dervish. "Choose which ten you please."

It did not take me long to make a selection and put them on the road to follow my others. I had not imagined the dervish would be so easily persuaded to part with his camels. As a result my greediness increased and made me think it would be no hard matter to get ten more. Therefore, instead of thanking him, I said: "Brother, the interest I take in your repose is so great that I cannot depart without asking you to consider how difficult a thing it is to govern even thirty loaded camels, especially for you who are not used to the work. You will fare much better to return to me as many more as you have already surrended."

My appeal had the desired effect on the dervish, who, without any hesitation, gave me ten more camels. He now had only twenty, while I was master of sixty and could boast of greater riches than any sovereign. You would have thought I might now have been content, but the more we have the more we want, and my success made me so greedy that I longed for the rest of the camels.

I redoubled my efforts and urged the dervish to grant me ten of the twenty, which he did with a good grace. As to the ten he had left, I embraced him, kissed his feet, caressed and entreated him, so that he gave me those also. "Make a good use of them, brother," said the dervish, "and remember that God can take away riches as well as give them."

Even yet I was not satisfied, though I had all my fourscore and knew they were loaded with gold and jewels. I had observed that before the dervish left the cave he took a small box, and after showing me that it contained only a sort of ointment, put it into his breast. It now occurred to me that this little box of ointment perhaps contained some treasure more precious than all the riches I had gained, and I determined to obtain it. I had bade the dervish adieu, but I once more turned back and said: "What will you do with that little box of ointment you got from the cavern palace? It seems a trifle not worth your carrying away, and I entreat you to make me a present of it. What occasion has a dervish, who has renounced the vanities of the world, for perfumes or scented ointments?"

The dervish pulled it out of his bosom, and handing it to me, said: "Here, take it, brother, and be content. If I can do more for you, you need only to ask me. I am ready to satisfy you."

When I had the box in my hand, I opened it, and looked in. "Since you are so good," said I, "surely you will not refuse to tell me the use of this ointment."

"The use is very surprising," said the dervish. "If you apply a little of it on the lid of the left eye, you will see all the treasures contained in the bosom of the earth, but if you apply it to the right eyelid, it will make you blind."

"Take the box," said I to the dervish, "and apply some of the ointment to my left eyelid. You understand how to do it better than I, and I am eager to experience what seems so incredible."

The dervish had no sooner done as I requested than I saw immense treasures and such vast riches that it is impossible for me to give an account of them; but as I was obliged to keep my right eye shut with my hand I asked him to apply some of the ointment to that eye also.

"I am ready to accommodate you in this matter," said the dervish; "but you must remember I have warned you that if any is put on your right eyelid, you will immediately be blind."

Far from being persuaded of the truth of what the dervish said, I imagined there was some wonderful mystery which the application of the ointment would reveal. "Brother," I responded smiling, "I am convinced that you wish to mislead me. It is not natural that this ointment should have two such contrary effects."

"I tell you simply the truth," declared the dervish, "and you ought to believe me."

But I persisted in my obstinacy and at last he reluctantly put a little of the ointment on my right eyelid. Alas! I ceased at once to distinguish anything with either eye, and became blind as you see me now. "Ah, dervish!" I exclaimed in an agony of dismay, "that of which you forewarned me has come to pass. I am sensible of the misfortune I have brought on myself by my fatal curiosity and greedy desire of riches; but you, dear brother, who are so charitable and good, among the many wonderful secrets with which you are acquainted, have you not one that will restore my sight?"

"Miserable man!" answered the dervish, "you might have avoided this calamity. Your punishment is only what you deserve. The blindness of your mind was the cause of the loss of your eyes, and the restoration of your sight is beyond my power. God gave you riches of which you were unworthy; and on that account He takes them from you, and will by my hands give them to men not so ungrateful as yourself."

The dervish said no more, but left me overwhelmed with confusion and grief and after collecting my camels he went away with them toward Bussorah. I cried out loudly as he was departing, and entreated him not to desert me in my unhappy condition. It seemed to me that he might at least conduct me to some inn; but he was deaf to all my appeals. Thus deprived of sight and of everything I had in the world, I should have died with affliction and hunger, if the next day a passing caravan had not charitably received me and brought me to Bagdad.

After this manner was I reduced, without remedy,

from a condition of great wealth to a state of poverty. I had no other way to subsist except by asking alms, which I have done ever since. In order to expiate my crime against God, I enjoined on myself, by way of penance, a box on the ear from every person who should pity my condition.

This, Commander of the Faithful, is the motive which caused me to make so strange a request of you. I crave your mercy once more, but am ready to receive any chastisement you choose to inflict.

"Baba Abdallah," said the caliph, "your sin has been great; and yet your self-inflicted penance proves your sorrow. Pray to God for pardon without ceasing; and that you may not be kept from your devotions by the necessity of getting your living, I present you henceforth four silver derhems* a day, which my grand vizier shall give you each morning with the box on the ear you have imposed on yourself."

At these words Baba Abdallah prostrated himself before the caliph's throne, thanking him and wishing him all happiness and prosperity. Then he rose and stood aside, and the caliph turned to Cogia Hassan, and demanded of him the narrative of his good fortune.

---

*A derhem is a coin valued at about ten cents.

XII

HOW COGIA HASSAN ACQUIRED WEALTH

I OWE the good fortune I now enjoy to two dear friends, whose names are Saad and Saadi. The latter is very rich, and he was always of the opinion that wealth is essential to happiness. He declared further his belief that the real cause of a life of poverty is in most cases a lack of sufficient money to make a thrifty start. Saad doubted the truth of these sentiments. He affirmed that a poor man may become rich by other means as well as money, and that some have become rich by mere chance.

"Well," said Saadi, on one occasion, when they had been talking on this subject, "we will not dispute any more, but will test our different theories by an experiment. I will give a sum of money to an honest, but poor artisan, and see if he obtains with it wealth and ease. If I have not the success I expect, then you shall try some other way and we will see whether that proves more effective."

A few days later Saad and Saadi passed through the street where I was working at my trade of rope-making. It was no hard matter for them to guess my poverty by my dress and appearance. Saad pointed to me and said to his companion: "There is a man, whom I remember seeing at work here in the same destitution for a long time."

The two friends came to me and Saadi asked me my name, and I replied that it was Hassan. He then expressed surprise that with all my industry I had not contrived to extend my trade and save money.

"Sir," said I, "you will no longer be amazed at my condition when I tell you that, let me work as hard as I can from morning till night, I find difficulty in supplying my wife and five children with food. They lack many things which it is a hardship to do without. So how is it possible that I should save money?"

"I am not so much astonished as I was," responded Saadi, "now that I understand your situation. But if I was to present you with two hundred pieces of gold, would you make good use of them, and do you think such a sum would enable you to become rich?"

"You seem to be too good a gentleman to banter me," I replied; "and I will say that I believe I could acquire wealth even if a considerably less sum than that you name were at my disposal."

The generous Saadi immediately showed me that he was serious in what he had suggested, for he pulled a purse out of his bosom, and putting it into my hands said: "Here, take this purse. It contains two hundred pieces of gold. God bless you and give you grace to make good use of this money; and, believe me, my friend and I shall both be greatly pleased if it assists you to become more prosperous than you now are."

When I got the purse my joy was so great that my speech failed me, and I could only thank my bene-factor by laying hold of the hem of his garment and kissing it. Then he and his friend pursued their walk.

As soon as they were gone, I returned to my work, and my first thought was what I should do with the purse to keep it safe. I had in my house neither box nor cupboard in which to lock it up, nor any other place where I could be sure it would not be discovered if I concealed it. In this perplexity I laid aside ten pieces of gold for present necessaries, and wrapped the rest up in the folds of my turban.

The principal expense I was at that day was to lay in a good stock of hemp for use in making my ropes, and afterward, as my family had eaten no meat for a long time I bought some for supper. I was carrying the meat home when a famished vulture flew toward me and would have taken it away if I had not held it very tight. But the tighter I held my meat, the more the bird struggled to get it, dragging me first this way and then that, till, in my exertions, my turban fell to the ground.

The vulture immediately let go its hold on the meat, seized the turban, and flew off with it. I cried out so loudly that I alarmed all the men, women and children in the neighborhood, and they joined their shouts with mine to make the vulture drop its prize; but our cries did not avail. It carried off my turban and was soon out of sight.

I went home very melancholy at the loss of my money, and as I was obliged to buy a new turban, that reduced still further the small remainder of the ten gold-pieces. What little was left was not sufficient to give me any hope of bettering my condition; and I was the more troubled over this because of the disappointment I knew it would occasion my benefactor.

While the remainder of the gold lasted, my family and I lived better than usual; but I soon relapsed into my former poverty, utterly unable to extricate myself from wretchedness. However, I never murmured nor repined. "God was pleased to give me riches when I least expected them," said I; "and He thought fit to take them from me, almost immediately, yet I will praise His name and submit myself to His will."

These were my sentiments, but my wife, from whom I could not keep secret the loss I had sustained, complained bitterly. In my trouble I told my neighbors that I had a hundred and ninety pieces of gold in the turban the vulture carried off; but as they knew my poverty and could not comprehend how I could have gotten so large a sum, they only laughed at me.

About six months after this misfortune the two friends were again walking through that part of the town where I lived and determined to call and inquire what use I had made of the gold Saadi had given me.

"You will undoubtedly see a great alteration in the man," remarked Saadi to his companion. "I expect we shall hardly know him."

Just then they turned into the street where I worked, and Saad perceived me at a distance. "I see Hassan," said he; "but can discern no change in his person. He is as shabbily dressed as when we saw him before, except that his turban looks somewhat better."

Saadi saw that Saad had spoken only the truth, and he wondered to what could be attributed this lack of change in my appearance.

"Well, Hassan," said Saad, "how have things gone with you since we saw you last?"

"Gentlemen," I replied, "I deeply grieve to tell you that your hopes as well as mine have not had the success you had reason to anticipate. You will scarcely believe the extraordinary adventure that has befallen me. I assure you, nevertheless, on the word of an honest man, that a vulture flew away with my turban, in which for safety I had wrapped my money."

Saadi rejected my assertion, and said: "Hassan, you joke and would deceive me. What have vultures to do with turbans? They only search for something to satisfy their hunger."

"Sir," I replied, "what I have told you is so publicly known in this part of the town that almost anyone can satisfy you as to the facts."

Saad took my part, and related a great many as surprising stories of vultures. At last Saadi was convinced,
and after bidding me be more careful in the future he
pulled out his purse and counted two hundred pieces of
gold into my hand. "These I present to you," said he,
"that they may win for you the advantages the others
should have procured."

I told him that this second kindness was much greater
than I deserved after what had happened, and that I
would surely be able to give a better report of myself
when he again came to see me. There was much more
I would have said, but he turned away and continued
his walk with his friend.

As soon as they were gone I put the gold in my bosom,
for lack of a purse, and then left off work and went
home. My wife and children were none of them in the
house, and I pulled out my money, put ten pieces
aside for present use and wrapped up the rest in a
linen cloth, which I tied fast with a knot. I next considered where I could safely hide this and at length
secreted it in an earthern pot full of bran that stood in a
corner of the kitchen. The pot had been there for a
long time and I imagined that no one would ever look
into it. My wife soon returned, and I told her I would
go to buy some hemp, without saying anything to her
about the second present from Saadi.

While I was absent there passed through our street
a peddler who sold washing-balls. My wife wanted

some and beckoned to him. She, however, had no money, and she asked him if he would exchange the washing-balls for a pot of bran. The peddler consented and the bargain was made.

Not long afterward I came home with as much hemp as I could carry, followed by five porters, also loaded with hemp. After I had paid the porters for their trouble I looked about me and could not see the pot of bran. I asked my wife what had become of it, and she told me of the bargain she had made with the peddler, which she thought was a very good one.

"Ah! unfortunate woman!" cried I, "you know not what injury you have done me, yourself and our children. You thought you only disposed of an almost worthless pot of bran, but in it were a hundred and ninety pieces of gold which Saadi this day gave me, with ten more, as a second present."

My wife was like one distracted when she knew what she had done. She cried, beat her breast, and tore her hair and clothes. "Unhappy woman that I am!" she wailed, "where shall I find this peddler? I know him not and never saw him in our street before. Oh, husband! you were much to blame for being so secretive in such an important matter."

"Wife," said I, "moderate your grief. By your cries you will alarm the neighbors, and there is no reason why they should be informed of our misfortunes. They will only laugh as they did before. We had better bear our loss patiently and submit to the will of God. It is true we live poorly; but what have the rich that we have not. Do not we breathe the same air, enjoy the same light, and the same warmth of the sun? They die as well as we. In short, the advantage they have over us is so very small we ought not to covet it."

My wife and I comforted ourselves with these reflections, and I pursued my trade with as much alacrity as before these mortifying losses which followed each other so quickly. The only thing that troubled me was the thought of how I should look Saadi in the face when he came and asked me what use I had made of his money.

After some time Saad and Saadi again called to inquire as to my progress. They still retained their former differing opinions as to the result of Saadi's repeated liberality. I saw them coming, but applied myself very earnestly to my work and did not lift my eyes again till they were close to me and had saluted me. Then I at once told them of my latest misfortune, and that I was as poor as ever. In conclusion I said: "Could I guess that a peddler would come by that very day to whom my wife would give in exchange for what she bought a pot of bran which had stood in our kitchen for years?"

When I had thus spoken I turned to Saadi saying: "I see, sir, that it has pleased God I should not be enriched by your liberality, but must remain poor. How-

ever, my obligation to you is the same as if your gifts
had produced the desired effect."

"I do not regret the four hundred pieces of gold I
gave you to raise you in the world," responded Saadi.
"The money was presented without any expectation of
recompense other than the pleasure of doing good, and
for the sake of an experiment I wished to make."

Then, addressing his companion, he remarked: "It
is now your turn to experiment and try to prove to me
that there are ways to make a poor man's fortune besides giving money to him. Let me see what you can
do with Hassan. I dare say, whatever you may give
him, he will not be made a bit richer than he was by my
two gifts of gold."

Saad had a piece of lead in his hand which he showed
Saadi. "You saw me pick up this piece of lead," said
he, "which I found on the ground. I will give it to
Hassan, with the expectation that in some way it will
come to be worth a great deal."

Saadi burst out laughing. "What is the value of
that bit of lead?" said he, "a farthing? How is it
possible for Hassan to make any use of it in winning
wealth?"

But Saad presented it to me and said: "Take it,
and let Saadi laugh. You will presently have news to
tell us of the good luck it has brought you."

I thought Saad was jesting and had a mind to divert
himself. However, I took the lead and thanked him.

The two friends then pursued their walk, and I resumed my work.

At night, when I pulled off my clothes to go to bed, the piece of lead, which I had never thought of since it was given to me, tumbled out of my pocket. I took it up and laid it on a shelf. The same night it happened that a fisherman neighbor was mending his nets and observed that a piece of lead was lacking. It was too late to buy any, for the shops were shut, and as he must either fish that night or his family go without food the next day, he called to his wife and bade her inquire among the neighbors for a piece of lead. She went from door to door of nearly every house on both sides of the street, but could not get any, and returned to tell her husband of her ill success. He asked her if she had been to my house.

"No indeed," she replied, "I have not been there. I know by experience they never have anything when one wants it."

"Nevertheless," said the fisherman, "you must go there; for though you have been a hundred times before without getting anything, you may chance to obtain what we want now."

The fisherman's wife went out grumbling and came and knocked at our door. I was awakened out of a sound sleep by the noise, and asked what was wanted. "Hassan," said she, "my husband needs a bit of lead with which to sink his nets, and I am come to see if you have a piece."

I at once remembered the lead I had received from Saad, and I told my neighbor I had some, and that my wife would give it to her. So my wife got up, and groping about where I directed her, found the lead, opened the door, and gave it to the fisherman's wife. The latter was much pleased, and promised that in return for the kindness we did her and her husband, we should have whatever was caught at the first cast of the nets.

This promise was fully approved by the fisherman, for he was no less pleased than his wife to get the lead, which he little expected. He finished mending his nets, and went fishing two hours before sunrise, according to custom. At the first throw he caught only one fish. It was, however, about a yard long, and thick in proportion. After he had done fishing he went home, and his first care was to bring this fish to me where I was at my work.

"Neighbor," said he, "my wife promised you last night whatever fish I should catch at the first throw of my nets. It pleased God to send no more than this one for you, which I desire you to accept."

"The bit of lead I let you have was such a trifle," said I, "that it ought not to be valued at so high a rate. Neighbors should assist each other in their little wants. I have done no more for you than you would have done for me in the same situation. Therefore I would refuse

The ropemaker's wife finds a wonderful gem

your present if I were not convinced you gave it to me freely."

After these civilities I took the fish and carried it to my wife. She was much surprised to see so large a fish. "What would you have me do with it?" she asked. "Our gridiron is only fit to broil small fish, and we have not a pot big enough to boil this one."

"That is your affair," answered I. "Prepare it as you will." I then went to my work again.

In cleaning the fish my wife found in it a hard, clear substance which she fancied was a piece of glass. She gave this to the youngest of our children for a plaything, and he and his brothers and sisters handed it about from one to another to admire its brightness and beauty. At night, after the lamp was lit, they were still playing with the clear substance taken from the fish, and they perceived that it gave forth light in the gloom, when my wife, who was getting supper, stood between them and the lamp. So they snatched it from each other to try it, and the younger children began crying because the older ones would not let them have it long enough in the dark.

I called to them to know what was the matter, and my wife told me they were squabbling about a piece of glass which gave a light. This interested me, and I bade my wife blow out the lamp so that we could determine whether the children were mistaken or not. We thus discovered that the piece of glass gave so great a light we could see to go to bed by it. So I placed it on the mantel and said: "Look, this will spare us the expense of oil."

When the children saw that the lamp was out and that the piece of glass supplied its place they shouted and made a great noise from astonishment. Before my wife and I could silence them we were forced to make a decidedly greater noise and put them to bed. They lay awake talking a long while about the wonderful light given forth by the piece of glass.

A very slight partition wall separated our house from that of our next neighbor. This neighbor was a rich jeweler, and the chamber he and his wife occupied adjoined the partition wall. They were both in bed when the noise my children made awakened them. The next morning the jeweler's wife came to mine to complain of their being disturbed out of their first sleep.

"Good neighbor," said my wife, "I am very sorry for what happened and hope you will excuse it. You know children will laugh and cry for a trifle. Come in and I will show you the cause of all the noise. See! it was this piece of glass which I took out of a fish."

"Indeed," said the jeweler's wife, "that is a piece of glass as you say; but as it is more beautiful than common glass I would like to buy it."

The children, who had been listening, now interrupted the conversation, crying and begging their mother not to part with it, and she, to quiet them, promised she would not. Thus the jeweler's wife was prevented from obtaining what she had at once recognized as a diamond of wonderful size and brilliance; but before she went away she whispered to my wife, who followed her to the door, that if she had a mind to sell it not to show it to anybody without informing her.

My wife's caller could not rest satisfied till she had told her husband what she had seen in my house, and she immediately went to his shop to acquaint him with her discovery. On her return home she came again to my wife and asked her if she would take twenty pieces of gold for the bit of glass.

But my wife would not make any bargain. She told the jeweler's wife she could not part with it till she had spoken to me. While they were talking at the door I came from my work to dinner. My wife stopped me and asked if I would sell the piece of glass she had found in the fish for twenty pieces of gold, which our neighbor offered. I called to mind the confidence with which Saad, in giving me the bit of lead, told me it would make my fortune. As I did not immediately reply, our caller fancied I considered the price she offered too low and said: "I will give you fifty pieces, if that will do."

As soon as I found that she rose so suddenly from twenty to fifty, I told her that I expected a great deal more. "Well," said she, "I will give you a hundred, and that is so much I know not whether my husband will approve of my offering it."

I knew then that what we supposed was a piece of glass must be a diamond, and I told her I would take nothing less than a hundred thousand pieces of gold for it. "You are well aware," said I, "that it is worth even much more than that, but because you and your husband are neighbors I will make this price to you. If you do not choose to pay it, some other jeweler, who will give a far larger sum, shall have the diamond."

The jeweler's wife confirmed me in my resolution by her eagerness to conclude the bargain. She came up at several biddings to fifty thousand pieces of gold, which I refused. "I can offer you no more," said she, "without my husband's consent. He will return home at night, and I would beg the favor of you to let him see the gem."

I promised to show it to him, and that evening he called. "Neighbor Hassan," said he, "I desire you would show me the diamond your wife showed to mine."

When I put it in his hands he looked at it and admired it for a long time. "Well," said he, "my wife tells me she offered you fifty thousand pieces of gold. I will give you twenty thousand more."

"Neighbor," said I, "your wife can tell you that I value my diamond at a hundred thousand pieces, and I will take nothing less."

He haggled a long time with me in hope that I would make some abatement; but finding I was positive, and fearing I would show the diamond to other jewelers, he at last concluded the bargain on my own terms. The next day he brought me the sum we had agreed on and I delivered to him the diamond.

I was now very rich, and I thanked God for His bounty, and would have liked to go and throw myself at Saad's feet to express my gratitude. In like manner I would gladly have gone to Saadi to whom I was first obliged, though his good intention had not the same success; but I knew not where either of them lived.

The next thing to settle was how to use the wealth that had so suddenly become mine. My wife proposed immediately to buy rich clothes for herself and the children, and to purchase a fine house and furnish it handsomely. I told her we ought not to begin with such expenses; "for," said I, "money should only be spent so that it may produce a fund from which we can draw without its failing. Therefore I shall start to-morrow to seek a profitable way of investing it."

I spent all of the next two days going to the people of my own trade, who worked as hard for their bread as I had done, and engaged them to work for me in the different sorts of rope-making, according to their skill and ability. This was easily arranged, for I promised not to make them wait for their money, but to pay them as soon as their work was done. Thus I became master of nearly all the rope business of Bagdad, and everybody was pleased with my exactness and punctual payment.

As so great a number of workman produced a large quantity of rope, I hired warehouses in several parts of the town to hold my goods and appointed over each a clerk to sell both wholesale and retail. By so doing I received a good profit and a generous income. At length, to concentrate my business, I bought ground and built the house you saw yesterday, which, though it makes so great an appearance, consists, for the most part, of storerooms for my rope.

Some time after my removal to this house, Saad and Saadi, who had scarcely thought of me since the day when Saad gave me the piece of lead, called to see me at my former habitation. There they were surprised by the information that I had become a great manufacturer, known as Cogia Hassan, and they immediately set out to visit me in my new abode. They knocked at the door, and the porter ushered them into the hall where I was sitting. When I saw my two friends I rose and ran to them, and would have kissed the hem of their garments; but they would not allow it. I invited them to be seated on a sofa which was placed in full view of my garden, and I sat down opposite them.

Then Saadi addressed me, saying: "Cogia Hassan I cannot express my joy to see that you have at last won wealth; and I feel certain that in some way this wonderful change in your fortune is due to the four hundred pieces of gold which I presented to you."

"Saadi," said the other, "I am vexed with you for

persisting in not believing what Hassan has already told us about your gifts. I am confident that he gave us a faithful account of those two accidents which befell him; but let him speak himself and say to which of us he most owes his present prosperity."

"Gentlemen," said I, "it will be my endeavor to declare to you the whole truth with the same sincerity as before."

I then related all that had happened since I last saw them; but my words had no effect on Saadi. "Cogia Hassan," said he, "what you tell us about the fish that had a diamond inside appears to me as incredible as the vulture's flying away with your turban, and the exchange made by your wife with the peddler. However, I am convinced you are no longer poor, and I rejoice heartily."

It was growing late, and they arose to depart; but I said: "There is one favor I have to ask. I beg that you will stay with me over night, and tomorrow we will go by water to a country house which I have bought. You will enjoy spending the day there, I think, and we will return in the evening."

"If Saad has no business that calls him elsewhere," said Saadi, "I consent."

Saad responded that there was nothing to prevent his staying, and I sent a slave to each of their homes to explain their absence lest their families should be anxious. While supper was being prepared, I showed my benefactors my house and storerooms. Then I brought them back into the hall, where they asked me various questions about my affairs, and I gave them such answers as satisfied them.

While we were conversing my servants came to tell me that supper was served, and I led my guests into another hall, where they admired the furniture and the manner in which it was lighted. I regaled them with a concert of vocal and instrumental music during the repast, and afterward with a company of dancers.

We agreed to set out early in the morning to enjoy the fresh air, and we were at the riverside by sunrise. A pleasure-boat was waiting for us, and in less than an hour and a half, with six good rowers, we arrived at my country house. As soon as we disembarked we went for a walk in the gardens, where we lingered longest in a grove of orange and lemon trees, loaded with fruit and flowers and irrigated by rivulets from a neighboring stream. The pleasant shade, the fragrant odors which perfumed the air, the soft murmurings of the water, and the harmonious notes of the birds, were so delightful that my companions frequently stopped to tell me how much they appreciated my bringing them to so beautiful a place.

Beyond the grove was a wood of large trees. Two of my boys, whom I had sent into the country with a tutor for the air, went into the woodland while we were strolling in that direction. They chanced to observe a nest which was built in the branches of a lofty tree and bade a slave who attended them to climb the tree for it. The slave, when he got to the nest, was much surprised to find it composed of a turban. There were some young birds in it and he brought it down, birds and all. My boys thought I might like to see a nest that was so uncommon and came running to show it to me.

The two friends and I were greatly astonished at the novelty; but my amazement far exceeded theirs, for I recognized the turban to be that with which the vulture had flown away. After I had examined it well and showed it to my guests, I said: "Gentlemen, can you remember the turban I had on the day you first spoke to me well enough to say whether this is the one?"

"I do not think that either my friend or I gave any attention to it," replied Saad; "but if the hundred and ninety pieces of gold are in it we can have no further doubts."

"Sir," I continued, "this is the same turban; for I know it perfectly, and I perceive by its weight that the gold is still in its folds. Observe well before I unwrap it that it is of no very fresh date in the tree; and the state in which you see it is sufficient proof that the vulture took it to the tree on the day it was seized."

While I was speaking I removed the young birds, pulled off the linen cloth which was around the cap of the turban, and took out the purse which Saadi knew to be the one he had given me. I emptied it before them and said: "There is the money."

They counted it and found one hundred and ninety pieces of gold. Then Saadi addressed himself to me saying: "I agree, Cogia Hassan, that this money could not have served to enrich you; but the other hundred and ninety pieces which you would have me believe you hid in a pot of bran might have done so."

"Sir," I responded, "I have told you the truth about both sums."

We now retraced our steps to the house, where we had dinner, and afterward we lay down for a siesta during the heat of the day. Later we talked together till it grew cooler, when we went into the garden and stayed till sunset. We then mounted horses, and a ride of two hours took us to Bagdad, which we reached by moonlight.

It happened, by some negligence of my grooms, that we were out of grain for the horses. The storehouses were all shut; but one of my slaves, seeking about the neighborhood, found a pot of bran in a shop and bought it. He carried his purchase to the stables and was dividing the bran among the horses, when he felt a linen cloth with something heavy tied up in it. He brought the cloth to me without undoing the knot, and I at once knew what it was.

"Gentlemen," said I turning to my two benefactors, "it has pleased God that you should not part from me without being fully convinced of the truth of all that I have told you. Here are the other hundred and ninety pieces of gold which you, Saadi, gave me. This is the very cloth in which I tied up the gold with my own hands."

Then I counted out the money, and after that ordered the pot to be brought to me. I knew it to be the one that formerly stood in our kitchen, and I sent it to my wife to ask if she recognized it. She returned word that it was the same pot she had exchanged full of bran for the washing-balls.

Then Saadi addressed his friend saying: "I yield to you and acknowledge that money is not always the means of becoming rich."

After he had so spoken I said to him: "I dare not propose to return to you the three hundred and eighty pieces of gold which it has pleased God should be found to undeceive you in your opinion of my honesty. I am sure you did not bestow them on me with an intention of getting them again; and if you approve of my proposal, tomorrow I will give them to the poor, that God may bless us both."

The two friends spent that night also at my house, and next day, after embracing me, went to their homes.

At the conclusion of this story the caliph said: "Cogia Hassan, I have not for a long time heard anything that has given me so much pleasure as your narrative of the wonderful way in which you acquired your riches. I recently bought that same diamond which made your fortune. It now is in my treasury, and I am happy to learn whence it came. I esteem it the most precious and valuable jewel I possess; and as Saadi may still have some doubts about it, I would have you take him and Saad to my treasurer, who will show it to them."

After these words the caliph signified to Cogia Hassan and Baba Abdallah that he was through with them, and they both prostrated themselves before the throne and retired.

XIII

THE FORTY ROBBERS

THERE once lived in a town of Persia two brothers, one named Cassim and the other Ali Baba. They belonged to a poor family, but Cassim married a rich widow and became a wealthy merchant. Ali Baba, on the other hand, married a woman as poor as himself and lived by cutting wood in a neighboring forest and bringing it on three donkeys into the town to sell.

One day when Ali Baba was in the forest, and had just finished cutting wood enough to load his donkeys, he saw at a distance a great cloud of dust approaching. He observed it attentively and soon distinguished a body of horsemen, whom he suspected might be robbers. So he determined to leave his donkeys, and after driving them into a thicket out of sight he climbed a large tree growing on a high rock. The branches of the tree were thick enough to conceal him, and yet enabled him to watch all that passed.

The horsemen numbered forty and were all well mounted and armed. They came to the foot of the rock on which the tree stood and there dismounted. Every man unbridled his horse, tied it to a shrub, and gave it a feed of corn from a bag he had brought with him. Then each took on his shoulder his saddle-bags, which Ali Baba could see were stuffed full of plunder. One, who was apparently the captain, came under the tree in which Ali Baba was hidden, and making his way through some bushes pronounced these words: "Open sesame!"

At once a door opened in the rock, and after the robber captain had made all his troop enter, he followed, and the door closed of itself.

The robbers stayed some time within the rock, but at last the door opened and the captain came out and stood to see all his troop go by him. As soon as the last man had passed out, the door closed, and they went and bridled their horses and mounted. Then the captain put himself at their head, and they returned the way they had come.

After Ali Baba had followed them with his eyes as far as he could see them, he descended from the tree. Remembering the words the captain of the robbers used to cause the door to open, he had the curiosity to try if his repeating them would have the same effect. Accordingly he went among the bushes, found the door concealed behind them, and said: "Open sesame!"

The door instantly flew wide open. Ali Baba, who expected to see a dark, dismal cavern, was surprised to find a spacious and well-furnished chamber admirably lighted from a strongly barred opening at the top of the rock. It contained many rich bales of silk, brocade, and valuable carpeting, great heaps of gold and silver ingots, and no end of money in bags. Evidently the cave had been occupied for ages by robbers who had succeeded one another.

Ali Baba boldly collected as many bags of the gold coins as he thought his three donkeys could carry, and when he had put these on the animals' backs he laid wood on top in such a manner that the bags could not be seen.

He now made the best of his way to town and drove his donkeys into his little yard. After throwing off the wood that covered the panniers he carried the bags into the house and emptied them, which made such a great heap of gold as dazzled his wife's eyes. Then he told her the whole adventure from beginning to end and asked her to keep it secret.

The wife rejoiced greatly at their good fortune and wanted to count all the gold, piece by piece. "You would never get done," said Ali Baba. "There is no time to be lost. I will dig a hole and bury it."

"Very well," replied she, "but let us at least know somewhere near how much we have. I will borrow a measure and measure it while you dig the hole."

So away she ran to Cassim's house, and addressing herself to his wife, desired the loan of a measure for a little while. Her sister-in-law inquired whether she would have a small or a large measure, and she asked for a small one.

The sister-in-law knew Ali Baba's poverty, and she was curious to learn what his wife wanted to measure. So before bringing the measure out she put a little dab of tallow in the bottom with the expectation that a portion of whatever was measured would stick to the receptacle and be brought back when it was returned.

Ali Baba's wife went home, set the measure beside the heap of gold, and continued to fill and empty it till she had done. She was very well satisfied to find the number of measures amounted to so many as they did, as was also her husband, who had now finished digging the hole. While Ali Baba was burying the gold his wife carried the measure back, but without taking notice that a piece of gold had stuck to the tallow in the bottom. "Sister," said she, "you see I have not kept your measure long. I return it with thanks."

As soon as Ali Baba's wife was gone Cassim's wife looked into the measure and was surprised to find a piece of gold sticking there. "What!" she exclaimed, "has Ali Baba gold so plentiful as to measure it? Whence has he all this wealth?"

When her husband came home from his warehouse she said to him: "Cassim, I know you think yourself rich, but Ali Baba is infinitely richer than you. He does not count his money, but measures it."

Cassim begged her to explain this riddle, which she did by telling him of the stratagem she had used to make the discovery, and showed him the piece of money, which was so old they could not tell in what ruler's reign it was coined.

Since he married the rich widow, Cassim had never treated Ali Baba as a brother, but neglected him; and now, instead of being pleased, he envied his brother's prosperity. He could not sleep all that night and went to him in the morning before sunrise. "Ali Baba," said he, "you pretend to be miserably poor, and yet you measure gold."

Then he took from his pocket the old coin, and added: "My wife found this at the bottom of the measure you borrowed yesterday."

Ali Baba, perceiving that Cassim knew of the wealth he had discovered, confessed all and offered his brother part of the treasure to keep the secret.

"I must know exactly where this treasure is," declared Cassim, haughtily, "and how I may visit it myself when I choose. Otherwise I will go and inform against you, and then you will not only get no more, but will lose all you have, and I shall receive a share for my information."

So Ali Baba told him all he wanted to know, even to the words he was to use to gain admission to the cave.

At daybreak the next morning Cassim set out for the forest with ten mules bearing great chests which he designed to fill with gold. He followed the road Ali Baba had described to him, and it was not long before he reached the rock with the large tree growing on it, of which his brother had told him. He pushed through the bushes to the entrance of the cavern and pronounced the words: "Open sesame!"

The door immediately opened, and when he was in, closed on him. He quickly laid at the door of the cavern as many bags of gold as his ten mules could carry; but his thoughts were now so full of the great riches he would possess that he could not think of the necessary word to make the door open. Instead of "Open sesame*," he said: "Open barley!" and was much amazed to find that the door remained fast shut. He named several sorts of grain, but still the door would not open.

Cassim had never expected such an incident, and was so alarmed at the danger he was in that the more he endeavored to remember the word "sesame," the more his memory was confounded, and he had as much forgotten it as if he had never heard it mentioned. He threw down the bags he had in his arms and walked distractedly up and down the cave, without having the least regard to the riches that were around him.

About noon the robbers returned. As they approached the rock they saw Cassim's mules straggling about with great chests on their backs. Alarmed at this, they galloped full speed to the cave, and with their naked cimeters in their hands went directly to the

---

*Sesame is a small grain.

door. Then the captain spoke the proper words and the door opened.

Cassim, who heard the noise of the horses' feet, at once guessed the arrival of the robbers and resolved to make an effort for his life. No sooner did he see the door open than he rushed out with such violence that he threw the robber captain down on the ground. But he could not escape the other robbers, who, with their cimeters, cut off his head.

The first care of the robbers after this was to examine the cave. They found all the bags which Cassim had brought to the door, and carried them to their places, but they did not miss what Ali Baba had taken away before. Then they held a council and tried unsuccessfully to imagine how Cassim had learned the secret words by which alone he could enter. In order to terrify any accomplice who might also know the secret, they agreed to hang Cassim's head just within the door of the cave on one side and his body on the other. This they did, and then closing the place of their hoard they mounted their horses and went to beat the roads again and attack the caravans they might meet.

The day passed and Cassim's wife became very uneasy. She ran to Ali Baba in great alarm and said: "I believe, brother-in-law, that you know Cassim has gone to the forest and on what account. It is now night, and he has not come back. I am afraid some misfortune has happened to him."

Ali Baba told her that she need not frighten herself, for Cassim would certainly not think it best to come into the town till the night was pretty far advanced.

Cassim's wife, considering how much it concerned her husband to keep the business secret, was easily persuaded to believe her brother-in-law. She went home and waited patiently till midnight. Then her fear redoubled, and her grief was the harder to bear because she was forced to keep it to herself. She repented her foolish curiosity and cursed her desire to pry into the affairs of other people. After spending all the night in weeping, she went as soon at it was day to her brother-in-law and his wife, telling them by her tears the cause of her coming.

Ali Baba did not wait for her to ask him to go to see what had become of Cassim, but begging her to moderate her affliction, departed immediately with his three donkeys. When he came to the rock in the forest, having seen neither his brother nor the mules on the way, he was seriously alarmed at finding some blood near the door of the cave. On pronouncing the proper words the door opened and he was struck with horror at the dismal sight of his brother's body. He was not long in determining what to do, and he had soon carried the body to the panniers of one of his donkeys and covered it over with wood. The other two donkeys he loaded with bags of gold and piled wood on top so that the bags should not be seen. Then he came away, but stopped some time at the edge of the forest that he might not go into the town before dark. Presently he reached home, and drove the two donkeys loaded with gold into his yard. There he left them in care of his wife, while he led the other to his sister-in-law's house.

When he knocked at the door it was opened by Morgiana, an unusually clever and intelligent slave maiden. He came into the court, unloaded the donkey, and taking Morgiana aside said: "You must observe close secrecy. I have brought your master's body. It is necessary that we should all act as if he had died a natural death. Go now and tell your mistress. I leave the matter to your wit and skilful devices."

Ali Baba helped to place the body in Cassim's house and then returned home with his donkey.

Morgiana went out early the next morning to a druggist and asked for a sort of medicine which was considered efficacious in the most dangerous disorders. The apothecary inquired who was ill. She replied with a sigh: "My good master Cassim, and he can neither eat nor speak."

In the evening Morgiana went to the same druggist again, and with tears in her eyes asked for an essence which was given to sick people only when at the last extremity. "Alas!" said she, taking it from the apothecary, "I am afraid that this remedy will have no better effect than what I got before, and that I shall lose my master."

Moreover, as Ali Baba and his wife were often seen going between Cassim's and their house all that day, and seemed melancholy, nobody was surprised in the evening to hear the shrieks and cries of Cassim's wife and of Morgiana, who gave word everywhere that Cassim was dead.

The next morning, at daybreak, Morgiana went to an old cobbler whom she knew to be always early at his stall, and bidding him good morrow, put a piece of gold in his hand, saying: "Mustapha, take your sewing tackle and come with me. But I must tell you I shall blindfold you when you arrive at a certain place."

Mustapha hestitated a little at these words. "Oh, oh!" said he, "you would have me do something against my conscience."

"God forbid that I should ask anything contrary to your conscience!" said Morgiana, putting another piece of gold into his hand. "Only come along with me and fear nothing."

So Mustapha went with Morgiana. After they had arrived at the place she had mentioned, she bound his eyes with a handkerchief and guided him to her deceased master's house, and she never unbound his eyes till he had entered the room where the body lay. "Mustapha," said she, "you must make haste and sew the parts of this body together; and as soon as you have done I will give you another piece of gold."

When Mustapha had finished his task she gave him

the money, blindfolded him again, and recommending secrecy to him, led him back to the place where she first bound his eyes. Then she pulled off the bandage and let him go home, but watched him till he was quite out of sight, to make sure that he returned toward his stall.

The next day four of Cassim's friends carried the body to the burying ground. The priest followed, reciting prayers, and behind him walked Ali Baba and several neighbors. Cassim's wife, uttering woful cries, stayed at home with the women of the vicinity, who came, according to custom, during the funeral, and, joining their wailings to hers, filled the quarter with sounds of sorrow.

The manner of Cassim's death was concealed and hushed up between his widow, Morgiana, and Ali Baba's family, so that nobody else in the city had the least suspicion of the real cause of it. Three or four days after the funeral Ali Baba removed his few goods in broad daylight to his sister-in-law's house, where it was agreed that in future he should live; but the money he had taken from the robbers he conveyed thither by night. Lastly, he entrusted his eldest son with the management of Cassim's warehouse.

While these things were being done, the forty robbers again visited their retreat in the forest. Great was their surprise to find Cassim's body taken away, with some of their bags of gold. "We are certainly discovered," said the captain. "The man we killed had an accomplice, and we must try to find him. What say you, my lads?"

All the robbers approved of the captain's proposal. "Well," said he, "one of the boldest and most skilful among you must go into the town, disguised as a traveler and a stranger, to try if he can hear any talk of the man whom we have killed, and endeavor to find out who he was and where he lived. The matter is one of the first importance, and for fear of treachery, I propose that whoever undertakes this business without success, even though the failure arises only from an error of judgment, shall suffer death."

Without waiting for the sentiments of his companions, one of the robbers started up and said: "I submit to the conditions and think it an honor to expose my life to serve the troop."

After this robber had been commended for his bravery by the captain and his comrades, he disguised himself, and bidding farewell to the troop that night, went into the town just at daybreak the following morning. He walked up and down, till accidentally he came to the stall of Mustapha the cobbler, who was seated with an awl in his hand about to start work. The robber saluted him, and perceiving that he was old said: "You begin to work very early. Is it possible that one of your age can see so well? I question, even were it somewhat lighter, if you would be able to stitch."

"You do not know me," replied Mustapha; "for old as I am I have extraordinarily good eyes; and you will not doubt it when I tell you that I sewed the head of a dead man on to his body in a room where I had not so much light as I have now."

"Where was that?" asked the robber.

"You shall know no more," answered Mustapha.

The robber felt sure he had discovered an important clue. He pulled out a piece of gold, and putting it in Mustapha's hand said: "I do not want to pry into any of your secrets. The only thing I desire of you is that you show me the house where you did this work."

"If I was disposed to do you that favor," responded Mustapha, "I could not. I was taken to a certain place, whence I was led blindfolded to the house, and I was brought back in the same manner. You see, therefore, the impossibility of my doing what you desire."

"Well," said the robber, "you no doubt have some remembrance of the way you were led. Come, let me blind your eyes at the same place. We will walk together. Perhaps you may be able to go where you did before; and as everybody ought to be paid for their trouble, there is another piece of gold for you. Gratify me in what I ask."

The two pieces of gold were a great temptation to Mustapha. He looked at them a long time in his hand without saying a word, but at last he pulled out his purse and put them in it. "I am not sure that I can remember the way exactly," said he to the robber, "but I will try what I can do."

To the great joy of the robber Mustapha rose and led him to the place where Morgiana had bound his eyes. "It was here that I was blindfolded," said Mustapha, "and afterward I turned this way."

He pointed out the direction, and the robber without further delay tied his handkerchief over the shoemaker's eyes and walked at his side till he stopped directly before Cassim's house, now occupied by Ali Baba. The robber marked the door with a piece of white chalk which he had ready in his hand, and then he pulled off the bandage from Mustapha's eyes and asked him if he knew whose house that was.

"I do not live in the neighborhood," Mustapha replied, "and I cannot tell."

The robber, finding he could discover no more from Mustapha, thanked him for the trouble he had taken and left him to go back to his stall, while he himself returned to the forest, persuaded that he would be very well received.

Shortly after the robber and Mustapha had parted, Morgiana went out of Ali Baba's house on some errand, and when she returned saw the mark the robber had made and stopped to observe it. "What can be the meaning of this?" said she to herself. "Somebody intends my master no good, I fear. At any rate, whatever the intention, I ought to guard against the worst."

Accordingly she fetched a piece of chalk and marked two or three doors on each side in the same manner.

By this time the robber had rejoined his troop. He told the others of his success, rejoicing over his good fortune in meeting so soon with a person who could inform him of what he wanted to know. The robbers listened to him with the utmost satisfaction, and the captain said: "Comrades, let us set off at once. We will go well armed, and that we may not excite suspicion we will enter the town in twos, and we will meet at the great square. Meanwhile I will go with our comrade who brought us the good news and find the house he has marked, that we may consult what had best be done."

They were soon ready and filed off in parties of two, and got into the town without being in the least suspected. The captain and he who had visited the town in the morning as a spy came in last and went to the street where the spy had marked Ali Baba's residence. When they came to the first of the houses which were marked, he pointed it out. But the captain observed that the next door was chalked in the same manner and in the same place, and showing it to his guide, asked him which house was the right one, that or the first. The guide was so confounded he knew not what answer to make, and he was still more puzzled when he saw five or six houses similarly marked. He assured the captain with an oath that he had marked but one and could not tell who had marked the rest.

The captain, finding that they could not distinguish the house the cobbler had stopped at, went to the great square where the robbers were to meet and told the troop that they had lost their labor and must return to their cave. So they separated in parties of two and returned as they had come.

When they were all together once more the captain explained the reason of their returning, and presently the robber who had acted as spy was declared deserving of death and was killed. But as the safety of the troop required the discovery of the plunderer of their cave, another of the gang offered to go and seek out the intruder's dwelling. He promised himself he would succeed better than his unlucky predecessor. His offer being accepted, he went and bribed Mustapha as the other had done, and being shown the house marked it in a place more remote from sight, with red chalk.

Not long afterward Morgiana, whose eyes nothing could escape, went out, and she saw the red chalk mark. Fearful that some evil was planned against her master, she marked the neighboring houses in the same place and manner.

The robber, when he returned to his company, prided himself much on the care he had taken, and the captain and all of them thought now they must succeed. They went into the town with the same caution as before; but when the robber spy and his captain came to the street where Ali Baba lived, great was the rage of the captain and the confusion of his companion to find several doors marked instead of one. Thus the troop was forced to retire a second time, and the robber whose efforts as a spy had been a failure underwent the same punishment as the first spy.

The captain, having lost two brave fellows, was afraid of further diminishing his troop if he pursued this plan to get information of the residence of their plunderer. It was evident that his men's heads were not so good as their hands on such occasions, and he resolved to take on himself the important commission.

Accordingly he went and addressed himself to Mustapha, who did him the same service he had done the other robbers. The captain did not set any particular mark on the house, but examined and observed it so carefully that it was impossible for him to mistake it. When he returned to the forest cave where the troop waited for him he said: "Now, comrades, nothing can prevent our full revenge, as I am certain of the house, and on my way hither I have thought of how to put the revenge into execution."

He then told his plan and ordered them to go into the villages about and buy nineteen mules, with thirty-eight large leather jars, one full of oil and the others empty.

In two or three days the robbers had purchased the mules and jars, and the captain put one of his men into each jar with the weapons he thought fit, leaving open

places in the seams to allow the men to breathe. Lastly
he rubbed the jars on the outside with oil from the full
vessel, so that they all had the appearance of being used
as oil receptacles, and no one would have suspected
what was really inside.

Things being thus prepared, the nineteen mules were
loaded with the jars containing the thirty-seven robbers,
and the jar of oil. Then the captain, as their driver,
set out with them, and reached the town by the dusk of
evening, as he had intended. He led the mules through
the streets to the house he sought, and found Ali Baba
sitting in the doorway to take a little fresh air. The
robber stopped his mules and said: "I have brought
some oil a great way to sell at tomorrow's market, and
it is now so late I do not know where to lodge. If I
would not be troublesome to you, do me the favor to let
me pass the night with you, and I shall be very much
obliged by your hospitality."

Though Ali Baba had seen the captain of the robbers
in the forest and had heard him speak, he did not know
him in the disguise of an oil merchant. "You are quite
welcome," said he, and immediately opened the gates
for the mules to go into the yard.

At the same time he called a slave and ordered him,
when the mules were unloaded, to put them in the
stable and feed them. Then he went to Morgiana and
bid her get a good supper for his guest.

After the captain of the robbers had eaten, he went

into the yard, took the lid off each jar, and gave his comrades orders what to do. Beginning at the first jar and so on to the last, he said to each man: "As soon as I throw some pebbles from the window of the chamber which I shall occupy, do not fail to come out, and I will immediately join you."

He now returned to the house, and Morgiana taking up a light conducted him to his chamber. Then she left him, and after putting out the light he lay down in his clothes, in order to be the more ready to rise.

Morgiana began preparations for the morrow's breakfast; but in the midst of her work the oil burned out of the lamp she was using. There was no more oil in the house, nor any candles, and what to do she did not know. Abdallah, a fellow-servant, seeing her very uneasy, said: "Do not fret yourself, but go into the yard and take some oil out of one of the jars the oil merchant has left there."

Morgiana thanked Abdallah for his advice, took the oil-pot, and went into the yard. When she came near the first jar the robber within said softly: "Is it time?"

Though much surprised at finding a man in the jar instead of the oil she wanted, she answered, without showing the least emotion, "Not yet, but presently."

She went quietly to all the jars till she came to the jar of oil, and as each robber in turn asked if it was time, she gave the same answer she had to the first. Thus she surmised that her master had admitted thirty-eight robbers to his premises, and it was evident that the pretended oil merchant was their captain. She made what haste she could to fill her oil-pot and returned to the kitchen, where she lighted her lamp. Then she took a great kettle, filled that also from the oil-jar, and set it on a large wood fire. As soon as the oil boiled she went and poured enough into every jar to stifle and destroy the robber within.

This action was executed without any noise, and when she returned to the kitchen with the empty kettle, she extinguished the fire she had made to boil the oil and blew out the light of her lamp. That done, she remained silent, resolving not to go to rest till she had observed through a window of the kitchen, which opened toward the yard, what might follow.

She had not waited long before the captain of the robbers got up, opened his window, and seeing no light and hearing no one stirring in the house, gave the appointed signal by throwing little stones, several of which hit the jars, as he doubted not by the sound they gave. After listening and not hearing anything whereby he could judge that his companions stirred, he threw stones a second and also a third time. He could not comprehend the reason that none of his men should answer his signal. Much alarmed, he went softly down into the yard, and going to the first jar, asked the robber if he was ready. Then he noticed the smell of hot boiled oil, and suspected that his plot to murder Ali

Baba and plunder his house was discovered. One after another, he examined the jars and found that all his gang were dead. His design had failed, and to save himself he forced the lock of a door that led from the yard to the garden, ran down a path, and by climbing over a rear wall, made his escape.

When Morgiana saw him depart, she went to bed, satisfied to have succeeded so well in saving her master and his family.

Ali Baba, after breakfasting the next day, looked from a window out on the yard and was much surprised to see the oil-jars. He wondered that the merchant had not gone with them at daybreak and he asked Morgiana the reason.

"My good master," answered she, "you will be better informed of what you wish to know when you have seen what I have to show you."

Morgiana then led the way to the yard and requested Ali Baba to look into the first jar and see if there was any oil. Ali Baba looked in, and seeing a man, started back with a cry of alarm.

"Do not be afraid," said Morgiana. "The man you see there is dead."

"Ah, Morgiana," said Ali Baba, "explain yourself."

"Moderate your astonishment," responded Morgiana, "and do not excite the curiosity of your neighbors by your loud exclamations. Look into the other jars."

Ali Baba examined all the other jars one after

another, and when he came to that which contained oil, found the oil nearly gone. He stood for some time motionless, looking at the jars without saying a word, so great was his surprise. At last he asked: "And what is become of the merchant?"

"Merchant!" answered Morgiana, "he is no more a merchant than I am;" and she told all she had done, from first observing the mark on the house to the destruction of the robbers and the flight of their captain.

On hearing of her brave deeds Ali Baba said to her: "God by your means has delivered me from the snares these robbers laid for my destruction. I therefore owe my life to you, and I give you your liberty from this moment. I will complete your recompense later."

Ali Baba's garden was very long and was shaded at the farther end by a number of large trees. Near these trees he and Abdallah dug a trench, long and wide enough to hold the bodies of the robbers. The earth was light and the burial was the sooner finished on that account. Then Ali Baba hid the jars and weapons, and as he had no use for the mules he sent them to be sold in the market.

Meanwhile the captain of the forty robbers returned to the forest. He did not stay long. The loneliness of the cavern became frightful to him. He determined, however, to avenge the fate of his companions and to accomplish the death of Ali Baba. For this purpose he returned to the town and took lodging at an inn disguised as a merchant. Under this assumed character he rented a shop opposite that of Ali Baba's son, and stocked it with a great many sorts of rich stuffs and fine linen which he brought secretly from the cavern.

The robber took the name of Houssain, and as he was both civil and well dressed he found it easy to make friends with Ali Baba's son. As time went on he often had the young man to dine and sup with him, and in every way treated him very handsomely.

Ali Baba's son did not have room in his own house to entertain Houssain in return, and he spoke of this to his father.

"Son," said Ali Baba, "tomorrow get Houssain to accompany you, and as you pass by my door, call in. I will order Morgiana to provide a supper."

The next day Ali Baba's son and Houssain went by appointment for a walk and passed through the street where Ali Baba lived. When they came to the house the young man stopped and knocked at the door. "This, sir," said he, "is the home of my father. From the account I have given him of our friendship, he has charged me to procure him the honor of your acquaintance, and I desire you to add this pleasure to those for which I am already indebted to you."

Ali Baba received Houssain cordially and begged he would sup with him. Houssain accepted the invitation, and presently Morgiana brought in the supper.

She knew the robber at first sight, notwithstanding his disguise, and looking at him very carefully perceived that he had a dagger under his garment.

When Abdallah had put the dessert of fruit and wine before Ali Baba, Morgiana retired, dressed herself neatly, girded her waist with a silver-gilt girdle to which there hung a poniard, and put a handsome mask on her face. She then said to Abdallah: "Take your tambourine, and let us go and divert our master and his son's friend."

Abdallah took his tambourine and played all the way into the hall before Morgiana, who, when she came to the door, made a low obeisance, by way of asking leave to exhibit her skill, while Abdallah left off playing. "Come in, Morgiana," said Ali Baba, "and let Houssain see what you can do."

So Abdallah played on the tambourine and at the same time sung an air, to which Morgiana danced in such a manner as would have created admiration in any company. Presently she drew the poniard, and holding it in her hand, began a dance in which she outdid herself by the many light movements and surprising leaps with which she accompanied it. At last she snatched the tambourine from Abdallah with her left hand, and holding the poniard in her right, presented the open side of the tambourine, after the manner of those who get a living by dancing, to solicit gifts from the spectators.

Ali Baba put a piece of gold into the tambourine, as did also his son, and Houssain had pulled his purse out and was taking a coin from it when Morgiana plunged the poniard into his heart.

"Unhappy woman!" exclaimed Ali Baba, "why have you done this to ruin me and my family?"

"It was to preserve, not to ruin you," answered Morgiana; "for see here what an enemy you had entertained;" and she opened the pretended Houssain's garment to show his dagger. "Look well at him, and you will find he is both the false oil merchant and the captain of the gang of forty robbers."

"Morgiana," said Ali Baba, "when I gave you your liberty I promised that my gratitude should not stop there, and as a proof of my sincerity I now make you my daughter-in-law."

Then addressing his son he said: "I believe that you will not refuse Morgiana for your wife. You see that Houssain sought your friendship with a design to kill me, and if he had succeeded no doubt he would have sacrificed you also. Consider that by marrying Morgiana you marry my preserver and your own."

The son readily consented to the marriage, and a few days later the wedding was celebrated with a great feast.

The captain of the robbers was buried with his comrades, and at length Ali Baba began to think of visiting the robbers' cave. But he did not go for a whole year, as he supposed the other two members of the troop, whom he could get no account of, might be alive. At the year's end, when he found they had not made any attempt to disturb him, he again journeyed to the place where the treasure was concealed in the forest. On arriving at the cave he tied his horse to a tree. Then he approached the entrance, pronounced the words: "Open sesame!" and the door opened.

He entered the cavern, and by the condition he found things in, he judged that nobody had been there since the captain had fetched the goods for his shop. It was quite evident that all the robbers who knew of the cave were dead, and Ali Baba believed he was the only person in the world able to open its door, and that all the treasure was at his sole disposal. He put as much gold into his saddle-bags as his horse could carry, and returned to town. Some years later he told his son the secret of the cave and taught him how to open the door. The son handed the secret down to his posterity, who, using their good fortune with moderation, lived in great honor and splendor.

XIV

THE ADVENTURES OF ZEYN ALASNAM

THERE was a sultan of Bussorah blessed with great wealth and well-beloved by his people. His only source of affliction was that he was childless. But after many years had passed a son was born to him, whom he named Zeyn Alasnam.

Zeyn was educated with the greatest care; but while the prince was yet young, the good sultan fell sick of a disorder, which all the skill of his physicians could not cure, and presently he died.

After the period of mourning for his father was past, Zeyn Alasnam ascended the throne. He, however, soon showed that he was unfit to govern a kingdom; for he only regarded what his subjects owed to him, without considering what was his duty toward them. He gave way to every kind of dissipation and conferred on his young and evil associates all the chief offices of the realm. Thus he lost the respect of his people and emptied the treasury.

The sultana, his mother, tried to correct her son's conduct, assuring him that if he did not change his habits, he would cause some revolution, which perhaps might cost him his crown and his life. What she pre-

dicted nearly happened. But when the people began
to murmur, and there were threats of a general revolt,
the sultan listened to his mother, dismissed his youthful
advisers, and committed the government to men of
years and discretion.

Zeyn, now that all his wealth was consumed, repented that he had made no better use of it. He became profoundly melancholy, and nothing could comfort him. One night in a dream he saw coming toward
him a venerable man, who, with a smiling countenance,
said: "Know, Zeyn, that there is no sorrow but what
is followed by mirth, and no misfortune but what in
the end brings some happiness. If you desire to termi-
nate your affliction, go to Cairo in Egypt, where great
prosperity awaits you."

The young sultan was much impressed by his dream,
and spoke of it very seriously to his mother; but she
only laughed. "My son," said she, "would you leave
your kingdom and go into Egypt on the strength of so
illusive a thing as a dream?"

"Why not, madam?" responded Zeyn; "do you
think all dreams are worthless. No, no, they often are
divinely inspired. There was something holy in the
aspect of the old man who appeared to me. I will rely
on his promise and am resolved to do as he advised."

The sultana endeavored to dissuade him, but in vain.
He committed to her care the government of the kingdom, and that night mounted his horse and privately

left his palace. He took the road to Cairo and after
much fatigue and trouble arrived at that famous city,
where he alighted in front of a mosque. As he was
much spent with weariness he lay down and fell asleep.
Then he dreamed that he saw the same old man who
had visited him in the former dream. "I am pleased
with you," said the old man; "for you have believed
me. You were not deterred by the length or the difficulties of the way. But I must now inform you that I
imposed this journey on you simply to test your character. It has proved that you have courage and resolution, and you deserve that I should make you the richest
and happiest ruler in the world. Return to Bussorah,
and you shall find immense wealth in your palace. No
other sovereign ever possessed so vast a treasure."

The sultan was not pleased with this dream. "Alas!"
thought he when he awoke, "how much was I mistaken!
That old man is the product of my disturbed imagina-
tion. It is no wonder I have seen him again, my fancy
has been so full of him. I will return to Bussorah.
What should I do here any longer? I am glad I told
no one but my mother the motive of my journey, else I
should become a jest to my people."

Accordingly, he set out for his kingdom, and as soon
as he arrived there he told his mother all that had happened. He showed such concern for having been so
foolish that the sultana, instead of adding to his vexation by reproving or laughing at him, tried to comfort

him. "Forbear afflicting yourself, my son," said she "and be contented. Apply yourself to making your subjects happy; and by securing their happiness you will establish your own."

Sultan Zeyn vowed that he would for the future follow his mother's advice and be directed by the wise viziers she had helped him choose to assist in the government. But the very night after he returned to his palace he, for the third time, dreamed he saw the old man, who said: "The period of your prosperity is come, brave Zeyn. Tomorrow morning take a pick-ax and dig in the late sultan's private room. You will find a rich treasure."

As soon as Zeyn awoke the next day, he dressed hurriedly and ran to the sultana's apartment. With much eagerness he told her of his latest dream.

"Really, my son," said the sultana, smiling, "this is a very queer old man; but have you a mind to believe him again? At any rate, the task now enjoined on you is not so bad as your journey to Cairo and back."

"Well, madam," said Zeyn, "I must own that this third dream has restored my confidence. Last night the old man pointed out to me exactly the place where the treasure is. I would rather search in vain than blame myself as long as I live for having, perhaps, missed great riches by being too unbelieving."

He left the sultana's apartment, caused a pick-ax to be brought to him, and went alone into the late sultan's private room. There he immediately began work, and took up more than half the square stones with which it was paved, yet saw not the least sign of any treasure. At length he stopped to take a little rest, thinking: "I am much afraid I have been deceived after all."

However, he presently resumed his labor and as he dug deeper uncovered a white slab. He lifted it, and there was revealed a marble staircase. After lighting a lamp he went down the stairs into a room, the floor of which was laid with tiles of chinaware, while the roof and walls were of crystal. This room contained four large tables on each of which were ten urns of porphyry; and when he removed the cover from one of the urns he was greatly surprised and rejoiced to find that it was full of gold-pieces. He looked into all the forty, one after another, and found them full of the same coin. Then he took out a handful and carried it to his mother.

She, as may be imagined, was amazed when he showed her the gold and gave her an account of what he had discovered. "My son," said she, "take heed you do not squander all this wealth as you have the royal treasure."

"Madam," responded Zeyn, "I will henceforward live in such a manner as shall be pleasing to you."

The sultana desired her son to conduct her to the wonderful underground place, which the late sultan had made with such secrecy that she had never heard of it. Zeyn led her to the private room, down the marble stairs, and into the chamber where the urns were. She observed everything with the keenest interest, and in a corner spied a little urn which Zeyn had not before seen. On opening it she found inside a golden key. "My son," said she, "this key will certainly disclose some other treasure. Let us search well. Perhaps we may discover the lock for which the key is designed."

They examined the chamber with the utmost care, and at length found a keyhole in one of the panels of the wall. The sultan immediately tried the key, and readily opened a door which led into a chamber. In the midst of this room were nine pedestals of massive gold, on eight of which stood as many statues, each of them consisting of a single diamond; and such a brightness radiated from the statues as made the whole room perfectly light.

"Oh heavens!" cried Zeyn, in astonishment, "where did my father find such rarities?"

The ninth pedestal redoubled his amazement, for it was covered with a piece of white satin on which were written the following words: "Dear son, it cost me much toil to procure these eight statues; but though they are extraordinarily beautiful, there is a ninth in the world, which surpasses them all. If you desire to possess it, go to the city of Cairo in Eygpt. One of my old slaves, whose name is Mobarec, lives there, and you will easily find him. Tell him all that has befallen you, and he will help you to obtain the wonderful statue."

After reading these words the young sultan said to his mother: "I will again go to Cairo; and I do not believe, madam, that you will now oppose my intention."

"No, my son," she responded, "and you can set out as soon as you think best."

The sultan soon made ready his equipage and started, attended by several slaves. On arriving at Cairo he inquired for Mobarec, and was informed that the person for whom he asked was one of the wealthiest inhabitants of the city, and that he lived like a great lord, but was very friendly to strangers and always glad to entertain them. Zeyn went at once to his house and knocked at the gate. A slave opened the gate and demanded: "Who are you, and what do you want?"

"I am a traveller," answered Zeyn, "who has heard much of the Lord Mobarec's generosity, and I am come to lodge with him."

The slave desired Zeyn to wait while he went to acquaint his master with the stranger's arrival. He soon returned with a request for Zeyn to come in, and he conducted him across a large court and into a hall magnificently furnished. There Mobarec received him very courteously, and after they had greeted each other Zeyn said: "I am the son of the late sultan of Bussorah."

"That sovereign was formerly my master," said Mobarec; "but I never knew he had any children. What is your age?"

"I am twenty years old," answered Zeyn. "How long is it since you left my father's court?"

"Almost two and twenty years," replied Mobarec. "But how can you convince me that you are his son?"

"I can quickly satisfy you as to that," was Zeyn's response. "My father had an underground place beneath his private room in which I have found forty porphyry urns full of gold-pieces."

"And what more is there?" asked Mobarec.

"Nine pedestals of massive gold," rejoined the sultan, "and on eight of these are as many diamond statues, but on the ninth is a piece of white satin containing directions how to procure another statue, more valuable than all those together. It is mentioned on the satin that you will help me to obtain this statue."

As soon as he had spoken these words, Mobarec fell down at Zeyn's feet, and then kissing one of his hands several times said: "I bless God for having brought you hither. You have convinced me that you are the son of the late sultan of Bussorah, and if you wish to possess the wonderful statue, I will go with you on the journey we shall be obliged to make to secure it; but you must first rest here for a short time. This day I am entertaining the merchants of the city. Will you vouchsafe to come and be merry with us?"

"I shall be very glad to be admitted to your feast," replied Zeyn.

So Mobarec led him under a dome, seated him at a

table with the rest of the company and served him. "Who is this person to whom Mobarec pays so much respect?" whispered the merchants one to another.

When they had dined, Mobarec directed his discourse to the company, saying: "My friends, this young stranger is the son and heir of the Sultan of Bussorah, my late master. His father bought me and died without making me free. Therefore I am still a slave, and all I have belongs to his son."

Here Zeyn interrupted him. "Mobarec," said he, "I declare before all these guests that I make you free from this moment, and that I renounce all right to your person and possessions."

Mobarec bowed low and thanked the prince most heartily.

The next day Zeyn said to Mobarec: "I have taken rest enough, for I came not to Cairo to indulge in pleasure. My design is to obtain the ninth statue, and it is time for us to set out in search of it."

"Sir," cried Mobarec, "I am ready to comply with your desires; but you know not what dangers you must encounter to gain this precious acquisition."

"Whatsoever the dangers may be," responded Zeyn, "I am resolved to make the attempt. I will either perish or succeed, and I urge you to accompany me."

Mobarec, finding that Zeyn was determined to go, called his servants and ordered them to make ready his equipage. Horses were brought and the sultan and he and such servants as were to go with them mounted and travelled many days. At length they came to a delightful spot where they alighted, and Mobarec said to the servants: "Remain here and take care of our horses till we return."

Then he said to Zeyn: "Now, sir, let us advance by ourselves. We are near the dreadful place where your father obtained the eight statues that are now yours, and you will need all your courage."

They soon came to a vast lake. "We must cross to an island in the midst of this lake," said Mobarec.

"How can we," asked Zeyn, "when we have no boat?"

"One will soon appear," replied Mobarec. "The enchanted boat of the Sultan of the Genies will come for us. But you must preserve a profound silence. Do not speak to the boatman; and whatever extraordinary circumstance you observe, say nothing; for I tell you beforehand that if you utter one word when we are embarked, the boat will sink."

"I shall take care to be silent," promised Zeyn. "You need only tell me what I am to do, and I will strictly comply."

While they were talking he spied a boat made of red sandalwood on the lake. It had a mast of fine amber, and a blue satin flag. There was only one person in it, and he had the head of an elephant and the body of a tiger. When the boat came to Zeyn and Mobarec, the

monstrous boatman took them up with his trunk, first
one and then the other, and put them into his craft.
He quickly carried them over to the island, set them
ashore, and then he and his boat vanished.

"Now we may talk," said Mobarec. "The island
we are on belongs to the Sultan of the Genies. Look
around you. Can there be a more delightful spot?
Behold the fields adorned with all sorts of flowers and
plants. See those beautiful trees, whose branches bend
down to the ground. Hear the harmonious songs from
a thousand birds of various sorts, many of them unknown in other countries."

Zeyn could not sufficiently admire the beauties with
which he was surrounded, and he still found something
new as he advanced farther into the island. At length
they arrived before a palace built of emeralds, and
encompassed by a wide moat. On the banks of the
moat, at regular intervals, grew such large and lofty
trees that they shaded the whole palace. The gate was
of massive gold and was approached by a bridge. At
the entrance to the bridge stood a company of tall
genies armed with great clubs of steel, who guarded the
portals of the castle.

"Let us at present proceed no farther," said Mobarec,
"lest we be destroyed by these genies. In order to
prevent them from assailing us we must perform a
magic ceremony."

Then he laid on the ground two large mats, on the

edges of which he scattered some precious stones, musk and amber. Afterward he sat down on one of the mats, and Zeyn on the other. "Now," said Mobarec, "I shall conjure the Sultan of the Genies, who lives in the palace that is before us. If our visit to the island is displeasing to him, he will appear in the shape of a dreadful monster; but if he approves of your design, he will show himself in the form of a handsome man. As soon as he appears before us you must rise and salute him, without going off your mat, for you would certainly perish should you stir from it. You must say to him: 'Lord of the Genies, I ask that your Majesty may protect me, as you always protected my father; and I most humbly beg you to give me the ninth statue.'"

Mobarec, having thus instructed his companion, began the conjuration. Immediately their eyes were dazzled by a sudden flash of lightning, which was followed by a clap of thunder. The whole island was covered with a thick darkness, a furious storm of wind blew, the ground was shaken with an earthquake, and the Sultan of the Genies appeared in the shape of a very handsome man; yet there was something terrific in his air.

Zeyn prostrated himself, and spoke as he had been taught by Mobarec. In response the Sultan of the Genies smiled and said: "I loved your father, and every time he came to pay me his respects, I presented him with a statue, which he carried away with him. I will gladly show you the same kindness. Some days before your father died, I had him write what you read on the piece of white satin, and I promised to receive you under my protection, and to give you the ninth statue, which surpasses in beauty those you have already. It was I whom you saw in your dreams in the form of an old man. I caused you to open the underground place where the urns and statues are deposited, and I know the motive that brought you here. You shall obtain what you desire on certain conditions. Return with Mobarec, but you must swear to come again to me and to bring with you a young maiden who has reached her twentieth year without ever having entertained a wish to be married. She must also be perfectly beautiful, and you must be so much a master of yourself as not to determine to keep her for your wife as you are conducting her hither. I will give you a looking-glass, which will clearly reflect the image of no other maiden except she for whom you are searching. Swear to me to observe these conditions, and keep your oath like a man of honor. Otherwise, I will take away your life, notwithstanding the friendliness I now feel for you."

Zeyn did not hesitate to take the rash oath demanded of him, and he swore that he would faithfully keep his word. The Sultan of the Genies then delivered to him a looking-glass and said: "You may return when you please. There is the glass you are to use."

After taking leave of the Sultan of the Genies, Zeyn

and Mobarec retraced their steps to the lake. The boatman with the elephant's head brought the boat and ferried them over and they joined their servants and went back with them to Cairo.

For a few days the young sultan rested at Mobarec's house, and then he said to his host: "Let us go to Bagdad to seek a maiden for the sovereign of the genies."

"Why should we go to Bagdad?" said Mobarec. Are there not beautiful maidens here at Cairo?"

"Certainly," responded Zeyn, "but how shall we get a chance to see them?"

"Do not trouble yourself about that," answered Mobarec. "I know a very shrewd old woman, whom I will intrust with the affair, and she will acquit herself well."

Accordingly he sought out the old woman, and she found means to show Zeyn a considerable number of beautiful maidens, twenty years of age; but when he had viewed them and consulted his glass, it always appeared sullied. Then the old woman brought more maidens until all in the city who were twenty years of age had undergone the trial. Yet the glass never remained bright and clear.

When Zeyn and Mobarec saw there was no beautiful maiden in Cairo of the desired age who did not wish to be married they went to Bagdad, where they hired a magnificent palace, and soon made acquaintance with the chief people of the city. There lived at Bagdad at this time a priest of much repute and noted for his charity, and Mobarec presented him with a purse of five hundred gold-pieces, in the name of Sultan Zeyn, to distribute among the poor. The next day the priest called on Zeyn to thank him. He was courteously received, and after several compliments had passed on both sides, the priest said: "Sir, do you plan to stay long at Bagdad?"

"I shall stay," answered Zeyn, "till I can find a maiden twenty years of age and perfectly beautiful, who not only has never loved a man, but never even desired to do so."

"You seek after a great rarity," affirmed the priest, "and I fear your search would be unsuccessful did I not happen to know of such a maid. Her father was formerly grand vizier; but he long ago left the court and has since lived in a lone house where he applies himself solely to the education of his daughter. She is twenty years old. If you wish, I will ask her of him for you, and I doubt not he will be overjoyed to have a son-in-law of your quality."

"Not so fast," said Zeyn. "I shall not marry the maid before I know whether I like her. But I only need to see her face. That will be enough to enable me to decide."

"You are skilled in physiognomy," remarked the priest smiling. "Well, come along with me to her father's, and I think I can arrange the matter to your satisfaction."

Zeyn accompanied the priest to the home of the vizier, who, as soon as he learned that the young man was the Sultan of Bussorah and was informed of the reason for his presence in the city, called his daughter and made her take off her veil. Never before had Zeyn beheld such a perfect and striking beauty. He pulled out his glass, and it remained bright and unsullied.

When he perceived that he had at length found such a person as he desired, he entreated the vizier to grant her to him. The vizier replied favorably, a magistrate was called in and a contract was signed. Afterward, Zeyn conducted the vizier to his palace, where he treated him magnificently and gave him valuable presents. The next day the wedding was celebrated with all the pomp that was suited to Zeyn's rank and dignity. As soon as this was concluded and the company was dismissed, Mobarec said to his master: "Let us now return to Cairo. Remember the promise you made to the Sultan of the Genies,"

"Yes, let us begone," responded Zeyn; "and I suppose I must be careful to do exactly as I agreed; yet I must confess, my dear Mobarec, that I obey the Sultan of the Genies with a good deal of reluctance. The damsel I have married is so charming I am tempted to carry her to Bussorah and place her on the throne."

"Alas! sir," said Mobarec, "take heed not to give way to your inclination. Whatever it costs you, fulfil your promise to the Sultan of the Genies."

"Well, then," said Zeyn, "you must be careful to conceal the lovely maid from me. Let her never appear in my sight lest I be shaken in my resolution."

Mobarec made ready for their departure. They returned to Cairo, and thence set out for the island of the Sultan of the Genies. When they arrived at the shore of the lake, the maid who had performed the journey in a horse-litter said to Mobarec: "Where are we? Shall we soon be in the dominions of my husband?"

"Madam," answered Mobarec, "it is time to undeceive you. Zeyn married you only in order to get you from your father with the intention of delivering you to the Sultan of the Genies.

At these words she began to weep bitterly. "Take pity on me," she begged. "I am a stranger. You will be accountable to God for your treachery toward me."

But her tears and complaints were of no effect. The boatman came and ferried them over to the island, and she was presented to the Sultan of the Genies. He gazed on her with attention and said to Zeyn: "I am satisfied. The maiden you have brought me is beautiful and good, and I am pleased with the restraint you have put on yourself to do as you agreed. Return to your dominions, and when you enter the underground room, where the eight statues are, you shall find the ninth which I promised you. I shall make my servants carry it thither."

Zeyn thanked the sovereign of the genies, and went back to Cairo with Mobarec. He did not stay long in Eygpt, and was soon on his way homeward. His impatience to see the ninth statue made him hasten his departure; yet he could not help often thinking regretfully of the young girl he had married and he blamed himself for having deceived her. "Alas!" said he to himself, "I have taken her from a tender father to sacrifice her to a genie. O wonderful beauty! you deserved a better fate."

Disturbed with these thoughts he at length reached Bussorah, where his subjects made extraordinary rejoicings over his return. He went at once to give an account of his journey to his mother, who was enraptured to hear that he had obtained the ninth statue. "Let us go to see it," said she.

So the young sultan and his mother went down into the room of the statues, where, great was their astonishment, to behold on the ninth pedestal, instead of a diamond statue, a most beautiful girl. Zeyn knew her to be the same maiden he had conducted to the island of the genies. "Your Majesty is surprised to see me here," said she; "for you expected to find something much more precious then I am. Doubtless you now repent having taken so much trouble."

"Madam," responded Zeyn, "Heaven is my witness that I more than once had nearly broken my word with the Sultan of the Genies by keeping you myself. Whatever be the value of a diamond statue, I would not exchange it for the satisfaction of having you. I love you more than all the diamonds and wealth in the world."

Just as he finished speaking, a clap of thunder was heard, which shook the underground place and greatly alarmed Zeyn's mother; but the Sultan of the Genies immediately appeared and dispelled her fear. "Your son," said he, "is one whom I desire to protect and help. I had a mind to try, whether, at his age, he could subdue himself. This is the ninth statue I designed for him. It is much more rare and valuable than the others." Then he turned to the young sultan and said: "May you and this, your wife, live long and happily, and if you would have her true and constant to you, love her always and love her only."

Having spoken these words, the Sultan of the Genies vanished, and Zeyn, enchanted with the beautiful maiden, had her proclaimed Sultana of Bussorah that same day, and they reigned in mutual happiness to an advanced age.

XV

SINDBAD THE SAILOR

IN the reign of the Caliph Haroun Alraschid there lived in Bagdad a poor porter called Hindbad. On a hot day, when he was carrying a heavy burden from one end of the town to the other, he stopped half way, and, being greatly fatigued, put his burden on the ground and sat down on it near a large mansion. He was much pleased that he stopped where he did; for an agreeable smell of wood of aloes mixed with the scent of rose water came from the house and perfumed the air. Besides, he heard a concert of instrumental music, and he concluded that some sort of merry-making was going on within. His business seldom took him to that part of the town, and he knew not to whom the mansion belonged. To satisfy his curiosity he went to some of the servants who were standing at the door and asked the name of the master of the house.

The servants gazed at him in surprise, and one of them exclaimed: "What! is it possible you live in Bagdad and do not know that here lives Sindbad the Sailor, that famous voyager who has sailed over every sea on which the sun shines?"

The porter had often heard people speak of the immense wealth of Sindbad, and he could not help feeling envious of one whose lot seemed to be as happy as his own was miserable. Therefore he lifted up his eyes to heaven and said: "Mighty Creator of all things, consider the difference between Sindbad and me! I am every day exposed to hardships and misfortunes, and can scarcely procure enough coarse barley bread to keep myself and my family alive, while happy Sindbad spends money right and left and leads a life of continual pleasure. What has he done to merit a lot so agreeable? And what have I done to deserve one so wretched?"

Scarcely had he finished speaking when a servant came out of the house, and taking him by the arm said: "Come with me. The noble Sindbad, my master, wishes to speak to you."

Hindbad was not a little surprised at this summons. Evidently his unguarded words had been overheard and he feared he had given offence. He tried to excuse himself on the pretext that he could not leave there in the street the burden which had been entrusted to him. However, the servant promised that it should be taken care of, and urged him so pressingly to obey the call, that at last Hindbad yielded.

He followed the servant into a great hall where a numerous company was seated around a table covered with all sorts of delicacies. In the place of honor sat a comely, venerable gentleman, with a long white beard, and behind his chair stood a number of domestics ready to minister to his wants. This person was Sindbad. The porter, more than ever alarmed at the sight of so much magnificence, tremblingly saluted the company. Sindbad beckoned to him, seated him at his right hand and served him.

When the repast was over, Sindbad turned to Hindbad and inquired his name and occupation. Then he said: "I wish you to repeat here what I chanced to overhear you say in the street a little while ago."

At this request, Hindbad hung his head in confusion. "My lord," said he, "I confess that my fatigue put me out of humor, and occasioned me to utter some indiscreet words, which I beg you to pardon."

"Do not think I am so unjust as to blame you," responded Sindbad. "But you are mistaken about me, and I wish to set you right. You doubtless fancy I have acquired all the wealth and luxury that you see me enjoy without difficulty or danger. On the contrary I have only attained this happy state after having for years endured more toil and distress than can well be imagined. I assure you my sufferings have been of such a nature as would deter the most miserly of men from seeking wealth at such a cost. Let me tell you something of my experiences."

THE FIRST VOYAGE OF SINDBAD THE SAILOR

I inherited considerable wealth from my parents, but being young and foolish, I wasted much of it in reckless and riotous living. Presently I became impressed with the fact that riches speedily take to themselves wings if managed as badly as I was managing mine, and I remembered also that to be old and poor is misery indeed. So I began to consider how I could make the best use of what property still remained to me. I sold all my household goods at public auction and entered into a contract with some merchants to go on a trading voyage. Not long afterward I embarked with them in a ship which we jointly fitted out.

We set sail and steered our course toward the Indies. At first I was troubled with sea-sickness, but I speedily recovered my health and since then have been no more plagued by that complaint. In our voyage we stopped at several ports where we sold or exchanged our goods; but one day we were becalmed near a small island that was only slightly elevated above the level of the water and resembled a green meadow. The captain ordered his sails to be furled and permitted such persons as were inclined to go on shore to do so. Of this number I was one.

We rowed thither in one of our boats and strolled about for some time. Then we lighted a fire and sat down to enjoy a repast we had brought. But suddenly we were startled by a violent trembling of the island. At the same time those of the crew who remained on the ship set up an outcry, bidding us come on board speedily, or we would all be lost; for what we thought to be an island was the back of a sea monster. The nimblest of us got to our boat, others betook themselves to swimming; but as for me, I was still on the island when the monster plunged into the depths of the sea, and I only saved myself from drowning by catching hold of a piece of the wood we had brought from the ship to make our fire. Meanwhile a breeze had sprung up, and in the confusion that ensued on our vessel in helping on board the men who were in the boat and those that swam, I was not missed. So the captain hoisted his sails and pursued his voyage.

All the rest of the day and the following night I was exposed to the mercy of the waves. Weary and spent, I continued to cling to my frail support, though I almost despaired of saving my life. Great was my joy when the morning light revealed land close at hand, and the waves carried me to the shore. High, rugged cliffs fronted the water, but luckily some tree roots protruded in places, and by their aid I climbed up to the top of the crags where I lay down more dead than alive till the sun was high in the sky. By that time I was exceedingly hungry, and I crept along and searched until I found some herbs fit to eat and a spring of clear water, which helped greatly to revive me.

The sea monster

Presently I advanced farther inland, and at last reached a fine plain, where I perceived a group of horses feeding. As I was walking toward them I heard the voice of a man, and the man himself soon appeared and asked me who I was. I told him my adventures, and he conducted me to a cave, where were a number of his companions.

They offered me some provisions of which I partook, and then I asked them what they did in such a forlorn place. "We are grooms belonging to the sovereign of this island," they said. "Every year we bring the king's horses here for pasturage, and we are to return on the morrow. Had you been one day later you must have perished, because the inhabited part of the island is a great distance off, and it would be impossible for you to go thither without a guide."

Next morning they journeyed toward the capital of the island, and took me with them. When we arrived I was graciously received by their king to whom I related my adventures. He was much concerned over my misfortune and ordered that I should be well cared for and provided with such things as I needed.

Being a merchant, I made friends with men of my own profession, and particularly inquired for traders who were strangers, that perchance I might hear news from Bagdad and find an opportunity to return. The prospects of soon returning seemed favorable, for the king's capital was situated on the seacoast and had a fine harbor to which ships came constantly from all parts of the world.

One day the ship arrived in which I had embarked at Bussorah. The captain was recognized by me at once, and I went to him and asked for my bales. "I am Sindbad," said I, "and those bales marked with his name are mine."

When the captain heard me speak thus, he exclaimed: "Heavens! whom can we trust in these times! It is true that a man named Sindbad was on my ship, but he and several other persons landed on what we supposed to be an island. In reality the island was the back of an enormous sea monster that was floating asleep on the waves, and no sooner did the creature feel the heat of a fire Sindbad and his companions kindled, than it plunged down into the ocean depths. I saw Sindbad perish with my own eyes, as did also the others on board my vessel, and yet you say you are that Sindbad. What impudence to invent so horrible a falsehood in order to possess yourself of property that does not belong to you!"

"Have patience," I responded, "and do me the favor of listening to what I have to say."

"Speak then," said the captain; "I am all attention."

So I told him of my escape, and of my fortunate meeting with the king's grooms, and how kindly I had been received at the palace. In the end the captain was persuaded that I was no cheat; for there came people from the ship who knew me and expressed great joy at seeing me alive. Then the captain recollected me himself and embraced me. "God be praised for your happy escape!" he cried. "You are at liberty to take your goods and do with them as you please."

I selected the most valuable articles in my bales and presented them to the king, who asked me how I came by such rarities; for he as yet supposed I had lost everything at the time I was cast up on his island by the waves. When I acquainted him with how my bales had been miraculously restored to me, he accepted my present and in return gave me one much more considerable. I then took leave of him, and after exchanging my goods for the commodities of that country, I went aboard the same ship on which I had begun my voyage. Among the things that I carried with me were camphor, nutmegs, cloves, pepper, and ginger; and I traded very successfully at the various ports where we touched. At last we arrived at Bussorah, whence I came to this city, with not a little wealth.

Sindbad now ordered the musicians to proceed with their concert, which his story had interrupted. Later, he sent for a purse of one hundred sequins, and giving it to the porter, said: "Take this, Hindbad, and return to your home, but come back tomorrow to hear more of my adventures."

The porter went away, astonished at the honor done

him and at the present he had received. The account of what had occurred proved very agreeable to his wife and children, who did not fail to express their thankfulness for what providence had sent them by the hand of their father's benefactor.

Hindbad put on his best clothes next day and returned to the voyager's house where he was heartily welcomed. As soon as all the guests had arrived, dinner was served, and they feasted long and merrily. At the conclusion of the banquet Sindbad addressed himself to the company saying: "Gentlemen, be pleased to listen to the adventures of my second voyage."

THE SECOND VOYAGE OF SINDBAD THE SAILOR

I had resolved, on returning from my first voyage, to spend the rest of my days at Bagdad; but I soon grew tired of a life of quiet, and longed to be again on the sea. So I procured such goods as were suitable for the places I intended to visit, and embarked in a good ship with other merchants whom I knew to be honorable men. We went from port to port exchanging our goods to great profit, but one day we landed on an island where we could see neither man nor animal. It abounded, however, with trees and grassy meadows, and we walked about gathering flowers and fruit. At length I sat down in a shady place near a brook to eat some provisions I had brought with me. I made a good meal and, lulled by the murmur of the brook, fell asleep.

How long I slept I know not, but when I awoke I perceived with horror that I was alone, and that the ship was gone. I rushed about like one distracted, beat my head and breast, and at last threw myself on the ground, where I lay in despair, ready to die with grief. A hundred times did I upbraid myself for not being content with the produce of my first voyage which might have sufficed me as long as I lived. But my repining did no good, and presently I got up and climbed to the top of a lofty tree, whence I looked about on all sides. In the seaward direction I could discern nothing except sky and water, but when I gazed off over the land my curiosity was excited by a huge white object, so far off that I could not distinguish what it was.

I descended from the tree, took what provisions I had left, and set off toward the white object as fast as I could go. As I drew near it, I thought it seemed to be a great white dome; but there was no opening on any side, and it was so smooth I could not climb to the top. I walked around it and counted fifty paces.

Suddenly the sky became as dark as if it had been covered with a thick cloud, and I saw with amazement that the gloom was caused by a monstrous bird. Then I remembered that I had often heard the sailors speak of a bird of vast size called the roc, and I concluded that the great dome which had so puzzled me was an egg, half buried in the sand. Sure enough, the bird settled slowly down on it, and I cowered close beside the shell to avoid being crushed. The day was drawing to a close, and the roc spent the night sitting on the egg. Just in front of me was one of the bird's legs, which was as large as the trunk of a tree. I tied myself strongly to it with my turban, hoping that when the roc took flight next morning it would carry me away from the lonely island. This was precisely what happened. As soon as the dawn appeared the bird rose into the air and I was borne up and up till I could no longer see the earth. How far the creature carried me I cannot say, but it at length descended with such rapidity that I lost my senses. When I recovered consciousness I found that the bird was on the ground, and I hastily untied my turban. I freed myself not a moment too soon, for the roc immediately flew away carrying in its bill a serpent of enormous length which it had just then seized.

The spot where it left me was encompassed on all sides by mountains that seemed to reach above the clouds, and so steep there was no possibility of climbing them. This was a new perplexity, and I doubted if I had gained anything by quitting the uninhabited island.

As I wandered about seeking anxiously for means of escape, I observed that the ground was strewed with diamonds, some of which were of astonishing size. This sight gave me great pleasure, but my delight was speedily dampened when I also saw numbers of horrible snakes, so large that the smallest of them was capable of swallowing an elephant. Fortunately, they spent the hours of daylight in their dens, and only came out at night, probably on account of their enemy, the roc.

When it grew dusk I crept into a little cave, and blocked the entrance, which was low and narrow, with a great stone to preserve me from the serpents. The stone did not fit so closely as to exclude light and air, and I sat down very comfortably and supped on the scanty store of food I had brought. But soon the serpents began to crawl to and fro outside, and the sound of their hissing so frightened me that I could not sleep. I was thankful when the day dawned, and the serpents retreated to their dens. Then I came trembling out of my cave and rambled about the valley once more; and though I can justly say that I walked on diamonds I felt no inclination to touch them. Of what use or interest were they to me, with no prospect but a speedy death, either as the prey of the serpents or by starvation? At length, overcome with weariness I sat down and in spite of my fears fell asleep, for I had scarcely closed my eyes all night.

I was awakened by the thud of some falling object close by, and when I looked saw on the ground a huge piece of fresh meat. As I stared at it several more pieces rolled down the cliffs in different places. I had always regarded as fabulous what I had heard travellers relate of the valley of diamonds and of the cunning method devised by the merchants for getting the precious stones; but now I found they had stated nothing except the truth. The merchants came to the neighborhood of the valley when the eagles, which nest in considerable numbers roundabout, have young ones and are therefore most eager in seeking food. They throw into the valley great joints of meat, and the diamonds, on whose points the meat falls adhere to it. The eagles, which are bigger and stronger in this country than anywhere else, pounce eagerly on the pieces of meat and carry them to their nests among the rocks at the summit of the cliffs to feed their hungry broods. Each merchant has chosen some nest which is recognized as his property and whenever meat is brought up to it from the valley he runs to the nest, drives off the parent birds by his shouts and takes away the diamonds that stick to the meat.

Until the moment that I was roused from my sleep I had supposed the valley would be my grave, for I had seen no possibility of getting out of it alive. Now, however, I took courage and soon thought of a plan which I believed would set me at liberty. But first I picked up enough of the choicest diamonds I could find to fill the leather bag which had held my provisions. After making the bag fast to my girdle I used my turban cloth to tie one of the largest pieces of meat to my back, and then lay on the ground with my face downward.

I had scarcely placed myself in this posture, when I

heard the flapping of mighty wings above me, and an eagle seized the meat and carried both the meat and me to its nest on the top of the mountain. This was exactly what I had expected. One of the merchants was close at hand, and he raised the usual outcries and scared the eagle away. Great was his amazement when he came to the nest and discovered me; but instead of inquiring how I came thither he began to abuse me and declare that I was stealing the diamonds from his meat.

"You will treat me with more civility," said I, "when you know my story. As for diamonds I have enough for you and me too. All that your entire company of merchants possess together would not equal mine in value. Whatever you have you owe to chance; but I selected for myself, in the bottom of the valley, enough of the finest to fill the bag that hangs at my girdle."

Several other merchants now came crowding around us, much astonished to see me; but they were still more surprised when I related my story. They conducted me to their encampment, where I showed them my diamonds which they agreed were the largest and most perfect they had ever seen. I told the merchant who owned the nest to which I had been carried that he might take as many as he pleased for his share. He, however, contented himself with one, and that by no means the largest. When I urged him to take more, he said: "No, I am very well satisfied with this, which will give me as great a fortune as I desire, and save me the trouble of making any future voyages."

I stayed with the merchants several days and then accompanied them on their journey homeward. We travelled to the sea, where we embarked at the first port we came to and sailed to the isle of Roha, famous for its camphor trees. I there exchanged some of my diamonds for merchandise, with which I traded to great advantage at other places where we stopped on our homeward voyage. At last we reached Bussorah, and I proceeded to Bagdad. The first thing I did was to bestow large sums of money on the poor, and then I settled down to enjoy tranquilly the riches I had gained with so much toil and pain.

Thus Sindbad ended the relation of his adventures on his second voyage; and after giving Hindbad another hundred sequins, invited him to come the next day to hear the account of his third voyage.

THE THIRD VOYAGE OF SINDBAD THE SAILOR

I soon again grew weary of a life of ease, and hardening myself against the thought of danger embarked with some merchants on another long voyage. We stopped and traded at a number of ports, but at length were caught on the open sea by a terrible wind which blew us completely out of our reckoning. The tempest continued for several days and finally drove us to the

shores of an island where we put into a harbor. After
we had anchored and furled our sails, the captain said:
"I greatly wish we could have avoided the necessity of
stopping here; for the islands in this vicinity are inhabited by hairy savages who are sure to attack us soon.
We must, however, make no resistance; because,
though they are dwarfs, they are more in number than
the locusts, and if we happened to kill one, they would
speedily destroy us."

We had not long to wait to find that the captain told
us the truth. A countless multitude of hideous savages,
about two feet high and covered all over with red hair,
came swimming to our ship. Chattering in a language
we could not understand, they clutched at ropes and
gangways and clambered up the sides of the ship with
such agility as surprised us. They hoisted the sails, cut
the cable, took the ship to the shore and made us all
get out. Then they went away with our vessel and left us.

We looked about and saw at a distance a vast building. Toward this we turned our steps and found it to
be a high and strongly built palace. We pushed open
the heavy ebony door and entered a large apartment,
on one side of which was a heap of human bones, and
on the other a great number of roasting spits. This
gruesome spectacle made us tremble with a deadly fear,
and before we had time to regain our composure a door
at the farther end of the apartment opened with a loud
crash, and there entered a horrible black man as tall as

a lofty palm tree. His teeth were long and sharp and his nails were like the claws of some great bird.

At the sight of so frightful a giant we were as motionless and silent as dead men. He sat down by the fire and looked at us. When he had considered us well, he stretched out his hand and took me up by the nape of the neck. After examining me, however, and perceiving that I was so lean as to be nothing but skin and bones, he let me go. He took up the rest, one by one, and viewed them in the same manner. The captain being the fattest, he roasted and ate him for his supper. After finishing his repast he stretched himself full length on the floor and fell asleep, snoring like the loudest thunder. There he stayed until morning. As to ourselves, it was not possible for us to enjoy any rest, and we passed the night in the most painful dread that can be imagined. At dawn the giant awoke, and went out, leaving us in the palace.

When he was gone we bemoaned our fate so loudly that the hall echoed with our despairing cries. We spent the day wandering about on the island, eating such fruits as we could find, and late in the day we returned to the palace, having sought in vain for any other place of refuge. At sunset the giant came back, supped on one of our seamen, then lay down and fell fast asleep. But during the day we had determined on a plan for revenging ourselves. As soon as we heard him snore, ten of the boldest among us each took a spit and thrust them into his eyes and blinded him. The pain made him give a frightful yell. He started up and stretched out his hands, in order to catch us; but we ran to such places as he could not reach, and after seeking for us in vain he groped his way to the door and went out, howling.

We immediately left the palace and hurried to the shore. Great quantities of timber lay there strewn about and during the night we made rafts enough to carry us all, each raft sufficiently large for three men. Day had scarcely dawned when we saw our cruel enemy coming, accompanied by two other giants who were leading him, and a great number more followed close behind. We at once clambered on our rafts, and put to sea with all the speed we could. Then the giants picked up huge pieces of rock, and wading into the water hurled them after us with such good aim that all the rafts, except the one I was on, were broken to pieces and their luckless crews drowned. My two companions and I, by working with all our might, gained the open sea. Here we were at the mercy of the wind and waves, which tossed us to and fro all that day and night; but the next day we found ourselves near an island on which we gladly landed.

Luckily we discovered an abundance of delicious fruits to satisfy our hunger, and when night came we lay down to sleep on the shore. A loud rustling noise presently awakened us, and, leaping to our feet we saw an immense snake gliding toward us over the sand. We started to run, but the snake overtook one of my comrades, and in spite of his struggles speedily crushed the life out of him in its mighty coils and proceeded to swallow him. "O Heaven!" I exclaimed, "to what dangers are we exposed! We rejoiced yesterday at having escaped from the cruelty of the giants and the rage of the waves; but now are we fallen into another danger equally horrible."

My remaining companion and I searched the next day for some place where we might hope to be safe from this new horror. About sundown we climbed into a tall tree, intending to sleep there. But shortly afterward the snake came hissing to the foot of the tree. It raised itself up against the trunk, until it found my comrade who was perched just below me. After swallowing him, it crawled away leaving me half dead with terror.

When the east began to brighten with the dawn, I came down from the tree with hardly a hope of escaping the dreadful fate that had overtaken my two companions; but life is sweet and I determined to do what I could to save myself. All day long I toiled with frantic haste and collected a great quantity of brushwood, brambles and thorns, which I bound into fagots. These I piled in a circle around a tree and slanted the upper ones inward to the trunk, thus forming a kind of tent in which I crouched like a mouse in a hole when it sees a cat coming. At nightfall the snake failed not to return, eager to devour me, and glided round and round my frail shelter seeking an entrance. Happily for me it was baffled by my prickly defences, and at last, when the sky paled with the approach of dawn the monster retired, but I dared not leave my shelter until the sun rose.

I had escaped for the time being, yet I felt so hopeless regarding the future, that in a fit of desperation I went to throw myself into the sea and end my troubles once for all. Imagine my joy and relief when I saw a ship in the distance. I called as loud as I could, and unfolding the linen of my turban, waved it to attract the attention of the people on the ship. This had the desired effect and the captain sent a boat for me.

As soon as I was on board the vessel I found myself surrounded by a wondering crowd of sailors and merchants eager to know by what chance I happened to be on that desolate island. After I had told my story they regaled me with the best of provisions, and the captain, seeing that I was in rags, gave me one of his own suits. When I observed the captain more closely, I knew him to be the person who, in my second voyage, had sailed away and left me on the island where I fell asleep, without sending to seek for me.

I was not surprised that he, believing me to be dead, did not recognize me. "Captain," said I, "look at me, and you may know that I am Sindbad whom you abandoned on that island."

The captain stared at me in amazement, but was presently convinced that I spoke the truth. "God be praised!" he exclaimed, embracing me; "I am glad to have that piece of carelessness off my conscience. I am glad, too, that I can deliver to you your goods, which I have taken care to preserve."

I received them gratefully, and as we went from one island to another traded for stores of cloves, cinnamon, and other spices. We continued our voyage for some time, but at last I arrived at Bussorah and returned to Bagdad with so much wealth that I knew not its extent.

Thus Sindbad finished the history of his third voyage. He gave another hundred sequins to Hindbad and invited him to dinner the next day to hear of the fourth voyage.

THE FOURTH VOYAGE OF SINDBAD THE SAILOR

After I had rested from the dangers of my third voyage, my passion for trade and my love of novelty soon again prevailed and I decided to make another venture. For the sake of variety I travelled this time through several of the Persian provinces and embarked at one of the more distant ports of the kingdom. The vessel put out to sea, and at first all went well; but at length we encountered a violent hurricane, our sails were split in a thousand pieces, and the vessel became a total wreck in spite of all that the worthy captain could do. Many of our company were drowned, but I and a few others clung to pieces of the wreck and were thrown up on the shore of an island. We scrambled beyond the reach of the waves and threw ourselves down quite exhausted to wait for morning.

At daylight we wandered inland, and soon saw some huts, to which we directed our steps. From these a great number of negroes ran forth as we drew near. They surrounded and seized us and dragged us away to their habitations. With five comrades I was taken into a hut, where our captors had us sit down on the ground and gave us a certain herb which they made signs for us to eat. My companions, not taking notice that the blacks ate none of it themselves, thought only of satisfying their hunger and devoured the herb with greediness. But I, suspecting some trick, would not so much as taste it. In a short time the effect of the herb became apparent; for I perceived that my companions had lost their senses, and though they chattered incessantly I could not understand a word they said.

The negroes now brought us large bowls full of rice prepared with cocoanut oil, and my crazy comrades ate heartily, but I partook very sparingly, fully convinced that the object of our captors was to fatten us speedily for their own eating. Within a few weeks they devoured my five comrades, but as I retained my reason, you may easily guess that instead of growing fat as the rest did I ate so little that I became leaner every day.

I was so far from being a tempting morsel that I was allowed to wander about freely. One day, when all the blacks, except one old man, had gone off on some expedition, I plunged into the forest, determined to make my escape. The old man called to me to come back, but the more he called the faster I ran. I hurried on until sundown, when I stopped to rest for the night. In the morning I resumed my flight, and I continued to travel for seven days. I avoided those places that seemed to be inhabited, and lived for the most part on cocoanuts, which served me both for meat and drink. On the eighth day I came near the sea and saw a party of white men gathering pepper, which grew abundantly there. Reassured by the nature of their occupation, I advanced toward them and they asked me in Arabic who I was and whence I came. Great was my delight to hear them speak my own language. I satisfied their curiosity by giving them an account of my shipwreck, and telling of my capture by the negroes and how I escaped from my savage captors.

The pepper gatherers welcomed me cordially and I stayed with them and helped them at their work. When they had as much pepper as they wanted they went on board their ship and sailed to the island whence they came. I accompanied them and as soon as they reached their own country they presented me to their king who received me very hospitably. To him, also, I related my adventures, and he ordered that I should be supplied with food and raiment and treated with consideration.

I soon learned that the island was full of people and that it abounded in desirable products. A great deal of traffic went on in the capital, where I soon began to feel at home and contented. Moreover, the king showed me many marks of special favor, and consequently every man in the court and city sought to oblige me.

One custom that seemed to me very extraordinary was the habit all the people had of riding their horses without bridle or saddle. The king was no better off in this respect than his poorest subject, and I determined to see him more comfortably mounted. I went to a workman and had him make under my direction the foundation of a saddle. This I wadded and covered with velvet and leather, and adorned it with gold embroidery. Afterward I got a blacksmith to make a bit according to a pattern I furnished, and also some stirrups. When the saddle and bridle were ready I presented them to the king, put them on one of his horses and showed him how to use them. His Majesty then mounted and rode about quite delighted. To express his gratitude he rewarded me generously. It was now necessary that I should make similar equipage for the ministers and principal officers of the king's household, and this not only gained me great reputation, but as they all gave me valuable presents I became a wealthy and important person in the city.

One day the king sent for me and said: "Sindbad, I am going to ask a favor of you. Both I and my subjects esteem you, and wish you to end your days among us. Therefore I desire that you should marry so that you will stay in my dominions and think no more of your own country."

I durst not resist the king's will, and I married a rich and beautiful lady whom he selected for me. My wife and I lived together happily, yet I could not forget Bagdad and I cherished the hope that I might sometime escape thither.

It at length happened that the wife of one of my nearest neighbors and best friends became sick and died. When I went to see the bereaved husband and offer my consolation I found him in the depths of woe.

"Heaven preserve you and grant you a long life," said I.

"Alas!" he responded, "what is the use of saying that when I have but a very short time left to live?"

"Come, come!" said I, "be not so melancholy. I trust that you may be spared for many years."

"No," he said, "the end for me is near. I shall be buried this day with my wife. That is the law in our island. The living husband is interred with the dead wife, and the living wife with the dead husband. It is thus our ancestors have done, and thus must we do."

While he was giving me an account of this barbarous custom, his kindred, friends and neighbors came to assist at the funeral and presently began their march to the place of burial. The husband, clad from head to foot in a black mantle, followed behind the open bier on which lay the body decked in rich robes and sparkling jewels. The procession took its way to a high mountain at some distance from the city, and when the destination was reached the body with all its apparel and jewels was lowered into a deep pit. Then the husband embraced his friends and bade them farewell. Afterward he reclined on another bier with seven small loaves of bread and a pitcher of water beside him, and he also was let down into the cavern. The ceremony was now over, the mouth of the pit was covered with a stone, and the company returned to the city.

I mention this affair more particularly because in a few weeks' time I was to be the principal actor on a similar occasion. My own wife sickened and died; and though I made every remonstrance I could to the king not to sacrifice me, a foreigner, to the inhuman custom of the island, I appealed in vain. However, the king and all his court sought to soften my sorrow by honoring the funeral with their presence. We went in solemn procession to the mountain, and soon I was lowered into the pit with the scanty supply of bread and water it was the habit to furnish. When my eyes became accustomed to the gloom I discerned by a feeble ray of light which shone down through a chink at the opening that I was in a vast cavern strewn with human bones and the jewels that had adorned the bodies buried there. For several days I lived on my bread and water, and just as they were on the point of exhaustion, I heard the tread of some animal, and the sound of its breathing. I turned to look, and dimly saw a shadowy form, which fled at my movement, squeezing itself through a cranny in the wall.

This roused a hope that there was some avenue of escape from the darkness and misery of the cavern. I hastily rose to my feet and pursued the animal as fast as I could. It stopped at intervals, but always resumed its flight when I approached. At last, after following it for what seemed to me miles, I saw before me a glimmer of light, resembling a star. As I went on I sometimes lost sight of the light, but always soon again brought it into view, and finally discovered that it came through a hole in the rock. I crept out and was overjoyed to find myself on the seashore.

The mountains roundabout sloped sheer down to the water, and the place was inaccessible except to boats. I did not doubt but that I could hail some passing ship and I was pleased that I was not likely to be seen there by persons from the city. Thus assured of my safety, I returned to the cavern and gathered up a rich treasure of the jewels with which it was strewn and brought them out to the beach. Shortly afterward a vessel came into view, and by waving my arms and uttering loud cries I attracted the attention of its crew. A boat was sent off for me and I and my bundles of treasure were transferred to the ship.

Luckily the vessel was voyaging toward Persia, and I at length arrived at Bagdad. Out of gratitude to God for His mercies I contributed liberally toward the support of several mosques and gave large sums of money to the poor, after which I enjoyed myself with my friends in festivities and amusements.

Here Sindbad made a new present of one hundred sequins to Hindbad, whom he requested to return with the rest of the company next day at the same hour to hear the story of his fifth voyage.

THE FIFTH VOYAGE OF SINDBAD THE SAILOR

All the troubles and calamities I had undergone could not cure me of an inclination to make new voyages. I soon wearied of the pleasures of a quiet life and therefore set forth once more. But this time I went in a ship of my own, for I wished to be able to call at whatever places I chose and stay as long or as short a time as I pleased. I therefore built and fitted out a vessel at the nearest seaport. When everything was ready I went on board with my goods; but not having enough to make a cargo I allowed several other merchants to embark with me.

We sailed with the first fair wind, and after a long voyage landed on a strange island. In looking about we found a roc's egg. There was a young bird in the egg just ready to be hatched, and its beak had begun to break the shell. The merchants, who were with me, in spite of all I could say to deter them, cut a hole in the shell with their hatchets, and killed the young roc. Then they lighted a fire, hacked off portions of the bird, and roasted and ate them, while I stood by aghast.

Scarcely had they finished their ill-omened feast when there appeared in the air at a considerable distance what seemed to be two great clouds. The captain of my ship, knowing by experience that the clouds were the parents of the young roc, urged us to get on board the ship with all speed.

This we did, and immediately hoisted our sails. Meanwhile the rocs had reached their despoiled nest, and at the sight of the mangled remains of their young one they hovered about uttering frightful cries. Then they flew back in the direction whence they had come and disappeared. We were flattering ourselves that we had escaped when they again came into view, and we observed that each of them carried in its talons an enormous stone. They were soon directly over our ship and one of them let go its burden; but thanks to the dexterity of our steersman the stone missed us. We had hardly time to draw a breath of relief when the other bird dropped its stone, and this hit the ship exactly in the middle and broke it in pieces. The mariners and merchants were all crushed to death or fell into the sea. I myself was among the latter. Fortunately I caught hold of a fragment of plank, and by holding on to this with one hand and swimming with the other I kept myself afloat. At last, with the help of the wind and a favoring tide, I got safely ashore on an island. There I sat down on the grass till I had somewhat recovered from my fatigue and then walked into the island to explore it. Truly I thought I had reached a garden of delights. There were trees everywhere gay with blossoms or ladened with fruits, and crystal streams rippled beneath their shadows.

Presently I saw an old man who appeared very weak and infirm sitting on the bank of a small river. At first I fancied he was some wrecked mariner like myself, and I went toward him and gave him a friendly greeting; but he only nodded slightly in response. I asked him what he was doing there, and he made signs that he wanted me to take him on my back and carry him over the river.

Because I pitied his age and feebleness I did as he requested, and when I reached the other shore bade him alight. I stooped that he might get off with ease, but instead of doing so, this creature, who had seemed to me so decrepit, nimbly hooked his legs round my neck. He sat astride on my shoulders with such a tight grip of his legs that I was well-nigh strangled, and this, added to my terror, made me fall insensible to the ground.

When I recovered, the ill-natured old fellow still kept his place, and as soon as he observed me reviving he prodded me adroitly, first with one foot and then the other, until I was forced to get up. Then he made me carry him about under the trees, while he gathered and ate the choicest fruits. He never left his seat all day; and when I lay down to rest at night, half dead with weariness, the terrible old man continued to hold on tight to me. At the first glimmer of morning light I was awakened by his pinching and prodding, and was compelled to resume my dreary march, with rage and bitterness in my heart.

This sort of thing went on for a week or more, until one day I found several dry gourds. I took up one of the largest, scooped it out and filled the shell with the juice of the grapes, which abounded on the island. Afterward I left the gourd propped in the fork of a tree. A few days later when I passed that way carrying the hateful old man I found that the grape juice had become very good wine. I drank some of it, and it gave me new vigor, and so exhilarated my spirits that I began to sing and dance in spite of my burden.

The old monster was not slow to perceive the effect which the wine had on me, and that I carried him with more ease than before. So he stretched out his skinny hand, seized the gourd, and cautiously tasted its contents. Then he eagerly drained all that was left. The wine was strong and the gourd capacious, so that he,

too, soon began to sing after a fashion. In a little while
I had the delight of feeling the iron grip of his goblin
legs unclasp, and with one vigorous effort I threw him
to the ground where he lay motionless.

I was extremely glad to be thus freed from the troublesome fellow, and I hastened to return to the sea shore.
There, by the greatest good luck, I encountered the
crew of a ship busy getting a supply of water for their
vessel, which lay at anchor not far away. They heard
the story of my escape with amazement. "You fell
into the hands of the Old Man of the Sea," they said;
" and it is a mercy that he did not strangle you as he has
everyone else on whose shoulders he has managed to
perch himself. The island is well known as the scene
of his evil deeds, and no merchant or sailor who lands
on it cares to stray far away from his comrades."

They took me with them to the ship, where the captain received me with great kindness. He soon set sail,
and some days later reached the harbor of a large and
prosperous town. One of the merchants on the ship,
who had been very friendly to me on the way, went
ashore with me, and introduced me to some people of
the town who gathered cocoanuts. "Go with them,"
he said, "and do as they do."

He furnished me with provisions for the journey, and
a large bag to fill with cocoanuts, and I went with them
to a thick forest of lofty cocoa palms. The trunks of
the trees were, however, so smooth and slippery that it

was not possible to climb to where the fruit hung. When we entered the forest we saw a great number of monkeys, big and little, which fled as soon as they perceived us and scrambled up to the tufted crowns of the trees with surprising agility.

My companions collected stones and began to throw them at the lively creatures. I did the same; and the monkeys, out of revenge, snatched off the nuts from the trees and cast them at us with angry, spiteful gestures. We gathered up the cocoanuts, pausing from time to time to throw stones in order to provoke the monkeys to furnish more cocoanuts. By this stratagem we filled our bags with very little labor.

We carried our spoils back to the town where we sold them; and I continued to be a cocoanut-gatherer until I had earned money enough to pay my way to my own country. Then I collected a goodly store of nuts to take with me and embarked on a trading vessel. We stopped at the isle of Comari where I exchanged my cocoanuts for pepper and wood of aloes, and went with other merchants pearl-fishing. I hired divers, who were very successful, and when I at length continued my voyage and arrived at Bagdad I realized vast sums on the pearls I brought. A tenth of my gains I distributed in alms, and then rested from my labors, and comforted myself with all the pleasures that my riches could give me.

Sindbad here ended his narrative, ordered one hundred sequins to be given to Hindbad, and requested that he and the other guests should dine with him next day to hear the account of his sixth voyage.

THE SIXTH VOYAGE OF SINDBAD THE SAILOR

It must be a marvel to you that I should again tempt fortune after having five times met with shipwreck and desperate perils. I am myself astonished at my conduct when I reflect on it; but evidently it was my fate to rove. So after a year of repose I prepared to make a sixth voyage, regardless of the entreaties of my friends and relations who did all they could to keep me at home.

I travelled through several provinces of Persia and India to a distant port where I finally embarked for a voyage. Some time after we started we encountered stormy weather which drove us so completely out of our course that for many days neither the captain nor the pilot knew where we were. When this uncertainty came to an end there was small reason to rejoice; for the captain cast his turban on the deck and tore his beard declaring that we were in the most dangerous region on all the ocean. "We have been caught," said he, "in a rapid current that is sweeping us to destruction. The ship will be wrecked in less than a quarter of an hour."

It happened as he said. The efforts of the sailors were of no avail, and we were driven with frightful

rapidity toward a high mountain that rose steeply out
of the sea. Our vessel crashed onto the rocks at the
base of the mountain, but did not go to pieces until we
had managed to get to the shore with our provisions
and the best of our goods.

"Now that we are here," said the captain, "we may
as well begin to dig our graves. We can neither escape
by sea nor ascend the mountain. Any vessel that ap-
proaches within a certain distance is drawn hither to
inevitable disaster, and from this fatal spot no ship-
wrecked mariner has ever returned."

The narrow strip of rocky shore was strewn with the
fragments of a thousand gallant ships, and the bones
of a host of luckless mariners shone white in the sun-
shine. We shuddered to think how soon our own bones
would be added to the rest. All around lay vast quantities of the costliest merchandise, and treasures were
heaped in every cranny of the rocks; but these objects
only served to augment our despair.

Soon after we landed, our captain divided equally
among us all the provisions we possessed, and the
length of each man's life depended on how long he
could make his portion last. I myself was able to live
on very little, and I survived all my companions. When
I buried the last of them I had so small an amount of
food left that I knew I also would die within a few days.

One very strange feature of the vicinity was a swift
river of fresh water that ran from the sea into a dark

cavern of the mountain. As I stood on the shore of this river I considered whether it were not possible that the stream might somewhere emerge. "Why should I not build a raft," I said, "and trust myself to the swiftly flowing current? It may convey me to some inhabited country; but if I be drowned, I only change one kind of death for another."

I immediately went to work and speedily constructed a stout raft using pieces of timber from the wrecks and tying them together with the ropes that plentifully strewed the beach. When it was finished I loaded it with chests of gold and jewels, and bales of rich stuffs selected from the wealth that so abounded there. I carefully balanced my cargo, fastened it securely in place, and went on board with two oars I had made. Then I cut loose, leaving the raft to the course of the river, and resigned myself to the will of God.

Once out in the current my raft was quickly swept into the cavern, and I was soon in total darkness, carried smoothly forward by the rapid river. Worn out with work and anxiety and weak from lack of food I presently fell asleep. When I awoke I was once more in the light of day, and a beautiful country lay around me. The raft was tied to the river bank, on which stood a crowd of friendly looking black men gazing down at me. I got up and saluted them. They spoke to me in return, but I did not understand their language. Overjoyed at my deliverance I murmured to myself in Arabic:

"Call on the Almighty, and he will help thee. Close thine eyes, and while thou sleepest Heaven will change thy fortune from evil to good."

One of the negroes, who understood Arabic, then came forward, saying: "Brother, we are inhabitants of this country, and water our fields from this river. We saw your raft floating down the current, and one of us swam out and brought it to shore. Here we fastened it and waited till you should awake. Tell us now whence you come and where you were going."

I begged them to first give me something to eat. They brought me several sorts of food, and when I had satisfied my hunger, I related faithfully all that had befallen me. They listened with attentive surprise, and as soon as I had finished, they told me, through the person who spoke Arabic and interpreted to them what I said, that I must go along with them and repeat my story to their king.

A horse was brought, they helped me to mount, and while some walked ahead to show the way, the rest took my cargo and followed. We marched until we came to the capital, and I then learned that I was on the great island of Ceylon. The negroes presented me to their king, and I saluted him by prostrating myself before him and kissing his footstool. He bade me rise, made me sit down near him, and then I told my story. At its conclusion my goods were brought in and displayed in his presence.

When I saw that he looked on some of the jewels with more than ordinary interest, I said to him: "Sir, not only my person but my goods are your Majesty's to dispose of as you choose."

He answered me with a smile: "Nay, Sindbad, I will take nothing of yours. Far from lessening your wealth, I design to augment it, and will not let you quit my dominions without marks of my liberality."

Then he commanded one of his officers to provide me with a suitable lodging at his expense, and sent slaves to carry my goods to my new dwelling place and wait on me there. I lived for some time thus cared for by the king, but after I had viewed the city and seen what was most worthy of notice in the region roundabout, I asked the king to allow me to return to my own country. He granted me permission in the most obliging and honorable manner and loaded me with rich gifts. When I went to take leave of him he entrusted me with a royal present and a letter for our sovereign, saying: "I beg you to give these to the Caliph Haroun Alraschid, and assure him of my friendship."

The ship set sail, and after a prosperous voyage I landed at Bussorah, and thence went to Bagdad. My first care was to take the King of Ceylon's letter to the Commander of the Faithful. When I had been conducted to the throne of the caliph I made my obeisance and presented the letter and gift. He read the missive and then demanded of me whether the King of Ceylon was as rich and potent as he represented himself to be in that letter; and he showed me what the monarch had written.

"I can assure your Majesty," said I, "that he does not exceed the truth."

The caliph dismissed me with a generous present, and I returned to my own house.

With these words Sindbad concluded his story, and Hindbad was given another hundred sequins and invited to come on the morrow to hear of the seventh and last voyage.

THE SEVENTH VOYAGE OF SINDBAD THE SAILOR

After my sixth voyage I was quite determined to go to sea no more. I had attained a sufficient age to appreciate a quiet life and had no desire to expose myself to such risks as I had hitherto encountered. My only wish was to pass the rest of my life in tranquility. But one day an officer of the caliph's came for me, and I returned with him to the palace.

"Sindbad," said the caliph, when I had been conducted into his presence, "I am in need of your service. You must carry a gift and a letter from me to the King of Ceylon."

The caliph's demand was to me as startling as a near and unexpected clap of thunder.

"Commander of the Faithful," I responded, "I am

ready to do whatever your Majesty thinks fit to ask; but I most humbly beseech you to consider what I have undergone. Besides, I have made a vow never again to leave Bagdad."

"But this is no adventurous voyage on which I am sending you," affirmed the caliph. "You have only to go straight to Ceylon and leave my gift and message, and then you are free to come back and do as you please."

I perceived that the caliph would insist on my compliance, and I therefore submitted to his will. He was delighted at having gotten his own way, and he gave me one thousand sequins to defray the expenses of my journey.

As soon as his letter and present were delivered to me, I went to Bussorah, where I embarked, and sailed quickly and safely to Ceylon. When I disclosed my errand I was conducted to the king with much pomp and he greeted me with great cordiality. "Sindbad," said he, "you are welcome. I have many times thought of you, and I bless the day on which I see you once more."

After thanking him for the honor he did me, I delivered the gift and letter from my august master. He was highly gratified at the caliph's acknowledgment of his friendship, and when he dismissed me he rewarded me handsomely.

I lost no time in embarking for Bagdad, but on the fifth day of our voyage we were attacked by pirates, who easily seized our ship. Some of the crew offered resistance, which cost them their lives. As for myself and the rest, who were not so imprudent, the pirates saved us and carried us to a remote island where they sold us for slaves. I fell into the hands of a rich merchant. He took me to his house and fed and clothed me very well. Some days later he had me brought before him to determine in what way I could be useful to him.

When I had informed him that I was skilful neither as a laborer nor as a mechanic he said: "Tell me, can you shoot with a bow?"

"Shooting with a bow was one of my youthful pastimes," I answered, "and practice might very likely again make me expert."

Then he gave me a bow and arrows, had me mount with him on an elephant, and we went to a thick forest some leagues from the town. We penetrated to its wildest part where we stopped, and he had me alight. Pointing to a great tree he said: "Climb up that. There is a prodigious number of elephants in this forest. Shoot at any you see passing by, and when you succeed in killing one come and tell me."

So saying he handed me a supply of food and returned to the town. I continued perched in the tree all night, but I saw no elephants. The next morning, however, at break of day, a large herd of them came crashing and trampling by. I began discharging arrows among them, and at last one of the great animals fell to the ground dead. The others retreated, and left me at liberty to go and acquaint my master with my success. He was much pleased and commended my dexterity. Presently we went back to the forest together and dug a great hole in which we buried the elephant I had killed. There we left it till it should decay and the tusks loosen, when my master would return and get them.

For two months I continued to hunt in the method I have described, shifting from one tree to another and from place to place as seemed best. Finally, as I was one morning watching an approaching herd, I was surprised that instead of passing by as usual they came straight to my tree. They were trumpeting horribly and there were such numbers that the ground shook under their heavy tread. My tree was soon surrounded with them, and there they stood with trunks uplifted, and all their eyes fixed on me. At this alarming spectacle I was so terrified that my bow and arrows fell to the ground from my trembling hands.

My fears were not without cause; for after the elephants had stared at me a few moments, one of the largest of them wound his trunk around the stem of my tree, and with a mighty effort tore it up by the roots, bringing me to the earth entangled in its branches. I thought my last hour had surely come; but the huge creature picked me gently up, and set me on his back,

There I clung while he led the way, followed by the rest of the herd, a long distance through the forest and out into the open country. At last the elephant stopped, lifted me down to the ground, and retired with all his companions.

When I had a little recovered from my fright I looked about me and found I was on a long and broad hill, almost covered with the bones and tusks of elephants. "This must be the elephants' burying place," I said to myself; "and they have brought me here that I might cease to persecute them, as I now know where to get their tusks without killing the live animals."

I did not linger longer on the hill, but made for the city as fast as I could go. After travelling a day and a night I reached my master's house. As soon as he saw me he exclaimed: "Ah! Sindbad, I was wondering what had become of you. I have been in the forest, where I found a tree newly uprooted, and your bow and arrows beside it. This made me despair of ever seeing you again. Pray tell me how you escaped death."

I satisfied his curiosity, and the next day we started together for the ivory hill. After arriving there we loaded the elephant which carried us with as many tusks as he could bear and returned to the city. When we were once more at my master's home he said to me: "The wild elephants of our forest have every year killed a great many of the slaves we send to hunt them. No matter what good advice we give the hunters they are sooner or later destroyed. You alone have escaped the wiles of those crafty animals, and you have procured me incredible wealth. Indeed, our whole city is enriched by your means, and we shall no longer sacrifice the lives of our slaves. After such a discovery I feel it is no more than your due that I treat you as a brother. God bless you with all happiness and prosperity. I henceforth give you your liberty, and I will also bestow a fortune on you."

"Master, I thank you," said I; "but the only reward I ask for what I have done is permission to return to my own country."

"Very well," said he, "ships will soon be coming for ivory. I will send you on your way in one of them, and you shall not lack something with which to pay your passage."

So I stayed with him until the expected ships arrived; and all the time we were adding to his store of ivory until his warehouses were filled with it. Meanwhile the other merchants had learned the secret of the ivory hill, but there were enough tusks for all.

When the ships came, and it had been decided in which one I was to embark, my master not only loaded half of it with ivory on my account, but obliged me to accept a present of some of the costliest curiosities of the country. The vessel presently sailed, and at the first port we touched on the mainland I left it; for I did not feel at ease on the sea after all that had happened to me in my various voyages. I disposed of my ivory to good advantage, bought numerous rare and beautiful articles which I intended to carry home for presents, and joined a caravan of merchants. Our journey was long and tedious, but I comforted myself with the thought that I was not exposed to many of the perils which had caused me so much distress in the past.

At last I arrived safely at Bagdad and immediately waited on the caliph to give him an account of my embassy. He assured me that my long absence had disquieted him not a little. What I told him of my adventure among the elephants astonished him greatly, and he declared he could not have believed it, had it not been for my well-known truthfulness. I took my leave of him more than satisfied with the honors and rewards he bestowed on me. Since that time I have rested from my labors and devoted myself to my family and friends.

Thus Sindbad finished the story of his final voyage, and turning to Hindbad, said: "Well, did you ever hear of anyone who has suffered more than I have? Is it not reasonable that, after all this, I should enjoy a quiet and pleasant life?"

At these words Hindbad kissed Sindbad's hand and said: "Sir, my afflictions are not to be compared with yours. You not only deserve a quiet life, but are worthy of all the riches you possess, since you make so good a use of them. May you live long and happily."

Sindbad then presented him with another hundred sequins and told him to give up carrying burdens as a porter. "Henceforth," said he, "I would have you eat at my table that you may all your life have reason to favorably remember Sindbad the Sailor."

The Sultan of the Indies could not help admiring the prodigious and inexhaustible memory of the sultana, his wife, who had entertained him for a thousand and one nights with such a variety of interesting stories. His temper was softened and his prejudices removed. He was not only convinced of the merit and great wisdom of the sultana, but he remembered with what courage she had offered to be his wife, regardless of the death to which she knew she exposed herself, and which so many preceding sultanas had suffered.

These considerations and her many other good qualities induced him at last to say to her: "I confess, lovely Sheherazade, that you have appeased my anger. I freely renounce the oath I had imposed on myself, and I will no more sacrifice any damsels to my unjust resentment."

The sultana cast herself at his feet and tenderly embraced them to show her gratitude; and the sultan then went to announce his decision to the grand vizier. Heralds soon made the news known throughout the city and couriers were dispatched to proclaim the tidings in the other portions of the realm, even to the remotest towns and provinces. Everywhere there was rejoicing, and the sultan and his beautiful consort gained the universal applause and blessings of all the people of the extensive empire of the Indies.

A Pronouncing Glossary

NOTE:—The accent and marking of the letters are in accord with Webster's New International Dictionary.

Abdallah, äb-dä′lȧ

Ahmed, ä′měd

Aladdin, ȧ-lăd′ĭn

Ali Baba, ä′lė̇ bä′bä

Bagdad, bäg-däd′

Beder, běd′ěr

Bengal, běn-gôl′

Bisnagar, bĭs-nŭg′ȧr

Bussorah, bŭs′ȯ̇-rä

Cairo, kī′rō

Cashmere, kăsh-mēr′

Cassim, käs′ėm

Caucasus, kô′kȧ-sŭs

Cogia Hassan, kō′gĭ-ä häs′ăn

Comari, kŏm′ȧ-rĭ

Dinarzade, dė̇-när-zä′dä

Euphrates, u̇-frā′tēz

Fareshah, fä′rě-shä

Fatima, fä′tė̇-mä

Ferozeshah, fė̇-rōz-shä′

Gulnare, gŭl-nä′rē

Haroun Alraschid, hä-rōōn′ ȧl-rȧ-shēd′

Hindbad, hĭnd′băd

Houssain, hōōs-sän′

Jehaunara, jě-hôn-ä′rȧ

Labe, lä′bā

Mobarec, mȯ̇-bä′rěk

Morgiana, môr-gĭ-ä′nä

Mustapha, mōōs′tä-fä

Nouronnihar, nōō-rŏn-ĭ-här′

Periebanou, pē-rĭ-bä′nōō

Roha, rō′hȧ

Saad, sä′ȧd

Saadi, sä′ȧ-dė̇

Saleh, sȧ-lě′

Samandal, sä′mȧn-däl

Shahriar, shä-rė̇-är′

Shahzenan, shä-zě-nän′

Shaibar, shī′bȧr

Sheherazade, shě-hä′rȧ-zä′dě

Sesame, sěs′ȧ-mė̇

Shiraz, shė̇-räz′

Sindbad, sĭnd′băd

Zeyn Alasnam, zān ȧ-lăs′ năm

āle, ăm, ȧccount, ärm, ȧsk, sofȧ; ēve, ė̇vent, ěnd; īce, ĭll; ōld, ōbey, ôrb, ŏdd, fōōd; ūse, u̇nite.